STAR JUMPERS

An Accidental Quest for Freedom

STAR JUMPERS

An Accidental Quest for Freedom

BERNETTE SHERMAN

MOUNT HOPE MEDIA

All rights reserved
Published by Mount Hope Media, LLC
Austell, GA
MountHopeMedia.com
BernetteSherman.com

2023 Paperback Print Edition ISBN: 978-1-954636-09-5

For every person who dares to be brave and stand for what's right.

For my children and my husband.

You May Also Enjoy
Light of the Dark Moon

BernetteSherman.com/LDM
Books2Read.com/Maradobu1

Chapter One

"Take your filthy hands off him!" I bark at the burly, masked man wearing a white full-body containment suit. There's no response at all to the sound of my voice. It figures he's deaf. He's just not blind – at least not yet.

He can see us through the gray cotton mask and clear goggles he wears, but he keeps his anonymity. Cowards. His eyes are probably close to the same faded blue as most of the other guards here who still have any sight. I struggle to see through the bars of the reinforced concrete cell they hold me in, looking for our father.

The other chair they use for these procedures is empty and I don't hear him in the cell beside me. That means they've already subdued him and taken him through the unmarked doors to the sterile, stripped-down hallway. I hate that hallway. It feels like the tunnel where time is lost. We've come and gone through them every day, but there are no guarantees how long that will last.

Our dad is either on his way, or already where they hold the Immunes for testing. Tezzi, our little sister, is somewhere else too. Hopefully she hasn't been taken for testing. But, after what I've seen today, I can't be sure. Too many have come through. We're the only ones left that I can see.

Before we were taken, we'd only heard rumors about what happened to Immunes; but since no one ever returned, we never knew if the rumors were true. They're still trying to find a cure for a disease that they helped create. They, along with the aliens we called Elitists who invaded our planet from Eliata. I don't even know what they really call themselves and it doesn't matter anymore. I hold them responsible for the disease that's been slowly killing the population for ten years, maybe longer.

I look back through the small, barred window at Morren, my brother, and the large man charged with restraining him. This is the small room they use to prep us and put us to sleep before beginning testing. Morren is already restrained in the chair and the tray with a large silver needle is in place beside him. We can't do this again. The drugs make you groggy for hours and the ravishing of our bodies for blood, enzymes, and micro-sized samples of tissue leave us too weak to do anything more than recuperate in the hard pallets we call beds. Not today. Morren needs to pull himself together if we're gonna do this. We aren't going down without a fight. If he goes down, I'll be alone – not something I want.

I kick against the door of my four by six-foot cell trying to get his attention. Morren's head turns slightly, and he glances in my direction.

"Dammit," I mutter. His eyes are unfocused.

He won't be able to jump in this state, and I won't jump without him. Besides, I need Morren to get Dad and Tezzi. They suspect her of being an Immune too, but they won't know for sure until she's around ten. If it's up to me, they'll never know. They won't even have the chance to run any more pre-tests to see if the markers for being an Immune are there.

"Morren! Morren! I'm here. I'm still here. We're still okay. Don't stop fighting!" I scream through the chamber. He has to hear me.

Morren steals another glimpse at me and this time he winks before returning to his semi-dazed appearance. The guard returns his focus to Morren and lifts the syringe.

My lip turns up in a one-sided smile and I look at the door behind Morren and nod. He continues to watch through partially closed eyelids as I put up three fingers. The oversized deaf man is trying to hold Morren down to give him the shot in his neck. Morren's tense muscles relax as he stops straining and goes still.

"Three."

The man serving as both a technician and guard turns Morren's head to the side.

"Two."

He picks up the large silver needle filled with the drug that will incapacitate Morren for hours. I've seen them do this to others.

"One."

With an abrupt motion, his hand comes near Morren's neck. The needle jabs into the black leather of the headrest where Morren's imprint still shows.

"Where are we going?" I call ahead to Morren as we sprint down another sterile hallway.

Blinding, fluorescent lights hang overhead for the benefit of those who still have their sight. Soon those lights will be useless too, unless you're an Immune.

We need to hurry. Someone is going to meet us to get us out of here, Morren sends me silently.

The gift to speak this way had been dealt to us on the mighty Mississippi when I nearly drowned, and it's been helping us ever since. I appreciate Morren's gentle reminder to not use our speaking voices. There are still some guards who have their hearing.

Morren's long, lean legs don't slow a bit. He has a few inches on me along with the speed of a sprinter like our mother. I don't have much speed, but can run farther. That doesn't matter. Right now, I need him to stop.

We can't leave. They have Dad and Tezzi. We have to go back for them. I stop running and look around. *There's gotta be a way to get to wherever they are, Morren.*

I rub my forehead, pushing back the curly coils. Walls in a dingy eggshell hue surround us, and there's nothing to tell one apart from another.

Morren ignores me. He turns a sharp right ahead of me, as if he's turned his second hearing on and has tuned into someone else. I run again, turning where he turned, not wanting to get lost or separated. I round the corner and slam into the back of my younger brother as he stands in front of her.

A scream tries to escape through my parted lips, but Morren turns and covers my mouth before the sound lets loose. I've never seen one of them, not in real life. We knew they'd come, bringing with them what would become the virus that decimated the human population. Since the virus hit us, we've been left with less than half a million survivors around Earth. Most of us who are still alive haven't escaped the effects of the virus. In ten more years that number will likely be only about one hundred thousand and all, but the Immunes, will be blind, deaf, and with nervous system disorders; or some combination. No one has survived very long once the virus has caused full deafness and blindness. She and her people are why we're here right now.

Intentionally loud enough for her to hear, I lean into Morren and say, "Why is that killer here?"

She can help us and she's not a killer. I sent a message for help and Eli answered. She can get us out of here. She can also hear us. Morren turns his head slightly over his shoulder.

Because of them our mother is dead, our sister has been detained for observation, our father is now being treated as a lab rat, and we're jumping and running!

Morren ignores the thoughts I shoot at him. He's gotten good at it - when he wants.

Morren? I insist while glaring at him.

What?!

There is no way I am willingly going with her or any of her kind. Not while I can still see, hear, taste, smell, or run. I look at Eli with narrowed eyes.

Morren doesn't take his deep eyes off Eli while he speaks as if I'm a child. *She can lead us out of here. We can find help and come back for Dad and Tezzi. We'll never find them on our own in this maze.*

I can't leave. We can't leave. Screw this, Morren. Let's go find Dad first. I grab his hand, but he pulls it away abruptly. I stare at him and wonder if he's lost his mind.

You're being unreasonable. It's a muttered response even in my head.

I'm not being unreasonable. This - this idea of leaving is unreasonable. It's a crazy stupid idea to leave Dad and Tezzi behind, to be lab experiments. We'll find them and then we can go.

Morren rotates to look me square in the eye.

"Dammit, Karana. We will all get killed. We don't have time to stand here. We need to get out of here or we won't be any good to anyone!"

He doesn't bother to keep his voice inside, despite using a loud whisper. His face is close to mine and while I'm sure no one else in the building can hear him, I don't miss any part of the message he delivers with added bass.

Faking confidence I plant my feet and fix my posture. "We get them, and then we leave. I promise."

I have no idea if it's a promise I'll be able to keep, but I need his help to find them.

It's time to test Eli's ability to hear me speaking silently. *Can you help us find our family? You know - the two who didn't die from the virus you brought.*

Morren sighs and shakes his head. All I can do is shrug. If we're in this with her, she needs to be able to keep up.

I hear her say, *Yes.*

Lead the way then. I wave my hand in front of me and give her a 'show me what you've got' look. She better not screw this up.

Chapter Two

With cat-like agility and speed Eli glides past us and down the hall. Periodically, she slows to a creep to sense where we should go next. It pisses me off that she can feel my dad and sister, but I'm too amped up and they're too drugged up for me to feel them myself. Needing her right now makes me want to wipe that smug thought bubble right out of her head.

Morren runs ahead of me and I'm left holding up the rear, again. My legs can't move any faster and the quick turns around the halls only make me more aware of my incompetence when it comes to agility. *Show-off alien.*

I want to grab her by one of her rope-like tentacle hairs, yank her back down to the floor, and stomp on her. But I can't even catch her and she knows what I'm thinking unless I'm careful to shield my thoughts. I don't even know if that will work since I can rarely shield them from Morren.

He shoots me another look. *Keep up. Shut up.*

I try to silence the backtalk in my head and follow them. I round another corner and again, run smack into Morren's back. I can see he's getting irritated with me.

"How was I supposed to know you stopped?" I ask defensively.

Shhh. They're in here. He sends me, ignoring my question.

Okay. What's the plan?

Morren looks at me as if he's surprised. *You're the one who always has the plan. I figured you were thinking up one while you took your time keeping up with us. Why else were you running so slowly?*

The alien, Eli, is waiting for me to do something, too. He's embarrassing me in front of her, and now they're both looking at me in anticipation.

Okay. I do have a plan. I nod like the bobble-head of Oprah Winfrey my mom used to keep on her dashboard.

I'm scrambling, but I don't have much choice. I look down both hallways and then share the plan silently through our thoughts. *We go in, lights off, and use our cat-like eyes to see in the dark.*

These are the same eyes we'd gotten from our father.

Morren waits for me to continue, but the plan is simple and complete.

He grips my arm before I can set the plan in motion. *Then what?*

You carry Tezzi out.

Tezzi is mostly normal, as far as we can tell. She doesn't have the special abilities Morren and I have; the abilities that made them hunt us down for testing. We've seen glimpses that she may be different, just not as different as Dad, Morren, and me. I know they're trying to save what's left of humanity, but it won't be at the expense of our freedom and lives. Some days I wonder if it's even worth saving.

Morren looks at me with a confused look and I realize he's hearing me again. *Get out of my head. Some thoughts are private.*

I shift my attention back to what we're doing now. We have to get out, but first we have to get in through the door that holds them. I push down on the metal handle.

Wait, Karana. What's the actual plan? He grabs my hand, and lets the handle slowly raise back up, careful to keep it from clicking.

Like I said, we go in and you get Tezzi.

That's not a plan, Morren protests.

Fine. We do that, and then we leave. You make sure no guards come after us. I look at Eli, standing there quiet and serene. It's like she doesn't realize we're in a life or death situation. *We run toward safety with your alien friend here.*

I pause and put my hand back on the handle. I can't let them hang their hopes on us and torture our little sister with tests until she's old enough to show whether she is an Immune or not.

The others like us vanished with no real explanation. They would go out for testing and never come back. No one would hear from them again; and there aren't many of us or regular humans left. My brother, father, and I might be the last three Immunes in any of the habitable places.

Morren shakes his head again in disappointment.

It's a straight-forward plan. I respond to the statement he hadn't made.

Because it's not one. I can see the disappointment in his face.

It's going to work, Morren. Trust me. I take a deep breath. *From three. Three. Two. One.*

Nothing. Morren and Eli stare at me, expecting some explanation, which I don't have.

Morren looks around anxiously. *What happened? Why didn't we get inside?*

Maybe Eli is blocking us. *Did you do this? Why can't we jump?*

I press down on the handle. Locked.

It's probably nothing, Morren sends. *I'll try. Three.*

Boots are approaching from somewhere too close for my comfort.

Two.

The sounds bounce off the walls making it impossible to tell exactly how far away they are. My guess is that they are around the corner and in seconds they'll be bearing down on us.

One.

The three of us escape the approaching guards, landing on top of each other on the other side of the door. Morren hustles to switch off the light. Dad must have had it on for Tezzi. The darkness and shadows still scare her.

The sound of slapping against the slick white tile floors is too close now. All it takes is one hearing guard and we're trapped.

My eyes adjust to the dark and I thank our dad again for passing on this trait.

Some of our abilities aren't from him, so we can only assume they're from our mother. But she was killed when Eli's people came. They said they came in peace, but our government wasn't taking any chances and attacked. The biochemical weapon was unleashed across the area of Greenland where the alien's ship crash landed. Our mother's jet was downed by an electro-magnetic pulse Eli's people sent as a reverse attack after the biochemical hit the air. None of the humans who tried to fend them off survived.

Morren and I were only five and seven then. Dad met Tezzi's mom not long after - before people started showing up with symptoms. They never married. They weren't expecting to get pregnant and the prospects for survival were low; but she did survive. It was still early in the days of the virus. The aliens created the virus when they reengineered our own biochemical weapon. It attacks the nervous system and takes out anyone with low or weakened immune systems first. Most pregnant women and their babies didn't survive at all.

Tezzi's mom survived only long enough to get through birth. I believe Dad's genes were Tezzi's saving grace. Her survival is probably why they think she's also an Immune. It's why rescuing them is a must. Where we'll go once we have them, I don't know. There are no safe places we can get to on foot. I still have to trust that we can get out of here and find somewhere to start over since outside of these walls the world as we knew it is all but ended.

I consider this for a moment; what life was like before we arrived back in Atlanta and were captured. Taking Tezzi out there where we scavenged for food, fought off the desperate, and hid in abandoned buildings where roaches and rats roamed room to room, competing with those still living to feed on the corpses of those who recently succumbed to death. Maybe we did need help to get out of here.

Morren comes back with Tezzi in his arms from the multi-room cell. A battery of wires still hang loosely from her head and wrists. Morren must have snatched everything from the machine. Dad's lethargic movements mean he is heavily sedated.

Eli and I wait by the door, ready to finish carrying out my plan. She looks at Tezzi and Dad before casting her gaze toward me. The shimmer of her tentacles dulls. Whatever she's thinking I can't get, but I still don't like it. I hear the faint beep of the sonar wand and press my ear to the door to be sure. Crap. I wonder if Eli is shielding us somehow, or if they're just now making their way to our door.

I touch Morren's arm and step back from the dented sheet of metal. Someone else had already tried kicking at it. We need to find another way out. The place will be on lockdown even more than usual.

Her tentacles dim even more.

What aren't you telling us? I finally ask.

She looks at me with an annoying calm. *How will you get out of this room?*

I think about it. We'd left Atlanta years before when everyone else started flocking here. It wasn't safe to be an Immune with so many people looking for answers. And now, we're back, trapped in concrete, with our dad the subject of scientific testing rather than the tester as he'd once been. That's what he'd become. What we'd all become. They want what we have, (whatever that is), and if we don't get out, they will have a chance to get it.

Dad's hair, once black with sprinkles of gray, is now all gone. They'd shaved it recently for whatever testing plans they had next for him. Morren and I would have the same fate and later Tezzi; if we stayed. His brown skin fades into the shadows in the same way mine and Morren's does. Tezzi's hair is held back by a tied piece of cloth. She doesn't deserve this – living her whole life on the run, trapped, and never feeling safe. She would never have someone to comb through her hair or sit her down with a movie to braid it. Never sleep in a real bed. We all have to get out of here. We'd come and gone from this city three times, and I am ready to do it once again – for the last time.

Morren holds Tezzi awkwardly, shifting the weight on his legs. *Karana?*

We're getting out of this room together, I say, cutting off any other thoughts he might have.

I look around at the windowless walls and the drop ceilings. That's it.

We have to climb through the ceiling and drop down in a room close to the exit door, I send to Morren and Eli.

First, we have to stay quiet, so the guards move on and search another area, Morren sends back to us.

Dad sits on the floor near the small inside room where Morren found him. They've already done testing on him and taken blood - too much of it. I peek at Tezzi in Morren's arms. Somehow, I'd missed it before this moment. She's asleep. Her head lies limp on Morren's shoulder. I touch her cheek but there's no response.

There is no way we will get them out like this. I look at Eli. She already knows. Her psychic superiority is irritating. I don't want to rely on her and I don't trust her. But we're stuck in a room and there is no way my dad and little sister will make an escape. I can't stop the tears from slipping down my face and into the crevice of my lips.

You can come back for them, Eli tries to assure me.

You have no right to give any suggestions. Not about this. So shut it! I shoot back.

Morren looks at me again. He hadn't heard her, only me, and assumes I'm being rude to Eli again. I am, but he doesn't understand how much she deserves it.

She thinks we should come back for them. Leave them. Here. I look around at the concrete room with a wall mounted toilet and sink. A dingy pillow on the floor serves as a seat. Leaving them here feels cruel.

Why? Morren looks at me, his brow crease revealing his apprehension at my answer.

Because...., I pause not wanting to admit the truth. *They won't make it. Dad is weak and so is Tezzi. The only way out is through the ceilings. We can't wait for them to gain their strength.*

Morren touches Tezzi's hair that grazes his chin.

They took too much blood and they've been through a lot already, he says.

Morren, the guards will come back. Maybe we can jump out of here, I suggest.

We've never jumped where we couldn't see or didn't already know.

We know the hall. Then Eli can get us out, right Eli? I look at Eli along with Morren, waiting for her to answer his question.

This isn't the question. The condition of your father and your sister are in question, Eli says.

I throw my head back, pretty sure we're screwed. *They won't let the fact that we vanished into thin air go without question. They'll come into every single room. I don't know what to do, Morren.*

Okay. Let's think. Can we jump with them?

We've done it before. We can try it again. I nod and then stop, my optimism fades. *It's just that the last time we tried leaping with her, she got left. We had to come back. Remember, that's how they finally caught us.*

I don't like to think about the botched escape that landed us here. The memory feels like it was weeks ago, but it may have only been days. With no clocks, sun, or windows, I have no idea how much time has passed in the compound.

Maybe it was a fluke. We weren't on the same page about where we were going. I think that's why it didn't work right, Morren rationalizes.

I'm not sure why it didn't work, and I'm scared of risking that again. What if she gets left and we can't get back?

They will be here soon, Eli says, interrupting our conversation.

Karana, do you think she might be like us? That one day she will be able to jump on her own?

Don't know. She is Dad's daughter, but her mother was ordinary. Maybe she has some traits, but right now she hasn't shown us anything that says she can jump. She hasn't come into her power. Besides that, she's too weak.

Morren inhales deeply, his chest heaving Tezzi up slightly. He's not saying anything as he studies the shadow of a man who'd once stood so strong. Given our father's condition, perhaps it has been longer than the mere days I want to believe it's been. Morren secures his hold beneath Tezzi's legs.

Even without saying anything to me, I know he's gauging whether he can carry her out of here, and how far. His eyes cloud with a sense of defeat as he's forced to adjust his grip on Tezzi again. At seven, she's too big for that, even if she is small for her age. We should all be bigger than we are given the size of Mom and Dad but eating every day is a luxury.

Karana, if we want to have any chance of surviving and saving both of them, we have to leave. We have to jump.

His words catch me by surprise.

Wait. Give me a minute to think of something. We don't even know where to go. We don't have any place safe, I say desperately.

Eli hasn't offered anything else useful since I shot her down. I wouldn't object if she tried again, but I won't ask. I know she's listening and understands our desperation.

We don't have a minute. We're gonna have to do our best. I want to take them too, Karana, but we can't, Morren says in a heavy voice. *I can't.*

We all turn at the sound of boots approaching quickly.

I look at Morren, then at Tezzi sleeping peacefully, and finally at Dad, who's nearly collapsed on the floor. I kiss Tezzi's cheek, which had never known the soft fullness kids should. She's just a little girl, barely older than I was when Mom died. She doesn't deserve this. I walk over to Dad and lean down to hug him.

"I love you," I whisper in his ear.

I need to say it out loud and let the vibration of my voice touch him as much as the words. I help him up and back to the room as Morren walks Tezzi back to her cot. I know he's crying too.

We will be back. I promise you, Dad. I promise you, Tezzi. We will be back. They can't hear me, but I tell myself because I must. I must make the promise and keep it, as much for them as me.

The sound of at least four pairs of boots stops in front of the door.

I hear Eli's voice in my head. *We must go.*

I know. On three?

She bobs her tentacles and begins. *Three.*

Two.

There is a moment of silence and then the door clicks.

One.

Chapter Three

We're catapulting through darkness and space. It's supposed to be instantaneous. In the blur, I reach out, trying to feel for Morren.

"Morren!"

My voice is lost in the rush of speed.

Morren! I scream out in my head.

"I'm here," he says and reaches for me. I feel his fingers lightly against my arm.

You're going to be okay. You can make it back home once you are ready to return. Eli's voice again intrudes into our conversation.

Shut your purple pie hole, you stinking, lying monster! I rip back.

I open my mouth to say more about how I feel, and something hits me hard in the chest, knocking the wind out of me. The sensation of water under me brings me back. We've arrived. Somewhere. I struggle to cough and get air back into my lungs. Gagging for air I catch the scent of the water and taste it as it seeps past my lips. Metallic. I raise my face up from the shallow shore where we've hit. The grains of sand remind me of crushed bricks. Water and sand mean we've landed on a beach, solid ground.

Morren lies fifteen or so yards from me and is gagging from the impact as well, having landed face first into the water. I struggle to get up and run over to him. Where is that slimy Eli? I look around wondering where she wound up as I drag Morren further onto the beach. I see her lying near the water's edge, like a wet ragdoll tossed aside. She's like an octopus, she should be just fine.

Wherever we are looks like another country, like we'd somehow jumped across continents. Maybe we'd be safer. But I can't be sure. Geography was never my thing.

A glimpse of movement catches my eye as Eli squirms on the beach like a whale slithering up the sand. Her round head crowned with what looks like octopus tentacles with sensors on them. The rest of her aqua blue body emerges from the water. I hate that the rest of her looks so much like us, except for the freakish blue skin and the lack of ears. And her eyes, while they're the same shape as ours, have no hair – no lashes, no eyebrows. They're filled by spheres of blackness. Shiny like obsidian, always reflecting back like a mirror.

Maybe she knows where we are. She rests on her forearms and looks over to where I stand next to Morren. I'm sure she can tell how I feel, and despite her exterior calm I'm pretty sure she's not that stoic to not feel the same way about me.

I march on the slippery sand to where she lies. My boots are soggy with water and my clothes still drip. My jeans grip my legs uncomfortably and the plain white t-shirt issued by the compound clings to my chest. I'm cold, wet, angry, and getting hungry. I can't wait to tell her exactly what I think.

I stop, my toes narrowly missing one of the long tentacles that drags on the sand. All five feet nine inches of me towers over her where she steadies herself a couple feet off the ground.

"Where are we? Why are we here? And how are you gonna get us back home? And don't even think of playing any mind games or tricks or I'll rip one of those slimy tentacles right out of your effing head! Do you hear me, you little alien princess?"

I can feel the fire rising behind my eyes. I don't want to hurt her - not yet. Despite being pissed off, we still need her.

"I'm still getting oriented, but I think we are on Baselonica Xuna in the first star system."

"What the heck? Basil what in the where?!"

"Baselonica Xuna. It's a planet in the first star system."

"You brought us to another planet!? You were supposed to take us to a safe place on Earth!" Morren says from where he's crouched on his knees.

I look up and take notice that it's far too different from Earth. We've had red skies but nothing like this. A sun and several other large celestial objects can be seen in the sky when I look past Morren's head. Perhaps moons. Or were those other planets?

"You piece of octopus slime. You tricked us. You looked right at us, knowing what was about to happen. You didn't say two words. Didn't give us any warning! You said nothing and let us jump to another star system. Some planet in the middle of…how the heck would I know where we are?"

"I didn't know we'd come here. We were supposed to jump to the other Immunes. You're supposed to be attracted to them." Eli's black eyes steady on mine, unflinching as she stands to her feet, making me suddenly feel much smaller.

"So what happened? How'd you screw up and bring us here?" My eyes are wide as I mimic her confidence and stance.

"One of my people must've brought an Immune here. Maybe a few years ago when they started hunting you. Or another one of them might have found an Immune like I found you recently. I don't know for sure. I can't think of anything else. You'll have to find them. But even when you do, it may not be safe to go back to Earth. They are still hunting you."

"Do you hear this, Morren? Your friend Eli has transported us to another planet, and we can't get back home."

"That's not what I said," Eli says defensively and takes another step back from me.

"That's pretty much what you said."

"Are we stuck here, Eli?" Morren asks, his lips barely parting, and his eyes cast out to the ocean. It's his *"I'm trying to be calm even though I'm about to freak out"* look.

"Not permanently. You're on Baselonica Xuna and you can leave it - once you find whoever is here."

"You're kidding right, Eli? I trusted you." This time, he looks at Eli directly. It's her turn to look away from the disappointment in his eyes. He could do that to you. Make you feel your shame.

"I told you I would help you and that I'd help you save your family. This is how."

"See. She trapped us." I kick sand into the air, not sure how intentional my narrowly missing her really is.

"Just take us back, Eli," Morren growls.

"I can't. Only you can do that." She takes a few steps towards the water's edge as if the answer lay out there somewhere in the deep ocean.

I stand up and scan the red beach for something hard or sharp - a weapon. "I'm going to kill you. That's it. I'm gonna kill you and then you can be the one stuck on a planet in the middle of some unknown star system."

"Just because you don't know it, doesn't make it unknown," she says smartly.

"You don't get to do that. You did this. All of this. You need to fix this!"

Eli turns to face me and she almost looks remorseful. "Do you want to save your father and your sister?"

I look back at her incredulously. "Of course."

"Then you won't kill me. You need me." Eli takes a deep breath and I see her tentacles lift slightly before returning to their normal position.

Morren walks away from us. He is usually the calm one, but this is too much even for him.

Eli drops her head. Her tentacles, with their shimmering blues, purples, greens and specks of white that glimmer like diamonds, hang loosely around her. For the first time I realize her hair, if I can call it that, reflects her mood.

Morren and I aren't the only ones out here. She's with us, but I don't pity her. I can't. She brought this on herself and on us the moment they chose to land on Earth.

Hands on my hip, I march up to Eli, refusing to let her feel that any part of this is okay. "When can we go back? Where are the others on Earth? Can't we go where they are and wait?"

She doesn't look me in the eye, choosing instead to stare at the red sky. "I don't know when you can go back. That's not up to me. I don't know where the others are on Earth." Eli's eyes turn to Morren first, then me. "I am not attracted to other Immunes. You have to be an Immune to be drawn to an Immune. You were drawn here, so we know an Immune must be close."

Morren's optimism returns and he nods as if he gets it. "So there is the possibility that we can try jumping and end up back on Earth with the other Immunes?"

For a second, I almost feel hopeful too. "We need to hurry then. We can't lose focus if we're going to get back to Dad and Tezzi."

Eli stares off blankly toward the water and glances at the sky again.

"Eli? So we can try jumping back to our dad and Tezzi, right?" I repeat Morren's question.

"You can try…"

"Come on, Morren. Let's try to get back to Earth. We'll go back to the compound."

"It doesn't hurt to try, but we'll be back where we started," Morren says with concern.

"It's better than being off the planet," I say, glaring at Eli.

"Okay. Let's do it." Morren stands beside me and I nod my head and begin to count.

"Three. Two. One." I close my eyes to prepare for the rocky return but don't feel anything happening. I cautiously open one eye to see Morren and the red sky in the distance.

I fail miserably in holding back the rolling sound coming from my throat. "Aaaargggghhh!!!"

Morren rubs his hands past his temples stretching his face as he stomps one foot. The energy of his anger suffocated by the forgiving sand. Eli shakes her head as if there is a part of her that was hoping we'd do it; and that she was wrong. I wonder if she can jump out of here and leave us. At least she seems to know where 'here' is.

I back up a bit to give her some space as she stretches out her arms and her tentacles flare as if she's feeling the air. She leans over and runs her hand over the reddish, rough sand and lets it run through her long fingers.

"There is a reason I had to come get you. You, your brother, and father are the last ones we've found to be immune for sure. You might be able to save your planet. But only if they don't kill you," Eli begins.

Being quiet is too difficult and I can't help but shoot back at her, "Only because your people engineered a virus that killed us."

"Yes. That is true. For that I am sorry. Our intention was truly to come in peace. And we did come in peace, but it was not taken that way. When we were attacked, we had no choice but to defend ourselves. We knew your men of war would not cease their aggression upon us, and we do not ourselves keep men of war. For times such as that we have science. That is how we fight."

"Why not just surrender? You were the intruders." I wish my glare was intense enough to cut her, but it's not. It was her fault any of this was happening.

Eli yields a heavy frustrated sigh and paces slowly in front of where I stand with Morren by my side. "Do you think they would have let us live? We did not have the option to leave. Our ship crashed on your planet, trapping my people. Not everyone is like me, as not all of your people are like you. I have the ability to move like you but only a few of us can do this. Only a few of your people can do this. When the virus devastated your world, we tried to save those of you who were strongest in order to rebuild it. Some of your people were rescued before the experiments, but most were rescued from that building."

"Then where are they?" I can't even pretend to hide what I feel for her.

I look at Morren impetuously. *I don't trust her. I never will.*

"We know that there must be some settlement on Earth but, unfortunately, we haven't located it…yet." She crosses her arms and begins to walk away from the water, forcing us to follow her as she talks. "As I said, we believe that Immunes are attracted to other Immunes. A group of our jumpers took Immunes to an island, but they never returned. We had confirmation that they'd dropped the Immunes off and were on their way back, but we never heard from them again. We believe they were killed or captured."

"But for some twisted reason, we weren't brought there." Morren's confusion matches mine.

"You were pulled here. That means there is at least one Immune here. It is possible that one of our jumpers made it here with an Immune if they felt threatened."

I sigh loudly. Tezzi and Dad need us back on Earth, and instead someone pulled us to another star system.

"Are you staying with us here to find this Immune?" The question comes out whiny.

Morren is back by my side now, listening to the exchange. Surely, he doesn't trust her anymore either. I wish I could speak to him without Eli hearing, but I haven't figured out how to shield my inner conversation from her.

"Can we get to finding them so we can get home?" he asks.

The look in Eli's black eyes tells us it won't be quite that easy.

Finally she speaks slowly, carefully; considering every word and tone. "I have brought you to safety. I have followed what I must do to aid in preserving humankind. Not the humans that were, but the humans that will be. I must go ahead of you to prepare a place suitable for your return. Otherwise, it will be in vain. Coming back to Earth as it is now could mean genocide of the beings of an entire planet. We cannot...I cannot allow that. But the survival of your species does not rest only on me. You two must be part of a new start. You, along with the other Immunes. Get the Immune who is here and then you can get back to Earth and the other Immunes."

"Genocide? New start? Our sister is not an Immune? What are you gonna – "Morren cuts me off as he tries to regain his calm.

"What happens next?" He's struggling to maintain his composure.

"I don't know. I cannot tell what you will choose or what you will do," Eli answers without commitment.

My eyebrows furrow as I realize she may still be lying to us. "Why didn't the others get drawn here if they are Immunes?"

"Maybe because you are the only two who weren't secured, and what you two have is what is needed to bring all Immunes together."

Chapter Four

"Wait. You said you have to prepare a place for us. Does that mean you're leaving us? And you expect us to go on some goose chase on this oven of a planet for an Immune that may or may not even exist?" I can feel a strange sensation just under my skin. Warmth. Anger. It could just be the temperature, but it feels like it's coming from the inside.

"If you were drawn here, the Immune exists," Eli answers calmly.

"This isn't home. This is a whole other planet neither of us has ever heard of. They've got like four moons and a blazing hot sun and water that looks like someone put rust in it. Not to mention we have no idea who we have to find to get back! Even their birds look like crazy creatures out of a sci-fi movie. Like that one! It's coming this way and it has teeth. Birds don't have teeth just like humans don't belong on Baselonica Xuna! Do something!" I cover my head as the menacing flying monster speeds overhead, turns sharply, and dives into the ocean. It comes back up holding a moss-colored creature that looks mostly like a fish.

I try to hold back the tears born from anger, frustration, and even fear. *We made them a promise, Morren.*

"Eli, we have a world, and we have people there who need us. That's where we need to go and you're gonna help us." Morren plants his feet as best he can in the sand and crosses his arms.

I grab one of her tentacles and pull it. The feel of sliminess in my hands makes me immediately regret it, but I don't let go.

"That hurts, doesn't it? All those nerves getting squeezed. I. WANT. TO. GO. HOME. NOW! Take us back to Earth!"

"I know you can get us back home. Just do it. Let's not waste time. We needed to escape the compound, not the planet," Morren says, his tone softer after my attack on Eli.

Eli grabs my hand and squeezes my wrist, forcing me to release my grip. She is much stronger than I am, which upsets me even more.

Her eyes look up at the sky yet again as if expecting something to magically happen. "The compound, and whatever island the Immunes are on, is all that is left. We haven't found people who've survived and aren't affected."

"But you haven't searched everywhere." Morren's eyes light up with his brand of hope.

"This is true," she nods.

I don't know whether to cry or yell or just collapse on the shore, but my body begs for some emotional release. My fingers tremble as I speak. "So there are others like us. All we have to do is find them when we get back. Okay. It's gonna be okay. We'll get our dad and sister. If this thing works like you said, we should jump to wherever the other Immunes are."

I stand straighter, trying to make myself taller beside Eli.

"You cannot go there. There is nothing there for you. We are searching for the location so we can prepare it. When it is ready and you have the other Immune, you will be drawn there."

"Listen, Eli! We're not going on your wild space hunt. We're going home. If this is your guilt trip, then why don't you take it? You can take us back where we came from!" I push her back, causing her to stumble, but I don't take her down.

"No. Not now, you aren't." She is aggravatingly calm.

I want her to get mad back. Instead she's standing here like it's all okay. I look at Morren for support and then back at Eli.

"Eli, stop being difficult and take us back," Morren says in his charming way.

That charming talk doesn't work with aliens.

Eli shoots me a sharp look and then turns to Morren. "Look. We can keep arguing about this out here in the open," she says and tilts her head up at what appears to be a sky with a few scattered clouds against the red backdrop. "Or we can try to find some shelter before the storm."

"What storm? You're trying to change the subject!" The air is still, the clouds holding their places. It doesn't feel like a storm.

"The storm that is on its way. I will help you find somewhere to rest and begin your search before I go. I will also explain why it has to be you and who you are looking for." She begins walking again further up the beach and we quicken our steps to keep pace.

A loud rolling sound like a freight train rumbling makes its way through the clouds and is met by a spark of electricity across the sky. Then the wind comes, howling and pushing the once stagnant clouds quickly.

"We need to hurry. On Baselonica the storms are strong and can be deadly. They seek out the weak and fearful. The people aren't much different. The Immune you seek may have already been impacted by the planet's atmosphere. You must be careful not to let it affect you," Eli pauses for a moment and her eyes scan past the beach. "We lost a few of our people here."

"How do you know about this planet?" I ask, sincerely curious.

"We explored it once as a possible home. The atmosphere is not suitable for pleasant living." Eli starts to say something else, but instead closes her pouty lavender lips and leaves it at that.

I roll my eyes at her as I follow her toward the dunes that line the beach.

What's she gotten us into, and how are we gonna get out of it? I ask Morren, not caring that she hears it too.

Morren shrugs and shakes his head as he runs. His jaw is clenched and he's looking around at everything from the burnt sky to the mirroring sea. His hands are balled into tight fists, and I think he may finally be past politeness with his so-called friend.

These two questions play on repeat in my head as we sprint toward an old, leaning wooden shelter. Its boards are barely held together by loose nails and holes the size of my feet gape in the roof and sides where the splintered wood has given way, or those evil looking birds have torn into it. Of the two shelters I can see, this one is in better condition. Even still, it looks as if the slightest breeze could bring it crashing on top of us. Perhaps her intention of dropping us here is to ensure we have a painful and certain death.

I pull Morren back before entering the shelter. "I still don't trust her," I whisper out loud, while giving her my best stink eye.

She'd still be able to hear even if I told him without speaking.

You don't trust anyone, she says back to me using her inner voice so I know she can hear all that we're saying.

Touché. I cast a look of contempt before entering the shack that might be our burial ground if the storm brewing outside is as bad as it sounds.

It's not that I don't trust anyone. It's that everyone I ever trusted except Dad, Tezzi, and Morren are dead. Some at the hands of people we were supposed to be able to trust. Mom is gone because Eli's people invaded Earth and killed her.

The skies have turned a crimson red. Streaks of pink clouds break up the red and remind me of blood I've seen spilled on the concrete. I step back into the corner, avoiding Eli and huddling next to Morren. He is always so balanced and sure. Always trying to 'understand' and give the benefit of the doubt - like he's trying to do now.

What if she is telling the truth? Had we stayed we would be useless. All of us would be trapped in that underground prison.

I roll my eyes at him. So much for the fire and passion I thought I was going to see. He's trying to talk to me, maybe to make me feel better but I don't want to hear him now. His reasoning isn't helping, and the choice has already been made.

The lightning strikes outside the shed with cackles and shrieks. The sound lingers like that of screaming in fear, culminating in the cacophony of a drumline gone awry. I've never experienced anything like it as each attack of the storm drives into my chest and my head, pounding like a hammer on a marshmallow. Overkill. The rain is coming down in blinding sheets. The water is further up on the beach and with each wave it gets closer.

"We can't stay here." Eli peers out the doorway. The door has long since come from the hinges.

I wipe at the brownish liquid dripping down my face, "Really? Did you realize that all on your own or are you stealing my thoughts?"

Morren throws his head back, "Give it a break, Karana." He's just as wet as I am.

You're defending her now? Look at us, Morren.

I can't believe it. She's the one that's supposed to be our mutual enemy. He is a little too friendly with her. Too forgiving of what she's done to us and our family.

"Karana, we need to survive. Otherwise, no one else will."

He can be annoyingly sensible considering he's only fifteen. I'm the big sister. I'm supposed to be the mature one.

Chapter Five

Eli peeks out the door of the shed. She's searching for a safe place to go during this brief lull.

"Do you see anything?" Morren asks.

"I need to feel it out. The city isn't far, but it's too far to run before the storm picks back up. We can jump, but only if we can do it without being seen by the Baselonicans."

"What do you mean feel it out?" I ask her as I slap at periodic drips on my cheeks and forehead.

"When we came here before we had to establish a connection with Baselonica. We left energetic markers in certain locations, a few of them were safe houses. One near the beach, one in the city, and one on the other side near the ridge. I am trying to feel the one near here. It's the one I've been in."

"Oh of course. That makes perfect sense," I lay the sarcasm on thick. "Let me look out there since it doesn't seem like you're feeling much of anything. If that energetic marker was so great, we should have landed there to start with."

It's Eli's turn to be frustrated at me. "It doesn't work like that. It's not like you and Morren with your jumping."

Following in the direction Eli is looking, I see a tower of some kind in the distance. Through the light rain and mist I make out several other buildings.

"How well do you remember this place?" I'm skeptical of what she can really offer.

"Enough to know it isn't very friendly. Before we get to the city, you two need to understand more about Base X and who you're looking for."

"First, we need to hurry up and get somewhere because the rain is starting to come down harder." Morren cuts his eyes at me again, as if to say, "Give it a break."

"Wait. I'm getting it. Let me check for signs of life." Eli pauses and ignores my toe tapping. "It's clear. I'm not picking up any life signs coming from that house."

"Then let's get out of here before this place blows away with us in it," Morren suggests, his voice hurried. He presses his back against the leaning side as the winds outside begin to pick up again.

"You both ready?"

"Once there we can get a better understanding of Base X. It'll help you get back home. Okay, Karana?"

"Fine. Let's go."

Eli looks at both of us and then counts. "Three. Two. One."

Where are you? I call out to Morren.

Nothing.

Morren, where are you?

Inside the house. Where are you?

I don't know. I'm standing in front of door surrounded by a mound of dirt.

That's a house here. Eli responds.

Then I'm outside. Let me in.

Morren opens the metal door that looks odd on the clay-like house. I step into an open room. It's bigger than it looked from the outside. Everything is tinged with red as if it seeped into every fiber of the planet and can't be taken out.

"Didn't you hear me the first time?" I asked him as I scanned the room.

"No. I guess not."

He's probably ignoring me again, like he does when he's irritated or annoyed. We haven't always been able to communicate like this. The first time I heard him in my head we were crossing the country in a last effort to reach Atlanta and the Centers for Disease Control and Prevention. Dad had been a research scientist there and when the epidemic began to spread, he was reassigned to research the disease. He'd hoped there were still some answers there.

The rickety boat we used to cross the Mississippi swayed, and I instinctively reached for Tezzi, managing to yank her from the edge, but tumbled in myself. Morren's voice was muffled, as if speaking through foam, but it was him, telling me to swim up and lift my arms. Dad grabbed my fingers as I thrashed, and I recall saying 'what happened?' in my head while hacking the water from lungs. I know I hadn't spoken through my mouth. I couldn't; but Morren had heard me. This ability has helped us more than I can count since then.

Stools line what must be a living room, and the sight of the kitchen reminds me that we haven't eaten that day. Against a wall is a metal door that I guess is a refrigerator with no noticeable way to open it. The sink is more normal looking. I try to turn the handle, finally figuring out how to get the water going.

"Ugh! It's dirty! The ocean, sure; but how am I supposed to drink this?"

"It's the soil. It won't hurt you," Eli says as she studies the room.

"It's that dingy red dirt. I'm not whatever these people are. I can't drink this. We're gonna freaking die here."

"No, not if you are smart and don't waste time," she admonishes me.

"Wait. How are we supposed to get around this planet without being seen? Without being killed or captured because we're human?"

Eli scans the modest house once more before, beckoning with her long fingers. "Follow me."

She walks down clay steps into another level of the house. In front of her is a bathroom. We walk inside and a light turns on. I jump back.

"Calm down, Karana. It's a light," Morren teases.

"Get back! They're here!" I yell to Morren and Eli.

Three aliens are standing right in front of us.

Morren puts up his hands to fight and the alien in front of him perfectly mirrors him.

"Those aren't aliens. Well, technically, they are. Those aliens are us. We have taken on the form of the planet we're on," Eli whispers.

"Holy crap!" I shriek.

The beings looking back at us are humanoid, but have a redder undertone. Pronounced markings on our faces are intriguing and I touch mine. Instead of markings, I find that they're veins protruding out from our foreheads starting between our brow and going up. Three of them. Our eyes are slightly closer together and smaller.

"How? How did we change?" Morren feels his face with his thick long fingers.

"We see what we want to see, then we see what we are willing to see. Finally, we see what we need to see. You are seeing yourselves as is best for you to see. They will see you as is best for them to see.

"So how do we see ourselves now like an alien?"

"Because at this moment you need to see how you will survive here. It is not by appearing in your human form," Eli explains. "Come now. Let's sit."

We return the way we'd come and land upstairs in the room with the stools. Eli sits first and then I hop onto one of the hard metal surfaces. My mind is reeling and fear is beginning to set in.

"You must find the immune Earthling here. It could be more than one. I don't know if it's a male or female, but you need to do it within three days. Otherwise you risk being consumed by the planet's atmosphere, or found by the leading Zo Clan."

"What? Consumed by the atmosphere?" Morren asks.

"This planet has a very strong pull. It's an angry planet and very tempestuous. Not everyone is consumed. Those who keep to themselves, not drawn into it all, have managed to not be fully consumed."

"Okay. So we go in, find this person or these people, and get out within three days while keeping to ourselves as much as possible," Morren summarizes.

"Yes. Luckily your Earth day and a Baselonica Xuna day are only a one to thirty ratio, approximately. Still, don't waste time."

"Wait! What? That's thirty days to one day. Is that what you mean?" Morren's forehead pulses.

"This is ridiculous. We're gonna lose three months! How are we supposed to find them?" *You see how ridiculous this is, Morren?*

"Whoever this person is must be an Immune like you. You will feel a pull. Follow it." Eli seems in a better mood since getting inside.

"Like it got us here," Morren nods.

"You also need to know there is no guarantee this person will willingly return. If they have been here a while, they may consider Baselonica Xuna home."

"Wait. They could have been here maybe five or six years already?"

"Yes."

"That means in Baselonica time they've been here less than two and a half months?"

"Yes, Karana. They could have already been impacted by the planet, but you won't know until you find them."

"How will we recognize them?"

"Will they look like humans, not Baselonicans?" Morren asks.

"They will appear as they need to appear for you."

"This isn't the time for you to be cryptic, Eli," I shake my head. "We just need to know what we're dealing with."

"Most of the younger people work in the mines. If it's a younger female, she may be employed in other sectors or fulfilling some of the required duties."

I raise my eyebrow.

"The mines are on the other side of the city. Otherwise, the Immune could be anywhere. Let yourself be attracted to the Immune and be pulled there. Unfortunately, the fact that you weren't immediately drawn to them means there is a good chance they have been affected by Baselonica Xuna."

"So we can jump to the other side of the city, find them, and jump out?"

"That's the idea. But remember that this planet has a powerful pull. You'll have to rise above it and not get trapped by it."

"How would we be trapped? We get this Immune and jump out. Simple as that." I glance at Eli and the irritation begins to rise up again. "We don't need your negativity."

"I'm not trying to be negative, Karana. It's not quite that simple. If you somehow fall into the trappings of Baselonica, you won't be able to make the jump off. And remember, when you're talking to anyone here, they call it Base X."

Shaking my head I study Morren's face. His eyes are drawn to my stomach as it makes a loud garbling sound. I don't want to talk to her anymore.

"I want to go home and if this is the only way, let's get started. Every day here is a month Dad and Tezzi are locked in that place of torture."

"There are guards who work for the Zo Clan and who work the mines," Eli tells us.

"We avoid the guards, get the Immune and get out. Got it," Morren slaps his leg and stands.

There's something else Eli isn't telling us.

"They trade with other planets, but don't like uninvited guests here. If they capture you and put you in jail for deportation, you still can't jump from the planet as long as you are being pulled here by the other Immune."

"This is impossible - like we're being set up to fail - to be trapped on a planet that doesn't want us," I protest. Instead of commiserating, Morren ignores me.

"What do we need to know about the people here?" Morren asks in his responsible way.

Eli peers into Morren's eyes and then mine. Her black orbs somehow holding a limitless depth I can't begin to fathom. Before she even speaks a word, I know none of this will be easy. "There are few Baselonicans who will help you out of their generosity. So you will need something to give in return. They value money. They are strong and physical. If you come up against one in a fight, I suggest you get out of their way. Your strength is no match for them. You can tell who has power by their clothing. Those with more money don't associate with those who have less. Money or not, they are vain and it shows in their appearance. They are fit either from labor or from procedures. Don't count on them to believe in anything greater than what they can experience with their five senses."

"Not much different than home, except the fit part," I joke nervously.

"Oh but they do have religion, sort of. They believe they must pay for their sins. If you are found guilty of one of the three sins, you must offer a penance, which is a payment of money to the Zo Clan who will absolve you of the sin. Obviously, the wealthy can sin more."

"We don't have any money."

"We don't know what the three sins are," Morren adds.

"When the Zo Clan overthrew the former leading clan about twenty Base X years ago, they designated three sins. The first is a failure to work. If you don't work, not only do you not eat but you have no money to pay your penance. If you don't work you may end up in an endless loop and held as laborers for the mines to pay off your penance."

"Work. Got it." It's clear to me that it's the most important thing.

"Females must procreate. If by the age of twenty-five Base X years you haven't produced a child, you will be sent for testing. If there is no evidence why you cannot become pregnant, you will be kept for impregnation."

"What? But what if I don't want a kid?"

"It's the law. They must keep the workforce supplied." Eli manages to say this without a hint of emotion in her voice, but her eyes don't hide how she feels.

"We have to get through however long we are here without breaking these laws, Karana. What's the last one, Eli?" Morren says.

"I don't plan on being here long enough for it to matter," I mutter in frustration as I tap my heel against the stool leg.

"The third sin is speaking or acting against the Zo Clan. It carries the most severe penalty. The first infraction is a high penance along with thirty days in their jails. The second offense is life-long penance and depending on the severity of your action, death."

"Death?" I ask, abhorred by the ridiculousness of the punishment. "For saying something bad about their leader?"

"Possibly, yes," Eli answers. She thinks about it a moment. "It does seem severe."

"Wait. You can do anything else? That's it?" Morren asks.

"Those are the three sins under the Zo Clan's rules. According to them, the punishment for failure to pay penance continues even after death, for eternity" Eli answers.

"I guess in the grand scheme of a universe of laws, those three are pretty simple ones. They may be dark, crazy, and scary, but at least there are only three," I say, feeling a little better.

"There are still civil transgressions. You shouldn't steal or kill anyone, but those are minor offenses compared to the three I mentioned. Oh, and don't get caught as an illegal alien – which we are."

"Yeah, you mentioned that," Morren says.

"I must return to Earth to prepare the place for the Immunes. Let us look through the window so I can show you which way you'll go. I suggest you hold hands when you jump so you are certain to land in the same spot next time."

We stand up and walk to an oblong window. The storm is finally passing, and the sky is clearer, like when we came.

"Over there is the city. On the other side are the mines. There are guard posts set up, and if they see you they may ask for identification. You don't have any, so don't let them see you."

"How will we speak to them?"

"Your words will be their words and you will understand them."

"Where on the other side are we going?" Morren asks.

"There are two main mines on that side. They both mine clay for minerals and building but one is the free mine, and the other is not."

"What do you mean?" I ask.

"One mine is worked by people who are free and aren't working off their penance debt. The other mine has the penance workers."

"Which one will the Immune be in?"

"I don't know for sure. If they were able to get identification they will be free. If they aren't there, they'll be in the penance mine."

"What if they aren't working now?"

"Then they'd be in the city where most people live." Eli begins to move about. She seems antsy.

"Are you leaving now?" Morren already knows the answer, just like I do.

"I am. Immediately after you jump, I will return to Earth."

"What if we need you?"

"We have a connection. Should you need me, call on me. Once you have this Immune, leave. Don't wait around, no matter how tempting."

"I don't think we have to worry about being tempted," I snort back. "By the way, who thought of this idea for saving our people? Was it your people?"

"When a planet, a system has fallen out of alignment, out of order, the only thing you can do is restore balance. You have to figure out what's wrong and fix it. Earth is a failing system."

"It was fine until you got there," I remind her.

"Not necessarily. Your people were already poisoned by something no one could see, and it was festering. The biochemical introduced only gave a physical reality to what already was. It destroyed humanity as you understood it on Earth, but people like you can start new. Better."

"Who says it'll be better? Everyone is dead or dying…or used in experiments. How do we bring our planet back with some aliens and what, a few Immunes?"

"You can. There are enough Immunes to start again," Eli says reassuringly.

"Oh, great. Kill all our people and then give us the burden of repopulating humanity."

"Be quiet, Karana. We can't waste time. Every hour is precious," Morren says.

He's handling this better than I am. I try to ignore the veins that seem to pulse in his forehead as I notice them pulsing in my own.

"You need to try to remain calm on Base X. It invites anger and fear and then feeds on it," Eli informs us.

But I'm not thinking about being calm. I'm thinking about Tezzi and Dad. Being here for one day or three days means that much more time that they can be tortured. It's extra time for the monsters back home to hurt them, maybe even kill them so they can find out what's in our blood. Morren looks at me knowingly.

A tear falls down my cheek. "They're gonna use Tezzi to try and save the few wretches still left in the human population."

Morren looks off toward the city. He'd always felt like he needed to protect her. The storm lightens and I know we must prepare to go. I'm scared for what is out there. For everything Eli has warned us about. Scared of losing myself and never getting home again.

"When you make your jump from this atmosphere, let me know. Then I can meet you in the place you land, wherever it is. I have been connected to you."

Suddenly I don't want her to go.

"What are your people called, Eli? I mean what do you call yourselves?"

I am an Eliatar. This is why you may call me Eli. My home planet was Eliata Setaraus in the fourth star system. It is no more."

"What happened to it?"

Her tentacles flag and she averts her eyes to find something else to rest her gaze on besides us. "Late in our planet's life two groups formed. There were different ideas about how we could continue to meet the energy needs. In short, we blew our planet up. The reactor that was supposed to harness energy from Eliata's core overreacted and those of us who'd been able to escape did. We'd been searching for a home since then, until we landed on Earth."

"So you destroyed your planet and then came to Earth and destroyed our planet?" I couldn't help myself. I kept my eyes on Eli as Morren glared at me.

"It isn't like that." It was the first time she seemed to sound truly defensive.

"It is exactly like that," I argue.

"Those of us who escaped on that ship were against the core reactor program. We were greatly outnumbered. There were less than three hundred of us altogether. We saw it coming. We tried to tell them the risks. In the end, we barely made it out."

"I'm sorry, Eli," Morren says.

"That sucks." I almost feel bad for her. "But you still brought your problems to Earth and made them ours."

Morren looks embarrassed as he turns to me. "We gotta go, Karana."

I look once more at Eli. I don't hate her, but I'm certain that I still don't like her either.

"Okay." I try not to let my fear of what waited for us get to me. "Let's jump. Hold my hand." Morren's fingers grip mine. "Three. Two. One."

Chapter Six

I spit the clay dirt out of my mouth as Morren and I roll down the side of a hill. When we finally come to a stop, I look around. I don't see anyone.

"I think we're safe. Do you see anything?" I whisper.

His eyes meet mine. *Are you really talking out loud at a time like this?*

I suddenly feel stupid. Someone is nearby. We move to the low bushes near the bottom of the hill. It's a kid carrying a bucket of dirt.

Follow him, I say, careful not to blow our cover by talking out loud, again.

Once the boy is ahead of us, we begin to move slowly. He's our best chance for finding the mines. He vanishes around the corner of a square building made of red clay bricks. Morren and I begin to follow, but the voices coming from the other side send us scrambling to the ground.

"How's your mona? She's six months full with your son now, right?" one of the guards says.

"She's healthy. Strong. Next month our son will be here. Didn't take her long either. We'll be right back at it for the next one soon."

"Good thing. We need more boys."

"What about your mona? Is she going to procreate? You've been partnered for more than three years already."

"It's hard to believe that much time has passed since she became my mona. We go for testing again if she isn't by next month. She'll be twenty-five."

I look at Morren in shock. Eli wasn't lying.

Morren looks at me with a hint of frustration. *We're gonna have to get around some other way. These two are just walking back and forth like they've got nothing better to do.*

Let's jump to the other side of the building. Together. Three. Two.

Come on. Stay close to the wall, Morren sends.

I hear people. I try to determine where they might be.

The low hum of a song doesn't get past me. The song is lively, but what I can understand from the words saddens me.

This is the penance mine. I'm certain.

Then we need to find the regular one.

Look over there. On the other side of that ridge. It looks like another building. Same as this one.

Worth a shot, he agrees.

We jump again, landing on the side of the wall. I wish we could jump like this back home, but these are mini-jumps in the same area, places holding similar vibrations and frequencies and visible. Where I want to go, home, is out of reach because of two people whose pull is stronger than my sister's, my dad's, or Earth's.

We crouch our backs against the wall. It's quieter than the other mine. We creep to the front of the building and I peek around the side to report.

One guard. He's sitting and reading some muscle magazine. He's on our side of the door. Let's go to the other side.

Once there, we can see around the corner to the front.

Wait. We don't have any identification and we don't work. How are we gonna get inside?

You're so smart, Morren. We gotta jump inside.

We can't go jumping in there unprepared! We have no idea who or what's in there. There could be guards at the front door - security.

We can wait until they come out for the day, I half-joke.

Good idea. We'll wait.

Fine, I sigh.

My mind wanders back to my stomach. Eventually, we will have to eat. Dirty water wasn't going to be enough.

Do you think we'll recognize them? Morren asks.

I hope so. I hope they look like us. I mean human us, not Base X us. Maybe they'll see us as humans and not Baselonicans.

What if the Immune isn't in the free work area but in the penance mine? I wonder.

We'll find out when they leave here. I'm not going into the penance mine unless we absolutely have to.

We sit on the side of the building for what feels like three or four hours waiting for their work day to end. The deep sound, like a gong, cuts the quiet. It rings out three times and then we hear them. They're finally leaving.

Come on. We need to blend in. I stand and grab Morren to come along.

As the crowds of people leaving the mine spread out, we begin walking alongside them. Some head up the steps to the street, and others to a covered area where what looks like a large bus waits. Morren and I scan the crowds as quickly as we can for any sight of a human.

I think I see them! Morren sends me, the excitement coming through strong.

Them? As in more than one?

Yeah. Two of them. Boy and girl. I can't tell if they're related.

I look where Morren is looking and spy them too.

Yeah. That's them. Come on, let's catch that bus.

We get in line with the others boarding the bus. I try to make eye contact with the girl who sits by the window. The boy is sitting beside her. The girl looks at me, her eyes wide for a moment before she leans over slightly and whispers something. I'm hopeful it means she recognizes that I'm human.

I step up on the bus behind Morren. There aren't any more seats, but that doesn't matter. The two people we need are on the bus. All we need to do is get them and get gone.

Morren begins walking down the aisle.

"Hey, you need to scan in," the driver calls back.

I panic. Scan what, I think.

Morren walks back slowly and glances at the Immunes.

"First finger right there."

Morren puts his thumb on the scanner.

"Your other first finger," the driver says impatiently.

Morren looks at the driver confused and then puts his pinky on the scanner.

"Try it again."

Morren looks at me and puts his pinky down once more.

"Nothing's coming up. Why aren't you coming up?" he asks with unmasked irritation.

"Not sure. I scratched up my fingers today. Maybe that's it."

"Get it checked out. I don't give handouts. You want to ride you need to pay. Get off the bus."

"I need to see someone on the bus real quick," Morren says.

"I don't care. See them when you can pay for your ride. I'm not a charity. You're holding up my line."

"We gotta go. Come on." Morren turns and he and I step back off the bus.

We watch as the driver closes the doors and waits for the last couple of people to sit.

"We'll have to follow this bus and see where it goes. We need some kind of money. Otherwise we aren't gonna be able to do anything here," I say.

"Let's hope we don't need to do anything. We'll follow this bus, get the Immunes, and jump out of this place."

The bus begins to pull off from the shelter and Morren and I follow it with our eyes. The only people around are down at the building, by the door.

"If we're gonna do this, we gotta go now," I whisper.

Morren knows what I'm talking about. We go to the other side of the shelter, our eyes still on the bus.

Three. Two. One, we say together.

"Oh shhhhhh!"

I catch myself as I nearly fall onto the boy's lap.

He looks at me, shocked, and pushes me off before looking around at everyone staring at us. The fear in his eyes is undeniable.

"You shouldn't be here. You shouldn't be here," he says angrily near my head.

"We gotta go. We gotta take you back home, now, before anyone stops us," I whisper back quickly.

"Hey, what are you two doing on here? You sneaking on the bus without paying?" the driver yells back.

"Eton, we can't go with them. We'll get in trouble." The girl beside him avoids looking at us as she gives her warning. She keeps her voice low, but I still hear it trembling.

"No. It's okay. We're going back home." They are probably as shocked as we are.

"Hey! Did you hear me? I don't remember getting any payment up here from either of you! Soon as I find a place to pull over, you're off. And you better believe you'll be detained," the driver yells back to us again.

"We know what you mean. He's stopping the bus and what do you think he's gonna do to you? To us?" Eton asks.

Eton is still avoiding looking at me directly. Instead, he is trying to avoid any association with us, speaking to me while looking out the window. I don't blame him. If we don't leave soon, we'll be arrested and given how things are going, we'd take them down with us.

They don't want to go with us, I send to Morren.

They don't have a choice.

"We're not going anywhere, Reyn. We're safe here." I can't believe Eton is saying this. Has he been brainwashed already?

What are we gonna do? How are we gonna get them to go, if they don't want to?

Morren studies Reyn and Eton. Reyn stares straight ahead to avoid looking at me. The bus is stopping now. We are nearly out of time. Morren is behind me and everyone is watching our every move.

They're coming with us. Like I said, they don't have a choice.

Hurry up, Morren. I'll reach over and get Reyn, you get Eton. Three. Two.

Chapter Seven

It's dark and damp. Whatever planet we landed on still reminds me of Baselonica Xuna. Ugh. But we did it.

Karana? You there?

Yeah. Right here. I can't see you.

I'm in the cell next to you.

What?

What did he mean by cell? We should've leaped out of here. We'd done what we came to do.

They got us, Karana.

Who? What do you mean? Where are we?

They're coming back. The guards.

I panic. Had we put ourselves back on Earth by mistake? I try to remember if we had successfully jumped. If not, where were we? If so, how'd we wind up back in the testing compound?

"Get the boy. He's been awake longer," the gruff voice of a man called out through the shadows. I hear the clinking of keys, and then high-pitched screeching of metal across the hard floors. My eyes begin to adjust to the dim light that dangles from the ceiling. This isn't Earth, at least no part I'd seen.

How long had I been out?

Where are they taking you, Morren? I send out, hoping he'd hear me.

I don't know. Don't talk. Don't say anything to anyone.

I wonder if Eli is anywhere around. Does she know what happened? That we'd been captured? That we'd failed.

Did you try to tell Eli what happened?

Silence.

Morren?

Morren?

"Morren!" I scream out.

He still doesn't answer.

"Where are you taking him?" I yell into the darkness.

I hear snickering coming from the direction they'd disappeared.

"So…what did you do?" the sound of a young woman comes from somewhere close by.

I ignore her. We don't know these people and any of them could be the reason we're here. We can't leave without Reyn and Eton, so wherever we are, we have to get out.

"I've been in here three days now. I'm waiting for a transfer."

Despite my curiosity, I'm not taking the bait.

"Yeah, then I'll be outta here and on to a whole new life, working my magic somewhere else."

My curiosity has me biting the tip of my tongue. Don't say anything to anyone, I remind myself.

"I know you're over there. I saw you when they brought you in. They said you weren't registered. A female and not registered. Whew! I'm not sure how you pulled that one off. Especially since you look old enough to be a mona. How'd you manage for no one to claim you for their partner? Be careful. If you don't become a mona or a pola and they'll have you readied for the institute."

I hum inside my head trying to drown her out. If what she said is true, this might be my way out. I am unregistered and there isn't anything I can do about that. But I'm also a female, and maybe I can use that to my advantage.

"My name's Willa. Twenty-one years young and I'm off this base today, tomorrow at the latest. I'm not gonna be their baby-making machine, I made sure of that."

"Would you shut up?!" I couldn't resist it anymore and immediately regret it.

Willa laughs. "What'd I say?"

"I don't wanna talk to you, okay?"

"Why not? You already are. So, what's your name?"

"I said, I'm not talking to you."

"Your loss. So, like I was saying, I'm outta here in one more day, max. Waiting for my transfer. I can't make babies and since I made sure I can't, I'm like a criminal. Now I have two choices. The penance for breaking that law is higher than I'll make in two lifetimes, and since I don't have a sponsor that's why I only have two choices. One is the prison labor camp or what they call the penance camp. The other is to be rented out to other planets. At least I can be almost free and use my fricking brain and other skills."

"What?" I blurt out before I can catch myself.

"I got a pretty good deal. I am going to work in a factory, and I get to keep half my earnings. Base X keeps the rest. It's like a freedom tax. Whatever. I don't have to be here anymore."

"That doesn't make any sense. Why would they bother sending you somewhere else to work and only take half, when they could keep you here and have it all?"

"Look, that's what they tell me. That's what they do to those of us who did what I did."

"And you believe them?"

"Why wouldn't I? No one's ever told me different."

Stupidly optimistic, I think. These people are crazy.

I can hear the clopping of footsteps outside the cell again. They're back. A large figure towers in front of the bars. He shines a light down at his clipboard and then walks down to another cell.

"Willa Zouxia?" he says.

"Yep. Right here. Is my transfer ready?"

"Yup. All set. You can come with me."

I hear the grating of metal on the concrete floor again as he opens her cell.

They walk the other way, their footsteps fading but I can still hear Willa for a while before she's gone.

I don't know how long I sit in the cell waiting for someone. I can't leave and I can't hear Morren. I have no idea whether it's day or night, but as soon as Morren is back, we're getting out the same way Willa left.

"You're a pretty valuable commodity, aren't you? An unregistered female, young, pretty. I bet someone got a good reward for you. You'll make some nice offspring, and they won't even have to make you a mona. Wish I would've found you."

The creepy voice came from somewhere down the hall. I ignore him as he starts tapping something hard against the metal bars of his cell.

"They've got a real special plan for you."

I was listening now, though I still refused to speak. I needed to get out of here. I needed to find my brother. I needed to get off of Baselonica Xuna.

Loud laughter echoes off the walls and cells as several boots hit the ground.

"We got ourselves a wild one. You shoulda seen her fighting before we tranqued her up."

"She won't be fighting long once we get her all settled into her new home," another man laughs.

"Come on, let's get her up there to finish processing her. Keep her separate from the boy we brought up. They got some kind a way of communicating I don't get."

A man with wild red hair spiked into three separate sections like a triceratops stands in front of the cell. His reddish-brown leather uniform is different from the others, and he smells like the clay that they are famous for.

"Stand for Chapis Kun Zo," the other man said.

He was the same man who'd taken Morren.

"The Chapis wanted to come see you personally, before accepting you."

"Where's my brother?" I shout.

"I said stand for Chapis Kun Zo." The man yells and bangs a long metal stick on the bar. I take a step back from the bars and glare at him. He turns to the other man and chuckles, "Told you she was a wild one."

"I like them wild. More fun to tame them. Yeah, I might like this one for myself. Take her up for processing, get her cleaned up, and then I want to see her."

"Do you want me to make her stand for you first, Chapis Zo?"

"No. That's fine. There'll be time for training her."

"Where's my brother?" I ask again, ignoring the comments.

"He's fine. He'll stay fine as long as you don't cause any problems."

Damn.

Eli? Eli, we need help here, I try to send out to wherever she was. I hope she's already back on Base X.

"You bite me again and I'll tranq you again, hear me? And this time, I'll make sure it hurts and you'll lose a full day, not just a few hours."

I lift my middle finger at him and he looks confused. Ugh. I don't remember biting him before, but maybe that was the problem. They'd made me lose that time. I had to reason the bus driver had gotten to us before we could count down. Reyn and Eton are still out there, and hopefully Morren is in this complex somewhere.

Chapis Zo hurriedly walks back the way they came, leaving me with the large brute. He pushes me in front of him as we move down the hall. I call out to Morren, repeatedly.

There is no answer. Something about this place has blocked me from communicating with him.

"Where is my brother?"

"Don't worry about him. Worry about yourself."

"Is he really okay? Is he hurt?"

"Why do you care so much? You're okay, aren't you?"

I look back at him, confounded by his question.

Chapter Eight

Streams of light cross my face as we climb the stairs. I glance through the glass pane on the door that leads to the stairwell. It looks like a lobby, and nothing like the dim and dank dungeon they'd brought me from.

He leads me up another flight of stairs before pulling the door open and shoving me through. It's bright. Large, circular, flat lights line the ceiling. The windows are set high up. The sky looks the same reddish color it had when we arrived. Another storm is probably brewing.

I narrow my eyes as I search for Morren.

"You can stop looking. Your brother isn't here."

A woman in a white pair of pants and jacket walks over to me and shines a bright light into each of my eyes.

"Age?" she asks.

I don't answer. I look at her crisp clothing labeled with the name Goede. The letters are strange to me, but somehow that's how I read it. *We see what we want to see.*

"Your age?" she asks again, looking at me directly this time.

"Seventeen."

"Hmmm. And why aren't you registered?"

"I don't know."

"You're seventeen and don't know why you aren't registered?" she asks, as if she doesn't believe me.

"Are your parents illegals?"

"I..I..I don't know," I stammer.

Eli warned us about how they don't like outsiders and we'd gone and gotten caught.

"Come with me. We have to get you cleaned up. Lucky for you we found you in Base City. Chapis Kun Zo has taken a particular interest in you. You said you're seventeen, correct?"

"Yes."

"Are you unregistered because you were shown to be incapable of basic processing skills?"

"What?" I was confused by her question.

"Uh huh. Hmmm." Goede taps something on the screen before she leads to a back room with a shower. She turns it on and closes the door.

"Get undressed."

"Pardon me?"

"I said get undressed. You don't have much time. The Chapis wants to see you soon and you need to be ready."

"I don't want to see the Chapis. I want to see my brother."

"You won't get to see your brother if you don't see the Chapis. Understand?"

"No. Why do I have to see the Chapis? Where is my brother?"

"Your brother is being held by the Zo Clan right now. They have found him particularly interesting. They have found you interesting as well. It's highly unusual to find two unregistered people of your age, at the same time. They want to keep a close eye on both of you, to make sure you aren't a threat."

"We're not. We don't want to bother anyone."

"Get undressed. Wash up and put this on. It should fit."

She doesn't look any older than my mother was when she was killed. But there was a quiet resignation in her eyes.

"Are you a mona?" I ask as I slide off the scratchy pants.

"Of course. We must all do our part."

"Are you a mother?"

"No. But not for lack of effort. You will do your part now. You will not be a mona, but you can still contribute by either procreating or providing pleasure."

I look at her to see if she is as serious as she sounds. There isn't a hint that she's laughing anywhere – inside or out. A procreator? Pleasure? Here? That is not my plan.

"Can you turn around please?" I prepare to take off the last bits of clothing.

"No. Get used to not having any privacy. You don't belong to you. You belong to Baselonica Xuna and I act on behalf of Baselonica Xuna. Your water is comfortable now. Wash."

I slip out of the remainder of my clothes and let them fall to the floor before stepping backwards into the shower. The cold water shocks my body and I tense up. The water running down my face masks my tears. These assholes are not gonna get away with this. I'll jump a damn bomb back to them and blow up this whole place.

Don't do that. I hear Morren say in my head.

Morren!? Where are you?

I'm at a place they call Baseland. I'm with the Zo Clan. Don't mess with them, Karana. They don't know the meaning of mercy. They only understand money. Please, stay alive. We'll get out together, Morren tries to assure me.

How'd you get through to me? I've been trying to talk to you for who knows how long?

I'm not sure. I finally heard you. Where are you? Morren asks.

I'm where they brought us after they captured us. They're taking me to Chapis Kun Zo. I think the same place you are. Morren, I think they want to make me into some kinda baby maker slave or something.

We gotta get outta here. I have a plan to escape once they bring you here.

Last time you made an escape plan, it brought us here. I didn't bother trying to hide my displeasure at our predicament.

I know. But you gotta trust me. I've been studying them for the past day since you've been in there.

It's been a day since they took you? We were losing more time than I'd thought. *We need to do something fast, Morren.*

Yeah and yeah.

"That's enough. You're the slowest washing person ever. Turn the water off," Goede orders as she steps forward with a worn towel.

I have to get out the shower. I guess I'll be there pretty soon. Let's keep talking, Morren. Please.

She hands me the towel and reaches over to turn the water off.

I will. Remember to stay..., Morren's voice in my head fades to nothing as the last of the water trickles down around my feet.

"These clothes are desirable for Chapis Kun Zo. It is of utmost importance that you do whatever you must to please him. For your sake and your brother's sake."

I look at Goede again. There's something odd about her.

"How are you able to be here? You didn't procreate."

For a moment she goes somewhere else, remembering something perhaps, but it doesn't last. Instead, her words are quick. "I have a special exemption. There are things I am able to do that are considered highly valuable. Now come. We can't keep him waiting."

I put on the silky crop top that is a poor excuse for a bra. The silk boxers are acceptable but only until I realize what I must wear over them. The leather bustier barely contains my averageness and the high-waisted leather skirt in the same color as the Chapis' uniform, doesn't allow me to bend over to put on the ridiculous thigh-high thick-soled boots reminding me of a go-go girl from my grandmother's days. The print on the top and skirt I remember seeing elsewhere. An O with a Z crossing over it.

"What do these markings mean?"

"Whoever wears items with these markings belong to the Zo Clan."

"You mean are members of the Zo Clan?"

"No. I mean owned by them."

Chapter Nine

The movement of the vehicle I'm in jostles me awake. I don't remember getting into the ride, but I know where we're headed. Goede sits beside me. I can tell she's nervous. She turns her head to look at me as I sit up.

"We'll be there soon."

"What's gonna happen to me?"

"The Chapis will give you an audition to determine if you will join his pola team. If he decides to keep you, you will remain at Baseland. If he decides not to keep you, one of his council or staff will have an opportunity to claim you for a fee. If that doesn't happen, you'll be sent to the Institute to serve in procreation. Everyone works here, no exceptions," Goede answers, avoiding my eyes.

I shake my head in disbelief. This can't be real. I was going to be taken to a man to be a part of his harem, sold off to one of his minions, or forced to have babies. There had to be a way out of this.

The driver pulls through high, iron gates that twist up like vines and end in pointed stakes. They are painted red like the Baselonican clay that forms the walls of the building. The windows are long, narrow slits that stretch from the bottom of the building up the side, at least four stories.

The car stops abruptly in front of a beautiful formed statue made of a black material with specks of red dirt. The fountain around it sprays up before cascading down and around the figures. As I try to see the full statue, I draw back. The figures aren't embracing. She is being held tight around her chest, her hair securely in the man's hand, her hand stretching out. *Who in the heck puts a statue like that in a place like this?*

The driver opens up my door and the guard who'd brought me to Goede comes over. Above the building the sky is darker. I can hear the sound of thunder rolling. It is strange, as it seems to be centered above Baseland.

"I'm going to let you out of the restraints. Try anything, and I mean anything, and you'll wish I let you rot in that cell. Got it little girl?"

My saliva lands on his chin and slowly drips to the ground. He wipes it with his hand, turns the same hand back, and slaps it hard against my cheek. I stumble, landing against the side of the vehicle. Eli was right. They are strong.

"Stop. We cannot have her marked. The Chapis wouldn't like that," Goede calls from the other side of the car.

"You're lucky. You good for one thing and nothing else unregistered pola-wannabe."

Baseland looms in front of me like a tall tomb. I am afraid if I enter, I may not come out again. I wince at the sting I still feel on my cheek from the brute's strong hand. It was still worth it.

"Come on." Goede walks toward the building, intentionally staying between me and the brute.

I trudge slowly in the skimpy outfit as the guards reach their hands toward me.

"Nice. She'll make a good pola girl. If the Chapis doesn't want her, maybe I'll toss my bid in."

"Screw you!" I snarl.

"I hope so! I like'em feisty," the guard holding the door says as I walk through.

"No touching. The Chapis has first rights," Goede says defensively.

Can you hear me, Morren? I send out in desperation.

Again, there is no answer.

The room we enter feels like a night club more than a place of official business. Music plays from a corner and tables fill the floor. Loud talking and yelling fill in the gaps between the music being played by a band in the corner. Men sit around tables, holding strange purple colored drinks served by women walking around in less than I have on.

"This is the meeting room. Officials and business men use this space to meet comfortably and safely."

I begin to take a step forward into the room.

"Watch your head," Goede says.

A woman flies by on purple silken sheets suspended from the ceiling. She twists in the air before landing on a platform on the other side.

I hear the sound of a table crashing to the floor, and then laughter from others nearby. One man is pummeling another and yelling about being cheated out of a deal.

In the corners are tall cage-like boxes. Women dance slowly between the bars, covered only by two sheer strips of fabric tied around the cage. I've gotta get out of here.

Morren! I yell inside my head.

Morren!!!!

Damn. He can't hear me.

"Come this way, through these doors," Goede instructs.

She pushes the door and lets me go through. Brute walks closely behind her. There is too much to take in. I try to see the doorways and windows, but they are few and far between.

"When we walk into the next room, Chapis Zo will be waiting for you. You must audition. If you don't audition for him, you'll have to audition for one of his lower men or risk the punishment for being unregistered and unable to pay for your crimes.

"Wait! I can pay? You never said that."

"Well, others can pay. But you…you have no money. No credentials. No registration. For all purposes, you don't exist. So, no, you can't pay."

"But I can be punished?"

"You can be punished. Yes. And you have the option of earning your life."

"As a pola? I'm not free as a pola."

"You can be a pola or you can go to the Institute. At least as a pola, you know you exist."

"I'm sorry. I didn't do well in history. Has it always been like this?"

71

"Since I was a girl. When the Zo Clan took over, many things changed. My own mother remembers when things were – different. But we must do what we must, mustn't we?"

"And everyone is okay with this?"

Goede looks back at the towering brute behind me and her lips become tight.

"Enough questions. When you complete your audition, the Chapis will decide immediately what your status is. If he chooses not to keep you as his own, he will call me in to prepare you for the bidding. The bidding wouldn't take place until tomorrow evening to allow for all eligible men to have an opportunity to win you. Do you understand?"

I nod my head. I think I understood.

"Can I use the restroom before I go in there, please? I really need to wash my hands."

Brute grunts. "You're clean enough. He doesn't care about your hands."

"Let the girl wash her hands. If it makes her feel better, she'll do better," Goede says. "I'll take her."

Goede leads me to a door down the hall and pushes it in. Inside, scantily clad girls lean against the wall. Their eyes are empty, despite the heavy make-up on their faces.

"You the new pick, eh?" A pretty girl with big brown curly hair asks as she looks at my reflection in the mirror.

"I guess."

"I used to be, but then I got old," she says.

Her eyes show no sadness. She couldn't have been more than a few years older than me. I look around at the other girls in the bathroom. A hard knock sounds on the door.

"Time to get back out here. We aren't paying you to hold up bathroom walls," a woman says pushing in the door.

I turn back to the mirror and glance at Goede who watches me nervously. She doesn't fit in here with her stark white clothes and pinned up hair. She's uncomfortable and anxious. One by one, the girls file out of the bathroom, leaving me alone with Goede.

"You don't have to send me in there, Goede."

"I don't have a choice. Wash your hands and wipe the streaks from under your eye."

I look in the mirror. I must've been crying. Perhaps I didn't even know I'd been when I was unconscious back in the car. I turn on the water and slide my hands under. It's cool beneath my fingers.

Karana, Morren's voice comes through.

I glance at the mirror, eyes wide and hope Goede doesn't suspect anything.

I'm here, Morren.

Where? Where've you been?

I'm here. I'm at Baseland. I'm in a bathroom near that meeting party room. I'm scared. They're about to send me in with Chapis Zo. I can't do it, Morren. I can't.

Okay. I told you I had a plan. I do. Trust me. In the hallway near his suite is an emergency alarm. It shuts the main lights off and turns on emergency lights. An alarm will sound. Get to an exterior door as fast as you can. Firewalls come down to block off main sections. Do you hear me, Karana?

Yes. I hear you. Where will you be? How will I find you?

I'm on the third floor. There is a chute for garbage that leads outside. Get outside and to the garbage area. I don't know where that is, but find it.

Okay. Then we're gonna jump outta this sick place, I tell Morren.

No. We can't. We still have to find Eton and Reyn.

"I think your hands are clean enough, I said," Goede says firmly.

"What? Oh!" I was still scrubbing my hands and hadn't realized it.

I gotta go. I'll find you. I say we skip Eton and Reyn. They don't want us to get them anyway. We have to get outta here.

Goede walks over and shuts the water off.

"Enough time-wasting."

Morren?

Morren?

He's gone again.

Goede holds the door open as I walk back through and down the hall. Brute stands at the end, his arms crossed and the lines on his head pronounced. I scan the walls looking for the emergency pull Morren mentioned. The reddish-purple walls have a small break ahead. It's a nook on the right. I know once I pass the nook, I'll see the hall with one side leading to Chapis Zo, and the other side to my escape.

Brute stands between me and my only path toward the outside of the building. Crap. My breathing changes as Goede and I walk down the hall. I'm keeping to the right, where the pull is.

We near the pull for the emergency alarm and I reach my hand out quickly, yanking it down as hard as I can.

"What are you doing, you stupid girl?" yells Brute.

The emergency lights switch on. He charges toward me as Goede steps back at the sound of the alarm. There's no way I can get around him in that hallway. He's too big. I look back at Goede. She's looking at me now, wondering like I am, exactly what I'm going to do.

Brute's lumbering body clamors toward me and I don't run. I stand in the position my father taught me. If you can't run you better be able to fight, he'd told me. Brute stretches his arms out to grab me. One big-soled, thigh-high boot leaves the ground and lands in his crotch. He buckles, falling to the ground in pain. They aren't that anatomically different than us after all.

His large, writhing body blocks the hallway with his hands protecting his already injured parts from further assault. I kick him once again in his ribs. I start to go, but put my asinine boots to his ribs once more before jumping on him and over, running. Goede stands there, watching, her mouth agape.

Chapter Ten

I run the length of the hallway and back toward the meeting party room. I remember the doors on the side. I can't go back through the front where the guards would remember me.

I run alongside the other Baselonicans to the side door and join the stream leaving the building. I keep running, this time slower, trying not to draw attention to myself. I wonder where the garbage is.

I move along the side of the building I came out and then creep along the other side. Nothing. I hear the sound of a thud from around the corner and step back as I get low to the wall. What I wouldn't give for my pants.

Morren?

I peak around the corner looking for the source of the noise amidst the chaos. *Give me a break!* He's there. The spiked hair. The red leather uniform. In the light, I can see him better.

His brow connects in one long, red row across his veiny forehead. He's angry and yelling.

"Where is he? Find him dammit. And find her too!"

Chapis Zo's men spread out, searching the people standing around that side of the building. It's impossible to sneak around the corner now. *They're looking for me. They're looking for me*, I repeat to myself. *If he thinks I did this and he catches me, he'll probably send me to the Institute.*

Morren! I cry out once more.

Nothing. I risk looking around the corner once more, safely on my knees.

"Oh, baby. I like that position." A man with green hair he'd slicked into a low pony-tail puts his large palm on my rear. "You a mona or you tryin' to be a pola? I need a pola like you."

"I'm neither, sick bastard." I jump to my feet and look him in his blood-shot pupils.

"You don't talk to me like that, girl. Who do you think you are?"

I try to ease around the corner now that Chapis Zo and his men are dispersing. I need to find Morren and get off this planet, fast. The man reaches toward me again, tugging at the small skirt that skims at the top of my thighs.

"I didn't mean it like that. You just make it so I can't help it." He smiles confidently and tries once more to put his hand in places he shouldn't.

"And you think I'm the weak one. You lose your mind and all control over a skirt. Pathetic!"

He backs off a few inches after the seething response and my glare. Others are coming around this side now too and I can't cause a scene.

"You're taking me all wrong. I'm not weak. Your pull is just so strong." He's still trying, but with a softer approach.

With as obvious an eye roll as I can muster with these strange muscles in my face, I look back at him. "I know exactly how you meant it. But right now, I have to go and find someone, you know with all this going on." I paste a tight smile on and leave everything else I want to say to myself. If he wanted to do anything in this crazy planet, I couldn't stop him. And I needed to get out of here alive and as in tact as possible.

"Stupid. You're not worth my time anyway," he says and walks in the other direction.

The pretty curly-haired girl from the restroom is running toward me waving her hand. I look behind me but realize she must be trying to get my attention.

"Wait. Wait. I gotta message for you," she says. In my head I've nicknamed her Curly.

"A message? From who?"

"Says he's your brother. Not like any of the men around here," she smiles.

"What'd he say?"

"He said he'll meet you back where you started out on Base X. Too many eyes here." She finishes and then asks, "What's he mean?"

"I know what he means."

"Can I come?" Her big brown eyes change in that moment, and I can see a hint of life.

"I don't know if I can take you. They'll be looking for me. They'll be looking for you."

"What else can happen to me that hasn't already? We get outta here, we can leave Base City for someplace safer."

"Like where? Never mind. I can't take you with me."

"I know you're different. I can tell. I don't know what it is, but you have to help me. You have to help us."

"Us?"

"You were brave enough to break out. I knew it was you. I've been working here since I reached the age of change."

"Change?"

"You know, when I truly became a woman. They'll keep me here until no one desires me anymore. After that they have no use for me. That's what happens to all of us."

I look at her and the other girls who've gathered around. I've never done a jump with more than two people. I finally had an agreed on destination to meet Morren and now she was asking me to take her too. But if I took one, I'd have to take all of them. And there were four others standing around us.

"Will you help us?"

"For the love of god why haven't you all gotten out of here before? All these years, what've you been waiting on?"

"We didn't know we could. No one has ever gone against the Zo before."

I roll my eyes and think of Goede. It was all they'd ever known.

"I don't know if I can do it with this many people. I never have before. And I'll be honest. I can't make any promises. I'm here for a reason and I gotta go soon. What you're asking could get all of you killed or sent to the Institute from what I hear."

"Or we could go with you," Curly says.

"I'll try to get you out of Baseland but that's all I can promise. You can figure it out from there. Everyone gather around me. Hold onto each other. This might get bumpy."

"There she is! What are you waiting for, you cretons! Get all of them!" Chapis Zo yells. "Don't you let that girl get away!"

"Three. Two."

Chapter Eleven

"One," I pant quickly, my eyes closed. I open them. *Crap!*

"I said get'em!" the Chapis yells again.

I open my eyes and run toward the way I came in. The fountain is straight ahead. I see something peeking from around the backside of the fountain. Could it be? Tentacles?

The sound of a gun goes off and hits the statue. I dive down, but there are only two of the girls with me now. The others have scattered.

"I said get them, don't kill them! They're worth too much alive. I can't use'em or sell'em if they're dead, you idiot!"

"Yes, Chapis."

"Now, put some tranq bullets in there and shoot them in their pretty little behinds."

"We lost Rache and Les!" Curly calls to me.

"We gotta get behind something quick!" There's only two who haven't run off and I'm hopeful we can get out of here.

The statue!" Curly points to a figure several yards away and then takes off.

It's where I thought I'd seen tentacles, but it's a risk to try to cover that much distance without ending up with a bullet in our butts.

The guard is fumbling with his gun. I mutter a 'thank you'. He must be out of bullets.

"Go. Now!" I yell to the other two girls. "We better run while we have the chance."

I dive into the fountain to escape the shot he fires. No one's behind me. *Where'd they go? Crap?*

It is her. Eli. I grab one of her hands, squeezing it and feeling her pulse in my body. I can't get my fingers to loosen their grip.

"Where've you been?"

"I've been trying to get closer but when I figured out where you were, the place was in chaos."

I look at her, a mix of relief and anger rising up. The veins in my head throb again, courtesy of the anger rushing through my veins. Her hand in mine keeps me from letting my emotions risk our survival.

"Are these the Immunes?" Eli asks confused.

Where are you? I hear Morren say.

I'm trying to get out. I don't know what happened. Where are you?

"No, they're not," I answer Eli.

Why do you hear me sometimes, and sometimes not? he asks.

I don't know. I need to get out. They're shooting at us. Eli's here.

"Come on, you two. Hold my hands. We're gonna try again." Eli speaks with a calm certainty.

I look at Eli who touches my shoulder. I grab their hands and squat down in the water as I hear Chapis yelling at his other men to join in.

"Don't you let them get away! Any one of you who can get one earns an extra week of pay. If none of them are caught, you'll pay."

"We're screwed," Curly says. "If we get caught now, our best chance is the Institute."

"Three. Two."

A dart lands in Curly's thick hair.

"Don't let go!" Curly yells as I scream "One!"

Falling to the floor, knees and elbows hit my back and sides. As I slowly open my eyes, it's to the sight of something like a squirming set of squid trying to detangle themselves, tentacles twisted and caught.

"I did it!" It's the house we'd last seen Eli in. We were back. Eli is sitting up looking around, and from the look in her eyes, she's searching for the Immune.

"Morren! Morren! Where are you?"

"Here! Right here, Karana!" His hand grabs me, separating me from the pile.

I follow the one set of legs and arms to the face that had escaped with Eli and me. Curly sits up on the floor, a look of awe and confusion printed across her face. It isn't every day you vanish from one place and end up somewhere else in little more than the blink of an eye.

"Why did the others run off when we were gonna get out?" I ask.

Curly shakes her head quickly and tries to regain composure as she processes what happened.

"They were so close," I whisper.

"Probably too scared to leave," she shrugs, still dazed.

She looks around the house and touches the floor, rubbing her hands against the woven fibers we'd landed on. Her curly spirals seem to form a crown, reminding me of mine, as she settles down, confused.

"Why? You said you needed help."

It's frustrating. After all that, she was the only one who'd come along.

"Sometimes it's hard to leave. Where are we?"

She's nervous and second-guessing her choice to escape. She's not the only one. It may be more trouble than it's worth if she's the only one who bothered to leave.

"I think it's the edge of what you call Base City. It's where we first came."

"Thanks for getting her the message," Morren smiles and looks at Curly. I wonder what his nickname is for her, given he can't help gushing. If I didn't know any better, I'd think he was actually blushing, too. If he is, he's lucky no one can tell under the ruddy Baselonican complexion.

"We need to get outta here, Morren. Now. They'll be coming for us, and I wouldn't doubt that they did something to us so they could find us."

"You're right. They probably did. Check the top of your foot. The ridge on your left foot is usually where they put it," Curly directs us.

She slips off her stiletto boots and shows me the thick meaty flesh.

Pulling my boot off, I run a finger along the same ridge on my foot.

"I feel something. How do I get it out?"

"You have to cut it out. It's why they put it on your foot so that it's harder to run if you take it out."

"Right. Cut it out – couldn't be an easier way, huh? Morren? Check yours too. If I'm tagged, you're tagged too. In fact, we all need to get these out."

I run to the kitchen and pull the drawers open quickly. They're left in various stages of being partially ajar as I search for a knife of any kind, that's sharp enough to do the job. I finally find a drawer with strange utensils. The handles are bent and the pointed end of the knife aims downward. It'll have to do.

"Where is the Immune?" Eli interrupts.

"Don't know. At this point, I really don't care. They didn't wanna leave this place. Seems like no one does."

"Karana, you do understand that we can't...you can't leave without them," Eli says.

"Morren, check the bathroom for something to disinfect this with." I can't deal with Eli right now.

He comes back seconds later with an orange bottle. "I think this is it?"

"That's it." Curly grabs the bottle, snaps the cap up, and pours some over the end of the knife. "Who's first?"

"I'll go first." I put my foot closer to her, causing my skirt rises even more.

"What are you wearing, Karana?"

"Shut up, Morren."

"Ready?" Curly asks.

"As ever." I wince as she cuts a small slit in the flesh and pulls out a tiny circle.

"You need to crush it. But first there is a very tiny wire on the inside. Pull it out, away from the tag. That disrupts the signal. Then crush it."

"How do you know this?" I ask, doing as she instructed.

"I used to help my brother with stuff like this before I got snatched up to work...there."

She digs her tag out and disconnects the wire before moving onto Morren.

"Tags out, which means we will be reported soon as missing. What's the plan?" Curly asks.

"First, what's your name?" I finally ask, feeling uncomfortable thinking of her as Curly when, surely, she has a name.

"I'm Lari Aincan," she says.

I grin at the notion of having called her Curly in my head all this time. Lari was much more appropriate for her.

"I know I wanted your help, but I have to admit, I'm not so sure about this," Lari says, not bothering to conceal her hesitation. "But... we couldn't stay there. I couldn't stay there anymore."

"I haven't been here but a couple of days, and I couldn't stay." The idea of spending a life like this went to my stomach, turning it slightly.

"Before you get too excited, remember, we still don't have the two people we need before we can leave," Morren says.

"You still want to bother with that crazy mess? After all this?" I throw my head back and look to the ceiling.

"We have to. If we don't, we can't get home. That's what Eli told us."

"I knew you two weren't from around here. What part of Baselonica Xuna are you from?"

I look at Morren and then at Lari.

"The other side."

"The other side? This is it. This is the only habitable place on Base X. Do you mean Base Ridge, the mountains? You must be rich."

The small ridges on Lari's forehead are pulsing. She's smart and from her body language, she probably knows I'm not being honest.

"Yeah, from over there," I nod absently.

"That means you could pay for our freedom. You could buy us out of trouble," she suggests.

"We aren't exactly rich."

"How'd you wind up there?"

"I guess we just did. Luck maybe," I smile.

Lari paces in front of us. "You wouldn't have been at Baseland if you were. Besides, no one lives on Base Ridge who isn't from the Zo Clan or wealthy."

"Well you got part of us figured out," I sigh. "We're not rich. We're not registered. We're nothing here."

"Not registered? Why? What happened?"

Explaining would be too much trouble and Lari would neither understand nor believe me. We have to get out of here and if Morren's right, jumping would lead us right back. Shaking my head and a shrug of the shoulders is all I can muster for an answer.

"There are a couple people who work at one of the mining factories we need to find. How would we do that?" Morren asks.

"If you know the factory, you could wait for them to get out. Then I suggest you follow them home."

"We tried that and got caught," I wince. "Can't we try looking them up on a computer or something?"

"Ha!" Lari laughs. "You're not even registered and you're far from Base Ridge."

I look at her confused.

"Oh. You're serious?" I ask.

"I saw them where they had me before I got sent to Baseland."

"Yeah, only the Zo Clan and their preferred businesses have access to computers that connect to each other. Any other computer isn't connected to anything," Lari says, more serious this time.

"I think following them will be our best bet, Karana. We can't risk going anywhere near the Zo Clan," Morren says sitting down beside Lari.

I look at my brother, sitting by Karana, closer than he needs to be and sigh. "Well at least we know we can jump here. We'll jump back to the mines when it's closer to when they get out."

The crackle of thunder overhead startles all of us.

"You may not be going anywhere anytime soon. This sounds like a big one," Lari sighs.

Chapter Twelve

"It's angry. Fuming," Lari says as she looks out the window toward the sky.

"What do you mean?" I ask.

"The sky is merely a reflection of the people. Chapis must have gotten his men, the people riled up against you. Against us. If the sky looks like this, it's not gonna be pretty for us." She sounds too certain for my comfort.

"Should we forget about them and leave?" I ask.

"You can't. I keep trying to tell you that you cannot leave without them," Eli reminds us.

"But what if they don't want to go?"

"You met them?" Eli asks with surprise.

"Yes, and they didn't want to have anything to do with us, at all," I say.

"I knew it was possible they'd be affected by this place, but that they wouldn't want to return is a problem."

"A problem, how?" Morren asks.

"Because you are drawn to them. Trying to jump away won't work because they are here."

"What about the others on…back home? Why aren't we drawn to them instead?" I ask.

"The pull here is much greater. It's like the Immune in you knows that these Immunes are lost or missing and must be returned."

"Wait. Wait. Wait!" Lari's eyes are wide with excitement.

"What is it?"

"I know you. Not you, but about you; from the legend."

A laugh escapes from my lips, unintentionally.

"Sorry. What do you mean?"

"When I was a little girl in training under my mother, she told me a story. It was a kids' story then, but it makes sense now. It makes sense." Lari shakes her head as if she doesn't believe it herself.

"What makes sense, Lari?" I ask.

"She said that one day the lost child of Base City would find the force of freedom. The child would know them, even though they appeared as us. She'd know they were different because they had an understanding not of our world. The force of freedom would rescue the people from the dark and raging monster. She said the force of freedom would be brave and have something we call prana. Prana has waned on Base X since…since the Zo took power. I am the lost child, and it was my destiny to find this force. It must be you. You two must be here to rescue the lost city of Base X!"

In silence, I wait for the joke, but she's not laughing. The word prana felt like it must mean something like love since they definitely don't have much of that here. Morren glances at me as I try to make sense of the meaning, feeling it went beyond my understanding of love.

"This makes sense. If it is your destiny to do this, that makes your pull here even greater. It would be why," Eli says, letting the rest of the thought fall off.

"Why what, Eli?"

She takes a deep breath, her tentacles rising slightly as she does. "It would be why the Immunes were brought here, as part of the answer to a call for help that someone here must have sent out to our people. How long ago did this call go out?

"It was years before I was born. I guess not long after the Zo took over. That's been twenty-five years."

"I guess your parents must have answered the call, Karana and Morren."

"Eli?!" Morren and I say in disgust.

"What?"

"Ugh. Besides, it's only a story her mom told her as a kid," I respond trying to get the other picture out of my head.

"Is that what you believe?" Eli asks.

"It makes more sense than us being some kind of rescuers or what was that? Force of freedom?"

"But what if you are the force of freedom? What if it's not just a story my mother told me?"

"Then you're pretty screwed." I walk over to look out the window.

The storm is giving off streaks of lightning across the sky.

Eli's eyes move in thought, processing this information. It's more than she'd understood before. It's something I'd never heard of before, and it was all ridiculous. Another distraction, keeping us from getting home.

"We have our business already. I helped you get away from Baseland, but we came here for a reason."

"We have to try, Karana. We can do both. There might still be a chance to reach Eton and Reyn if we can get them and talk to them," Morren says optimistically.

"You see? You have to help us," Lari pleads.

"I'm sorry, Lari. This legend? It's probably just a story your mother told you to give you hope. It's like the fairytales we had." I immediately see her expression sink, but can't let that deter me. "It's just not a compelling enough argument to risk our lives and our chance to get home as soon as possible."

"But it's not just a story or one of your fairy tales. It's not an accident that we're here. It's destiny."

"I know you think we might be this force of freedom. I understand why you might hope we are. But we're nothing but two people trying to get home. That's it."

"What if we are?" Morren asks me pointedly.

"Look, we don't have time for speculation. We get the Immunes and go from there." I have to stay focused despite his willingness to let his heart override his head.

"Go where? What happens to us?" Lari demands.

Her veins begin to pulse, and I can't tell if it's random coincidence that above our heads thunder cackles.

"Why haven't you saved yourself? You seem pretty capable," I challenge her. "You want us to risk everything. What have you risked?"

"I've lost everyone and everything. What you saw back there at Baseland; that's my life. Day in and day out. That's it. That's all it will ever be until I'm used up or too old, then they'll put me to work doing something else. I'll never be free. But Karana, believe me when I say I'll fight. I'll fight and I'll die if I must, but I can't do it alone. I know you don't think you're the ones. But even if you aren't, you're here now. You know what's happening. Are you gonna go get your friends and leave us to be consumed by the monster? Can you really go on back to your safe place and forget about what's happening here?"

"Our sister and father are waiting for us. They need rescuing too. Every hour here is time we lose." Even letting the words pass through my lips brings an unexpected pang of guilt.

"Maybe there is something we can do, Karana," Morren says, pulling me to the side.

"What if I get the Immunes and you help them?"

I know leaving them like this isn't the best choice, but I can't, we can't fight everyone else's battles, I send him, knowing even then he's right.

For whatever reason, we wound up on Baselonica Xuna. It's a screwed-up planet with two Immunes we're supposed to bring home. I don't know how and why, but we're here and I don't believe much in accidents." His eyes are so intense I look away, feeling guilty.

"Fine, Lari. But before we agree to help, I need to ask you something."

"What? Anything," she says eagerly.

"First, who are you in all this? And second, how do we bring down the Zo Clan?"

"I thought you'd never ask," she smiles.

Chapter Thirteen

"I am from the line of rulers who'd faithfully served Baselonica Xuna for several hundred years. It was the golden era of Base X. Many of the advances we had in equality and technology came during that time. The Aincan's developed trade with multiple star-systems, planets, and peoples. We flourished. At least that's what I was taught."

"What happened? Seems like your family was doing fine," Morren asks Lari carefully.

"There were freedoms. Everyone had a chance to live, not like we are now. It wasn't perfect. Nothing is. There were those who didn't benefit from the progress being made. That faction helped the Zo overthrow my family. A small group managed to take the power and take us back to before the Aincan's ruled."

Even with the shadows hanging over Lari's face, I can't help but utter in wide-eyed disbelief, "Wait. You're like…royalty?"

"I know you couldn't tell to look at it." She tugs at the top she wears and pulls her shoulders back. "My family has been out of power for the better part of twenty-five years, and it's time the Zo rule comes to an end. To the Zo, I'm a threat."

"He's got all the power. How are you a threat?" I ask.

"He runs an upside-down system and before him, his father did. I'm a threat to that system. I'm also his prized possession. Having me as his pola is both insult and injury to me. I'm in his harem! I wasn't even alive when this happened, but it has determined everything in my life. I have never forgotten my mother's stories. It's why I can't leave or ever truly be free."

"Can I go back one minute? I know how important all of this is, but can I confirm one thing? You're like a princess of some kind?" Morren smiles.

"Not exactly. Before the Zo took over, everything was different. The Aincan oversaw Base City, but like I said, there were freedoms. People had a voice, and everything wasn't based on your ability to pay or produce."

"What is it now?"

"The Zo are in charge. And only the Zo. They control all of Base City. Base City is the habitable land and includes from the water to ridge. Past the ridge is a wasteland. There is no way to survive out there. If you don't go along with them, they have no use for you, except for procreation. We can't produce enough to export without a labor force," Lari says.

"I'm sorry, Lari. I hear your story. I do, and it's horrible, but my home is literally dying, and I don't know what you expect us to do here." Helping them seems impossible, given how big the problem is and how long it's been going on.

"You don't understand. Since the Zo took over, no one has come in or out of Baselonica Xuna except for the Zo and their hired diplomatic hands – diplomats and businesspeople. We still trade with other planets, but us regular Baselonicans don't have any interaction with anyone from the outside. No one knows what's happening here. We have no way of sending for help. You're only here because of a message sent during the takeover. That message was sent years before you or your brother were even born."

I wait for her to continue, still unsure of what Morren and I can do, even with Eli.

"They know that if they keep us separate, we can't get enough people to care. All people see is the anger, the fighting, the monsters. But there are more Baselonicans like us than them. Even still, the monster has the power and that's what everyone sees. They believe that, and then they can justify seeing us as labor and resources," Lari adds.

"So, what is it you want?" I search her eyes, hopeful it's something that doesn't confirm my suspicion that it will be impossible.

"If others knew what was happening, they'd help. I know it. We need someone to tell them. To let them know about us. I am proof that the Aincan line lives and can be restored, but the other star systems believe us to be dead. We need someone to lead, to bring back prana, and prepare the people."

"Lead the Baselonicans?"

"Yes," Lari says with no uncertainty. Her eyes penetrate mine.

"Look. I'm sorry, but I'm not a leader," I study my hands and fingernails. "I'm only here so I can save my family."

"Fine. I understand if you don't want to help, but maybe Morren will. You can see what's happened," she turns her big brown eyes to my brother.

"What you're asking us to do is risky, Lari. Too risky. If we get caught again, we might not get out of here," he answers, guiltily. "We came here to get the Immunes so we could rescue our family."

"Maybe you can come with us for now," I suggest.

"Where?" Lari asks.

"Don't know yet," I say.

"Leave without knowing where? Leave all these people to the Zo?" Lari asks, her brow furrowed and the lines in her forehead more pronounced. "What if where you go is worse than this?"

The possibility of that idea is unsettling, but the notion of staying on Base X is even more so.

The skies are still dusted red, and the clouds that brought the storm shortly after we'd hit the sandy beach are full now. The rain begins to fall in loud, hard plops. The sound of lightning hitting something nearby reminds me of where we are. We can't stay here.

"Morren, can you find the Immunes and bring them here? Lari, if we agreed to help, do you have a plan? You've been here your whole life so you know better than I do what needs to happen. If we get the two we need to get, we can jump somewhere and get help. But I know nothing about the rest of it. Leading, preparing them – it's not my thing." I don't even try to hide my hesitation at the last part. She already knows this, anyway.

"They can't know who I am. Even Chapis Zo doesn't know my real identity. He knows I was in the household, but believes I was a child of one of the servants. After I was born, my mother had Rache's mom who'd just given birth a month earlier, take me out to Base Ridge. She claimed that's where she'd found me, unregistered. She offered to care for me and try to find a woman to nurse me. Well, they eventually found one. It was my mother, dressed in plain clothes. She was brought to Chapis Zo's father and made my nurse."

"Didn't they recognize her? She was one of the Aincans, right?"

"I don't remember what my mother looked like before the Zo took over. She said she went into hiding after the siege, and when she turned up at Baseland, three months later, she was barely recognizable as having facial features."

A tear slips down her ruddy skin.

"It was around the time I was six or seven that she told me she was actually my mother. But she didn't have to, I always knew. The old Chapis had come into the room my mother and I shared and summoned her out. I think she knew she wasn't coming back. She must have because she came back and touched my head with her lips. She told me to remember my bedtime stories. When she walked out of the room, her face was wet."

Lari's hand swipes across her own face, leaving her hand damp.

"It was the last time I saw her. They have murdered anyone who sympathized with the Aincan. I guess she must've said something or done something that marked her as a sympathizer. I cannot let anyone else know who I really am before they are out of power. Being the child of a trusted member of the household has been hard enough."

Words catch in my throat as I imagine her, a little kid like Tezzi, watching her mother leave for the last time. In that moment, I am even more certain that if anyone is to lead them, it isn't me. I look at Morren. *You could.*

He looks at me and nods. *We could.*

He's right, again. All our lives we've been stronger together. Survived together. We were a force.

In a somber tone he says, "I will get Eton and Reyn. In the meantime, we need a plan for after we have them. I don't want to spend any more time than necessary on Base X."

Lari almost smiles for the first time. The storm rages outside the clay house while we remain seated on the stools and hash out a plan to defeat Chapis Zo and the Zo Clan.

Chapter Fourteen

Eli has agreed to stay with Lari while Morren and I find Eton and Reyn. Going into the heart of Base City feels slightly better with us together, rather than him going alone. It's not ideal, but nothing about Base X is.

"It's almost time for the mines to empty out. The storm isn't passing, so you'll have to go out in it, if you wanna go at all," Lari says.

"We have to be careful, Morren. They're looking for us. And from what we see out there, they are mad."

"He's safer out there than you," Lari reminds me.

"Why?" I ask.

"He might be held as a hostage to get you but other than that, the worse he'd probably get is to pay penance in the mines or be transferred since he isn't registered."

"That's not good either," Morren objects.

"Better than being a pola or being sent to the Institute," Lari retorts.

"Girls get transferred too," I argue. "I met one in the jail they held me in."

Lari laughs nervously. "Yeah."

"She was being transferred. They took her out and I heard them say it."

"I'm sure she's being transferred, but not like what you think."

"Okay. I get it. Don't get caught. Either of us," Morren agrees.

Eli nods. I assumed she was female, but realize that I'm not completely sure. I see her as Eli, but what did the Baselonicans see her as? On second thought, I don't want the answer to that question. We'll put our plan to action before it matters; that's what's important.

We've already lost nearly two full days. Whatever is going to happen needs to happen in the next day if we hope to leave in three days as planned.

Eli looks at me again, her eyes downcast. I can hear her say, *It won't happen in the next day.*

"What do you mean? We're about to do it now."

"You're already at the end of your second day. Three days is ideal, but if it is more than three days, it is more than three days. The point is that you cannot be consumed by this place. Just as Lari has held onto something to give her hope, so must you," she shares an affectionate smile with Lari.

"Let's go, Morren. We need to hurry and come back. We have work to do." Entertaining Eli isn't high on my to-do list, especially since she seems to be trying to trick us again. I can only wonder if she knows something we don't.

Morren and I clasp hands.

"Three."

The look of optimism in Lari's eyes hits me and I understand it. Prana.

"Two."

These two Immune fools better not screw this up again.

"One."

***

"Shirt. Hanger. Iron. Table!" I yelp quietly as I hit a wall, banging the side of my head and shoulder. It's the same wall we'd hidden beside the first day.

We've made it in time, sparing only seconds. The sound of the gong begins to vibrate, signaling the end of the work day. Morren and I wait for the sight of Eton and Reyn in the crowd as they exit the building.

There. Morren points toward the stairs leading up from the mine, to the buses.

I see them. This time, we're gonna do it my way. They can be mad about it later, I say. *Follow me.*

We get behind the miners leaving work, blending in to climb the steps.

Stay close, Morren. You take Eton. I'll take Reyn, and don't wait. We get them and get right out of here.

Got it.

Staying a few people behind Reyn, I keep my head down as she and Eton march up the steps, having what seems like a tense conversation. Reyn turns around sharply, and I quickly duck behind a large male as she surveys the faces behind her. I wonder if she can sense us, and if our attraction is mutual?

Hurry, Morren. Get up behind him.

I look Morren in the eye, *Ready?*

Ready.

Three. Two, I begin.

Reddish brown fingers graze their shoulders and before either can fully turn around, I say, *One.*

We hit the floor of the little dirt mound house and Eton gets up, his arms swinging wildly. His eyes change, becoming darker, and the veins all over his arms and face bulge. He squares up to Morren and throws a punch landing on Morren's right cheek, drawing blood. The sight of the blood gives the effect of making Eton even wilder and draws Reyn up from the floor.

Her lips snarled and a growl rolling in her throat, she stands to her feet. They must both be feeding off the same energy because neither resembles the quiet people we'd encountered on the bus the first day.

"We don't want to leave," she screams, scratching at my face. I barely avoid one of her long nails trying to make contact with my cheek.

"We're here to rescue you. Calm down," I say.

"We didn't ask to be rescued. We've already been rescued from that sick underworld, and you want to take us back?" Eton says.

Reyn swings at me again, this time grazing my forehead as I duck.

"It's gonna be better," I argue.

Eton and Morren are now going to blows, their arms locked around each other's necks and pummeling each other in the stomach and face. I look around for Eli and Lari.

"A little help, please!" I call out.

There is no answer.

"Eli!" I yell. "Lari!"

No answer. I wonder where they are. They weren't supposed to go anywhere.

I look at Morren and pick up the stool in the sitting area. I hit Eton on the back and he finally lets go of Morren. They're both bloody and panting, though they seem ready to pounce on each other again. Reyn lunges toward me, and I push her back with the stool.

"STOP! This is crazy. This is what this planet does to you! STOP!"

Despite feeling fired up now, I am trying to be calm. Like the storm outside, I am getting angry and volatile, and it isn't much of a stretch for me. But Morren – he is always the calmer one, even if I can't tell that right now.

"I know you don't really want to be here. So…" I step back and to the side to avoid her knee. "So why are you fighting so hard to stay?'

Eton stands hunched over holding his stomach, fuming. Reyn glares at me as she glances around the sparse surroundings. I know she's looking for a weapon. I run over to where we'd taken out the tags. The small knife still sits on a little table where Lari had left it. I pick it up, stool in one hand and knife in the other, wanting this all to end.

"Now, enough fighting. Why don't you want to go home? This place is awful, the people are terrible, and everyone is on edge." I cautiously take a step back.

"Depends on your definition of awful and terrible. And when we left Earth, it was all those things too. At least here people here aren't dying because of an alien invasion," Reyn argues. "It's not perfect. It's actually pretty messed up in some ways – okay, a lot of ways; but no one is hunting us so they can test us in some secret compound!"

I won't give her the satisfaction of hearing me say it aloud, but she has a point.

"We're in this together, Reyn. We're not gonna do anything to you," I say.

I understand their resistance. They were at least mostly free here.

"How long have you been here?" I ask.

Eton and Reyn look at each other, thinking.

"I don't know exactly. Six or seven months, maybe," Reyn says, still thinking about it after answering.

"How'd you get here and be able to work?" Morren asks.

"We got brought in and someone helped us get registered so we could work. We took over the identification of a couple of orphans. The person who helped us sent the orphans to another planet where they could be free. I don't know why we couldn't go there. We got stuck here instead," Eton shrugs, clearly bitter.

Eyes bore into the side of my face. I know it's Morren, and I know he's trying to talk to me, but I really don't want another argument about this legend. Even without his intruding thoughts, my own mind is busy plaguing me as I try to be comfortable about this not being our problem. Maybe the legend is true, and this is the only way to get us here. Studying Reyn for a moment, I notice she's still in a fighting stance and I can't help but feel sorry for them. Defense mode has probably been their status quo since coming here.

"You've been here a while," Morren says as he walks slowly over to a stool and sits.

Eton keeps his position, legs spread far enough to run or fight – whichever was needed.

Reyn walks over to one of the stools and runs her fingers across the seat before resting her hands on it. I can't tell if it's so she can pick it up and use it as a weapon, or if she's not ready to get too comfortable. Either way, I'm glad she's taking a little off her defensive edge.

"Yeah, six months, seven months – either is definitely long enough. I'm surprised you came so fast. I figured we'd be here longer. Is Earth ready for us already?" she asks.

Chapter Fifteen

"Morren, can you try to reach Eli? They should be here. I can't imagine why they'd go out in the storm," I ask.

Reyn looks at Eton, visibly shaken now. "What's it like? Back home now?"

"I guess it's much worse, but that kinda means it has to get better," I begin.

"So it's not ready yet?"

"Not yet. But Eli and her people are getting it ready."

I can see the disappointment in Reyn's eyes.

"What are you bringing us back too, then?" she asks.

I don't have a good answer, realizing that my reasons were selfish. I needed them so we could get Dad and Tezzi. That was all.

"When we got here, we were the last of the known Immunes who hadn't gotten out and to the safe place. We were being held with our sister and father in the compound. They'd captured us about a week or so before and had started testing all of us. They knew Morren and I were immune to the virus, and that our dad was, too. Our sister is too young for them to be certain," I hesitate.

"Honestly, Reyn, things aren't great. The people who aren't immune to the virus hunted anyone down who wasn't sick so they could study us. You remember that first the headaches came, then the blindness and deafness. Then the breaking down of the nervous system, which meant no longer being able to move, eat, or swallow. It was terrible. I can't unsee it," Morren says, his eyes looking off.

"Are there any regular people left?" Eton asks.

"From what I know, people are either dying from the virus, or they are Immunes. There is no life outside the compound, except wherever the Immunes are hiding and in Greenland where the aliens landed. That's it."

"So again, why would we want to go back there?" Reyn's question is sincere, even as she holds her head down.

I don't have a good answer for her. I know why we need them to go back, but I can't think of how they benefit from returning to Earth.

"Did you ever plant a flower, or a vegetable, or anything?" I ask.

"Once. In elementary school I planted a pea plant in the back of the school. Why?" Reyn answers.

"So you had to break up the ground, turn it so it was loosened up, right? Before you could put your couple seeds in there, it had to be broken up."

"Yeah?"

"So Earth had to be loosened up, turned and shaken up so that it could grow again. We, the Immunes, are the seeds that are needed to replant Earth."

Reyn and Eton raise an eyebrow, both suspect of my analogy.

"We need you to bring Earth back," Morren tries to help my argument.

"What? You mean, make babies?" Reyn's eyes hold a look of cool steel.

I think about it and what Base X requires.

"Yeah, I guess that would be necessary too."

"So, again, not much different than here, but a whole lot more pressure since there's only a few of us."

The expression on Reyn's face when she says this is hard to read, but I know I'm not making my case. Morren isn't helping either.

"Morren?" I say.

He holds up a finger, making me wait. A few moments pass before he looks at me, Eton, and Reyn.

"We have to get Eli and Lari. They have someone else with them. Chapis Zo's men got them. Somehow, they found them here."

"Where are they?" I shoot off my stool.

"They're not going back to Baseland. Eli says that Lari thinks they're going to Base Ridge. She says there are two things on the Ridge. The top is where the wealthy live and the Zo have their homes. The Institute is on the way to Base Ridge."

"My bet is that they take them to Base Ridge to draw us out."

"You've got the Zo Clan after you?!" Eton shrieks. "That's something you might want to lead with next time!"

"We were doing okay. We were getting along. I was following the rules even; keeping my head down, being submissive. That's not easy, but I was doing it and I was safe. Now you come and mess it all up in what? Not even three days?" Reyn's brow ridge pulses.

I look at Eton and Reyn. Maybe we did screw up, but this wasn't how it would end. We needed to get off this planet, and we needed to get help. It wasn't part of the plan to do this without Lari and Eli. And now there was someone else.

"Can't Eli just jump with Lari and the other person?" I ask Morren.

"No. They're separated. Eli won't leave them. If she does, it'll bring too much attention to her."

I think of Tezzi. *We have people who need us, Morren. Are we supposed to sit around and wait?*

"We haven't been completely honest with you. We were brought to Base X because you're here. We're supposed to bring you back with us. We were told we can't come back without you. That as long as you are here, we will be attracted to where you are."

"So you wanna get home and we're your ticket," Reyn says bluntly.

"You make it sound bad when you put it that way."

"It is bad. You want to use us so you can see your family. I don't have anyone left there. Neither does Eton. We're on our own."

I cast my eyes to the floor, embarrassed. "I'm sorry."

"Well, now that you've apologized, of course we'll help you get back home," she says in a chipper voice.

"Really?" I ask, surprised.

"No! Are you crazy? Why would we help you? We don't know you, and we get nothing outta this deal besides being stuck on a virus filled planet with a few other weird humans. No thanks. I'd rather get back to my simple confining life right here. It's better than being a test subject, human incubator, or dead."

"She's got a point. We get nothing and you get to save your precious little sister and dad. You know what? No one saved my little sister, or my older sister, or my dad, or my mother. Nope. No one came back for them," Eton says angrily.

"We have the chance to rebuild Earth. To start fresh." I grasp for something that might matter to them.

"Not everyone wants to go back. I wanna forget," Eton says. "I'm not leaving. Sorry."

This isn't going right, for any part of the plan. We need them.

"This isn't all about going to Earth. It's about Base X, too. We need to help the people here who are under the Zo Clan control."

"You really don't know how to leave well enough alone, do you?" Eton asks. "The Zo are ruthless. They'll kill you, sell you, or put you in penance without blinking twice. We stay outta their way. If you're smart, you'll do the same."

"And what about you, Reyn? In a few years you will be expected to become a mona and procreate, regardless of anything else you might wanna do. Is that okay with you?" I ignore Eton as best I can.

From her glance to Eton, I can tell it's something that has crossed her mind before. He hasn't had to worry about it, but if she stays, it's a part of her reality.

"Is that what you want?" I press.

"It's better than nothing. Better than being tested on until you're sick with weakness, strapped down to tables, or in cells day in and day out."

I throw my hands up. This was the problem. This is what Lari meant. It had only been six months and already she was resolved to accept it. What did that mean for those who'd been here their whole lives? For those who never knew anything else? She needed off this planet and maybe she'd come to her senses.

"How about this? You help us to at least tell another star system about what's happening here so that help can come to Base X. That's it. If you don't want to go home after that, fine, you can come back here and stay."

Morren looks at me skeptically. I don't know if it means we have to stay too, but I can only take one step at a time.

"What do I get outta this besides trouble?" Eton asks.

"Maybe if someone knows what's happening, they can put pressure on the Zo to treat you all better. Pay you better."

The last part of what I said piqued his interest.

"Treat everyone better? Pay us all better?" Reyn asks.

"That's the idea."

Reyn looks at Eton again, as if trying to gauge whether she needs his permission.

"I'll do it. I'll help."

A smile crosses my face. Now we just need him.

"What? You can't go like that," Eton says with a look of anger.

"I can."

"You're not free as you think. They'll come after you. After us," he says angrily.

"It's why I have to go, Eton. If I don't, then I will never be free, and someone will always be coming after me. If I have to live on Base X, that isn't really how I want to live. If I want to get back to Earth one day, it's a step there."

Eton shakes his head in disbelief.

"What about you, Eton? Will you help us? You can come back," Morren asks.

"No. If I leave and miss work, I don't make my money. She's gonna miss it, too, and not make her money." Eton waggled a long finger at Reyn, "If you wind up short at the end of this week, how're you gonna pay for your room?"

"We share an apartment, Eton. If you won't go with us, you could at least help cover my share for missing a day or two of work."

"Why? Because you're mad you don't get paid the same as I do?"

"Eton!?"

"What? That's it, isn't it? You don't think it's fair so you wanna run off and tell someone. Lighten up. It's the way it is here. Don't like it – leave, but don't drag me down with you."

Reyn glares at Eton as he nurses his jaw. Maybe it's too late for him. He has it pretty good here.

"You think we can we do it without him?" I ask Morren and cast a sideways glance to Eton.

Morren is looking dumbfounded at Eton. He didn't hear me, forcing me to repeat the question.

"We can try. But I need to know what he's gonna do, before we jump outta here."

"I'm gonna go home. I'm supposed to be off work and relaxing, not scheming."

"Will you tell?" I ask point blank.

"Maybe. Maybe not. Give me a reason not to tell."

My neck tenses and I can feel the heat rise to my face. I want to bring a knee to him, like I'd done the brute, but that wouldn't help.

"We don't have anything to give you, Eton. Isn't it enough to know you are doing something good and right?"

"Ha! You think I care about that? I need something a bit more…tangible."

I look at Eton. He's gonna be a problem. Reyn smiles and pulls Eton to the side, out of our ear shot. I see her gently stroking the back of his neck, whispering in his ear, letting her hand glide down his back to his waistline. Her body is close to his as she talks sweetly. I can't hear her, but whatever she is saying, seems to be getting to him.

"I'll come. But I need to be back by morning. I don't like to be late for work," he says, smirking at Reyn.

Reyn smiles with a tilt of her head. "Now what?"

"I am confident that when we jump, we'll land exactly where we need to be. There will be someone who will listen and can help. We'll tell them what's happening, and you two have personal experience with it. You can vouch for what's going on. We come back here, rescue Eli and Lari," I say.

"And then?" Reyn asks.

"Wait. No one said I had to vouch for anything. I agreed to come. That's all." Eton steps back and folds his arms over his chest.

"If you want to be luggage, fine," I tell him.

Morren runs his hand across his head, trying to stay calm. "When we get back, we move forward with our plan."

"What if everyone here wants it to be like it is?" Eton asks. "It's not that bad, and what you have to offer might be worse."

"What I have to offer might seem worse, but in the end it'll be better for everyone…not just some."

"Are we ready?" I ask.

Morren, Reyn, and Eton nod as we grab one another's hands. I take a deep breath, unsure where we'll land, but secretly hoping it's better than Baselonica Xuna.

"Three."

Chapter Sixteen

"Two. One."

We roll into a field of grass and flowers of every color. It's a fragrant rainbow, delighting my senses; just as I remember from my childhood. *Have we died? Am I dreaming?*

No. Home, just as I remembered it, from before. The sun warms my cheeks and I reach to feel the earth beneath my fingers. Home.

Morren, we did it. I don't know how, but we did.

Somehow the Eliatars had not only made it okay for us to return, but they'd restored our home to the beauty of my childhood. I let my head fall back, taking in the blue skies dotted by clouds.

Amidst the clouds, I spot the faint silver moon and smile. Out of the corner of my eye I see another silvery moon.

Morren follows where I'm looking. *I guess we're not quite that lucky.*

It's foolish of me to be so hopeful. I push myself up from the grass, disappointed but appreciative of a place that feels familiar. I scan the area. Surrounding the field we'd fallen into are woods with tall thick trees. They must be old. A small creek divides us, and a small cottage on the other side. I can't help but wonder if there might be food there. We hustle over to the creek

"Water!" Morren says, excitedly.

"And it's not red," I say, gratefully. "For a minute, I thought we'd really gone home, Morren."

"Me too. But we can't think about that. Can't get distracted."

Reyn and Eton cautiously follow us.

"Do you even know where we are - you know before you start drinking strange water?" Eton asks.

"It reminds me of home. Not Base X, but Earth," Reyn says.

I detect a bit of nostalgia in her voice.

"It does, doesn't it? Blue skies are something I took for granted," I say.

"Fine. If you get sick, don't say I didn't warn you," Eton snorts, refusing to join us.

Reyn casts him a sideways glance and then joins Morren and I at the creek. As we kneel over the water, I try to see myself, unsure of what to expect. If we look like Baselonicans, we might be seen as an alien threat. If we look like the people wherever we are, we might not be believed.

I lean forward to see my reflection in the water. Morren does the same. We look at each other. This may not be as easy as we thought.

The creek reflects back another stranger. This time she is tinted green, and I can see no white in the eyes. There is no hair that I can tell, only a pronounced dark ring that extends over the crown. I touch my head and find that I'm not mistaken about the hair. My nose seems about the same size, but the area between my nose and lips connects with a flexible ridge that feels like the cartilage in my nose. I can't see or feel ears sticking out from my head, but since I can hear around me, they must be there somewhere.

"Let's go to the house. Maybe we'll find some food and figure out where we are," Morren suggests.

I study Morren again. The difference in our bodies is barely discernable. The same is true for Reyn and Eton.

Morren doesn't wait for an answer and walks along the water until it becomes narrow enough for us to cross. On the other side, I pick up a scent and my nostrils flare. It smells like something burning.

I hold my finger up to my lips. "We need to be quiet," I whisper.

We risk exposing ourselves out here, walking up to this house, I send Morren.

He nods. *We can jump closer so whoever might be there, won't see us.*

Good idea. "Eton and Reyn, we need to hold hands for this. Let's go to the side closer to the tree line," I say.

"Wait. What? Why not just walk up? You do know coming out of nowhere is creepy, right?" Eton jumps in.

"We can't be caught," I whisper back to him.

We all look up toward the sky. We're too late. What looks like a small drone comes down from where its sky blue surface had given it camouflage.

"Greetings. I am Skadot. How might I be of assistance?" the flying device asks.

"Ummm. We need to talk to someone in charge," I risk.

"Perhaps I can direct you to someone based on your specific need."

I sigh. "We need someone who can help us with humanitarian concerns." I'm unsure if that best sums it up, but it's the best I've got.

"Our humanitarian agencies include a wide range of resources, services, and solutions for the people of Anfar. There are agencies serving children, adults, our elders. Which population is your concern regarding?"

"Adults, mostly."

"Adults. For adults, we have agencies concerned with education, health, habitat, and general equity. Which concern would you like assistance addressing?"

"I don't know. I'm not sure where it fits."

"Before you can receive assistance, you must know what you would like to accomplish. In a short phrase of three to five words, what humanitarian concern do you have regarding the adult population?"

I roll my eyes. I didn't think I was going to have to talk to a flying computer to get help.

"Gender and income equity," Reyn pipes in, unexpectedly.

Eton looks at her, his eyes not hiding his intrigue. Reyn ignores his gaze and watches the flying computer.

"Gender and income equity is not understood. Please rephrase your concern," Skadot requests.

"Female and money equity," Reyn tries again.

"I'm sorry, but female does not register. Our Agency on Monetary Value of Labor and Welfare serves adults and is the closest match to your concern for money equity. Would you like information on contacting this agency?"

"Yes, and how to get there," I say.

The flying computer rattles off information quickly. "Director Jable Narp heads the agency and is responsible for any complaints and requests. The primary office is located on the main street in Sentursyd. Based on your current location, walking will take you approximately forty-seven minutes. The office closes in sixty minutes and will reopen tomorrow for regular business."

"Thank you," I say back to Skadot.

"Have I provided the assistance you need?"

"Yes."

"Is there anything else I may help you with?"

Morren looks at the rest of us, "Can you point us in the direction of Sentursyd?"

"I will guide you in the proper direction, and then you may continue. Your path will lead you through the trees. Sentursyd is on the other side of the trees. Nothing on Anfar is very far apart."

"Okay. Thanks," Morren says as we begin to follow the computer.

My head does it again. I'm swooning and off balance. My stomach feels ill, as if I've gotten on a spin ride at the amusement park. It doesn't make sense. We haven't done more than walk twenty yards and have been standing in one spot since then.

Morren looks at me oddly and then turns back to follow the computer.

"One more question, Skadot. You seem to have a lot of information."

"Yes. I am programmed to be helpful."

"Is a day on Baselonica Xuna longer than a day on Anfar?"

I look at him dumbfounded. Of all the things we need right now, that isn't one.

"Our Anfar day is shorter than Baselonica Xuna's."

"And how long is an Anfar day?" I ask, curiously.

"A Baselonica Xuna day is twenty-three hours, ours is eighteen. But you must take into consideration that we are not anywhere near each other, and therefore this information is non-consequential."

We'd gone farther into the deep of space and were losing time at a faster rate.

"Do you know what date it is on Earth at this time?" I ask hesitantly.

"One moment, while I make that calculation."

We all wait in silence, nervous about the answer Skadot would give.

"Today is October 3, 2038."

Morren, Reyn, and Eton all turn their heads at my audible gasp. That couldn't be right. "Can you double-check that, please?"

"One moment while I verify my calculations."

My stomach was heaving from the faster rotation and the date that couldn't possibly be right. How had we lost so much time? Where had it gone?

"Confirming the date of October 3, in your year two thousand and thirty-eight on the planet Earth."

I look at Morren who is visibly shaken, along with Eton and Reyn. Could it be possible that we'd lost more than two years when we'd only left Earth less than three days ago? My voice caught in my throat as I thought about what Tezzi and Dad must be thinking; if they were even alive.

Don't even think like that, Karana, Morren warns me.

I gasp for air and struggle to hold the vomit back from the bright green grass.

"Is there any further assistance Skadot might provide? Medical perhaps?"

"No. Thank you. That's all," Morren answers and throws an arm around me to help me balance.

"Continue in this direction, straight through the woods and you will be in Sentursyd. You will need to walk quickly if you wish to reach your destination before they close for the day. Thank you for allowing me to be of service."

"Thanks," Reyn whispers.

"Would you recommend Skadot to your fellow Anfarians?" the flying computer asks.

"Yes," Morren says quickly.

He waits for the computer to leave before saying what we're all thinking.

"We need to hurry and figure this out fast."

"Two years. More than two years. Morren, we've been gone for two Earth years. That means Tezzi is old enough for them to know."

"I know what it means, Karana. That's why we need to hurry and get to Sentursyd so we can get off of this planet and back home."

"Why didn't gender register with that thing?" Reyn asks. I can tell she's worried too.

"We'll figure this out. Maybe they call it something else." That's Morren, trying to remain rational.

Eton has been silent, as if he's taking it all in. I don't trust him. His reasons for coming along are purely self-interested, and even if ours are also, it isn't the same. It would be difficult for him to care any less about anyone else.

I try to read his face for whether knowing he's been gone from Earth for more than two and a half years bothers him at all. But his face is blank, and instead he gives me a look that says, "back off."

"Come on. Let's get going. I don't want to lose a night on Anfar because we got there after they closed."

"I wish we knew exactly where we were going so we could jump there. It'd be faster," I say weakly.

"Unfortunately, we could wind up anywhere, including right back here," Morren shrugs.

"Well then let's walk faster. I have work in the morning, and I don't plan on waiting until after work for my reward for doing this crazy trip with you," Eton says, walking ahead of Morren.

I frown, thinking that maybe we should leave him here. Then, I remember, we can't. He's connected to us as much as

Reyn. Our pace quickens as we try to stay straight in the direction the computer told us to go.

The woods bring me a bit of comfort and my nausea becomes bearable. I haven't been among trees like this in years. They are tall and full of vibrant leaves; though the leaves have a strange bluish hue to the green. I touch the bark on the trunk of what looks like an evergreen as I pass. I miss this. I miss the outside and fresh air. I miss feeling a gentle breeze without the fear that enjoying it without protective gear made me a target.

I want to go home. I want to get Tezzi and Dad. I want to find the other Immunes. As I breathe in the air around me, my eyes again catch a whiff of something far-off. I'm not the only one.

"What is that?" Reyn pins up against a tree, her eyes darting back and forth.

The crackle of breaking sticks makes us all lean into the trees, hoping our alien green appearance serves as camouflage. As I hug the bark my skin changes slightly, taking on a browner hue. I look around at Morren, Reyn, and Eton. It's the same for them. Chameleon skin. I hope it's enough.

We hear voices passing through. I remember what Eli told us. *We hear what we need to hear.* I marvel at the fact that we can understand what they are saying. It wasn't just Skadot.

"They've already given their recommendations to the Director. This doesn't help. It's risky us being here, meeting like this," the male says.

They are at least twenty yards away and don't seem to notice us. As they pass the area where we're hiding, the female looking Anfarian slows down and smells the air. Her eyes carry to the trees, the leaves, the ground, and the spaces between as she sniffs again.

"Someone's here. We need to get out of here," she whispers.

Chapter Seventeen

The sound of thunder from beneath grabs our attention. It's the sound of galloping. The two Anfarians turn and run.

From the safety of my crouched down spot beside the tree, I see one of the Anfarians - possibly a female. Riding on a creature with the body of a horse and head of a mutated eagle, she pulls out a long sword, preparing to attack. My eyes open wide. The others behind her do the same. The six horse-eagles chase the two through the woods. If we don't get ourselves together, they'll hear our heavy breathing and turn their attention to us.

We need to do something quick, I send to Morren.

We should run ahead while they are chasing those two.

I think we need to jump out of these woods and then find our way to Sentursyd, I counter.

Good idea.

"No! Don't. We've done nothing wrong." They've caught them.

I freeze in horror, afraid to know what's going on.

The Anfarians on the horse-eagles surround the two who'd been running, and the one with a symbol reminding me of a crown cracked down the middle speaks in a matter-of-fact tone. "By order of the lawful rule of Anfar you are hereby charged with violating Anfarian honesty code 2-1AN4. Anfar is a place of peaceful action and order. Violation of this code is punishable by just and swift action. You will hereby be detained and presented for the Sovereign Goyar. You will serve as a reminder to all Anfarians of our laws, customs, and norms. Do you understand?"

"Please. No! Not the Goyar! We'll do anything. Please. We were only trying to help." The male pleads to the Anfarian who managed to speak without emotion.

"Our laws are non-negotiable. Failure to abide by them is punishable by just and swift action. Do you believe you are above our fair laws?" I can't see the face of the leader speaking but imagine it to be as emotionless as the voice.

"We were on our way to seek immunity from the Agency on Monetary Value of Labor and Welfare. We did nothing wrong. I worked for those earnings, all of it. I did not steal by taking off an hour early as I was accused." The Anfarian who may have been female says argumentatively. She has enough emotion for the entire group.

"If you are being honest, you will be spared in the Goyar. The Goyar is just and administers justice swiftly and accurately. It does not err." The leader's head turns left and right, and I think we may have been sniffed out. "Get them up and will make our way to the Goyar."

"What is going on?" I mouth to Reyn who's in my eyesight.

She shrugs one shoulder, the other still pinned to the tree, and fear is locked in her eyes. I wonder what about this place brought us here to get help for the Baselonicans. *What kind of place delivers someone to a Sovereign Goyar because they took off an hour early from work? And what the heck is a Goyar?*

A place we don't want to stick around any longer than necessary. Morren heard my self-bantering. But whether I meant for him to hear it or not, he is right.

There they are again, crossing further ahead of us. The male and female Anfarians, bound and on the back of the horses with their captors. For the briefest moment I think she sees me, and I lean back. We have to wait for them to clear the woods before we can continue.

***

The walk through the woods is much more somber now. We don't know what to expect when we arrive in Sentursyd. Our moods have changed from feeling welcomed and optimistic to something else that I can't explain.

The trees give way to a small open park. With the exception of the chameleon like people, they are much like we were before the aliens came. Family groupings, friends, people leaving and going to places – a normalcy I find refreshing.

Children play and run, just as I once did. I smile briefly, thinking how nice it would be to live like this again.

Their clothes are simple, uniform. Gray button down tops with matching gray pants. I look down at myself. I hadn't noticed before that we have on what they do. From the edge of the park, we attempt to exit the safety of the woods unnoticed, but fail miserably.

A couple with a young child stops their playing to watch us, suspiciously. The one who appears to be male, takes out what looks like a phone and begins recording us. Soon, several others begin doing the same, as we try to make our way through the park.

"Excuse me," says a man with the same brown eyes as everyone else.

He wears a rimless cap with an emblem on his head. His shirt has the same emblem on the chest and sleeve.

He smiles uneasily before nodding at the people around us with their cameras, letting them know it is okay to put them down.

"You seem to be causing some distraction. Reports came in that a group of young people just exited from the woods. I'm sure you understand the concern, given the rules we have around that, don't you?"

I search out any meaning in his tone and voice, but am at a loss.

"I'm sorry, we were told to go through by Skadot." I couldn't imagine we'd gotten that wrong.

"Well, I'm sure Skadot must have thought one of you was an adult because teenagers entering the woods without an adult is an offense. You understand our need to remain vigilant against any deviant behavior. Now, where are your parents?"

He looks around for a responsible adult. I look around too; maybe Eli is around and can play the part for us. Unfortunately, she's not here and neither is anyone else. We are alone and need to get to the agency.

"Sir, I'm sorry. We were in a hurry to get to one of the agencies before it closes. We were told it was on the main street," I say innocently.

"Why would you be looking for an agency? In Sentursyd there are only the agencies for adults."

"We need to file a complaint or a request for help."

"I see. Is someone in trouble?" he appears genuinely concerned.

"Yes. Someone is. We just need to get there before they close."

"I'll escort you," the man with the rimless hat, whom I assume is an officer, says. He walks alongside us toward the main street.

Those who'd been recording us are back to their business, seeing we aren't a threat, or at least are no longer a threat. I notice there aren't any teens in the park, only adults and young children. *Great. Would've been nice for the flying computer to mention that.*

As we leave the park area for the sidewalk, I hear the clod of hooves - this time against pavement. They are approaching to my left. It's the same men and women from the woods. The male captive sits on the second horse-eagle behind a large burly male. The female rides behind them. They are coming toward us and for a moment I can feel the nerves tingle along my back on both sides. I wonder if she saw me in the woods or had I remained camouflaged.

As the caravan passes us, her head turns, and our eyes meet. She squints, before she takes a deep breath in through her nostrils. I can see them flare and know she's trying to match the scent from the woods.

"Where are they taking them?" I ask the officer.

"Probably the Sovereign Goyar. Justice is promptly executed."

I open my mouth to ask what this Goyar is and Morren shakes his head, warning me not to.

It's probably another piece of information a true Anfarian would know.

"We're almost to the agency. Do you have an appointment?"

I can feel us all hold our breath. "No, sir. It's an issue that came up suddenly," I answer.

"Oh. Well without an appointment, and at this time of day, there's no guarantee you'll be seen. At least you can get on the list and come back in the morning if his office is backed up."

There is silence. Not seeing him today was never considered.

What do we do if we can't get in today? I send Morren.

We go back to Baselonica and come back in the morning.

But our time is different there. We don't know what day it'll be here if we leave. Or what time.

Then we stay. Find somewhere to hide out for the night, he says, almost unconcerned.

How can you be so flipping calm?

I don't have a choice, Karana. What am I gonna do? What are we gonna do? Panic? And what will that get us?

I scowl and walk up the steps to the pearlesque stone building with large heavy wooden doors. The officer pulls one of them open and holds it for us. I assume he feels charged with making sure we stay together and keeping his eyes on us the entire time.

"This way," he says and points to a window in the corner with an unidentifiable Anfarian.

"I've got some young people who would like to see Director Jable Narp."

"Do you have an appointment?" the androgynous being asks.

"No. How busy is he today? Can they get in?" the officer asks.

"He's already backed up, and then he was called down for a special hearing at the Sovereign Goyar."

I am pretty sure the officer could hear me gulp. The man and woman in the woods were trying to get a message to him before they were caught.

"Can we get an appointment for first thing in the morning?" I ask.

"I can't do that. I have places to be in the morning," Eton says frustrated. "This is a waste of time."

"Now, young man. What's the problem? People your age shouldn't have such hopeless feelings," the clerk says.

"I'm not having a hopeless feeling. I'm just saying that this isn't gonna work. I have some place to be tomorrow," Eton says glaring at me.

"Is there any way he can see us today?" I ask trying to sound as calm as I can, despite the dizziness and nervousness.

"Well, he has one last appointment on his schedule today, but he probably canceled it to go the Goyar early. Depending on what you need, you might try going to the Goyar and waiting. I can let his assistant know."

I scan the others, and particularly Eton, to make sure they're okay with this.

"Can we get on his schedule for tomorrow, in case we can't see him at the Goyar?" I ask, feeling slightly more optimistic.

"You can. I need a name and contact information. You can enter it here. You can also see what times are available. There aren't many, but there are a couple."

The clerk hands a tablet shaped like an hourglass to me through the window.

"Oh, and I'll need your card."

"Card?" I repeat back.

"If you don't have the Anfar Max Connect card yet, you can still use your youth card."

"We had an urgent situation and left in a hurry. We don't have our cards." I try to mask the panic rising in my chest. *I should've let Morren do this part.*

"Hmmm. That is unfortunate. You all do understand the importance of following our guidelines, rules, and procedures, correct? Without order, there is chaos," the clerk says with a depth of sincerity that surprises me.

"It is expected that every Anfarian carries their card with them at all times. That was the agreement set during the internal chip resistance movement. Surely, you studied that," the officer chimes in.

"Yes. Of course," Morren answers, before I can say what I'm thinking.

The officer looks at us. I can tell he feels sorry for us. "Director Narp doesn't see anyone without us verifying their card. That means you can't meet him at the Goyar, but you can get on the schedule for tomorrow. Please remember your card. Otherwise, there's nothing we can do for you right now."

"Fill it out, come back tomorrow. It's your best bet," the clerk says before checking the clock on the wall that only goes to nine and putting things away.

Chapter Eighteen

Staring at the blank lines on the screen doesn't give me anything. It wants information I don't have. Information none of us have.

"Can we do all this in the morning? You're closing soon, so we should still be able to get in if we come first thing, right?"

The person looked at something I couldn't see and nodded. "You've got a good chance if you are here when we open."

"Thanks. We'll be back," I say and hand the tablet back, in the same state I'd gotten it - blank.

"So, where can I escort you to now?" the officer asks as we step back from the counter.

"We don't need an escort. We'll walk home, and we'll be sure to stay out of restricted areas," Reyn chimes in sweetly.

There is something about her I'm trying to wrap my head around. She doesn't speak much, but I can tell she's smart and resourceful. She managed to get off Earth and convince Eton the toad to come along, even if under what I hope are false pretenses.

"I'll walk you out. I like seeing young people be active," the officer says.

"Thank you," Morren says, still not letting me speak.

"And good luck tomorrow," the officer says.

He opens the door for us and waves bye to the Anfarian behind the window.

Outside, the sun seems to be going down quickly. Again, we're stuck on a planet with nothing besides ourselves. We need to ditch Officer Friendly and get a few things if we're gonna make it through the night and do what we came to do.

Standing on the steps I look at the street and smile. "Thanks again," I say.

He's waiting for us to leave first, so I start walking down the steps. Morren, Reyn, and Eton come down the steps. Together we head in the direction the caravan of horse-eagle creatures had gone.

"We've got a slim chance that maybe we can see Director Narp at the Goyar. If not, we're gonna need a plan to see him tomorrow."

"We don't have a slim chance tonight. He won't see anyone without a card," Eton says, his tone oozing with a righteous air.

"He doesn't know we haven't been vetted," Reyn says. "And from what they told us, all we need to do is get hold of some cards."

I smile. I knew it. She's resourceful and smart.

"Let's find whatever this Sovereign Goyar is and see what we can do," Morren says.

I stop and look around. Surely, there is some map or signage or something we can use to figure out where we are.

"What's that over there?" Morren asks.

"Looks like a transit stop," I say.

"It should have a map then, right?" he smiles.

He crosses the nearly empty street to what looks like a tram spot. Reyn and I follow him while Eton sits on the curb of the sidewalk. He isn't making me feel very good about the prospects of saving humanity alongside him.

The shelter has a map posted on the inside. A blue square marks where we are, with the agency building shown nearby. We follow the lines on the map to what looks like a ring with the label Sovereign Goyar.

"That's it!"

"This is helpful. Look. A tourist office is about three blocks ahead. Maybe we can find out exactly where and what it is and you two can use your powers to jump us there," Reyn suggests.

"Good idea. Come on. They're probably closing in five or ten minutes," I say, dragging both of them back to where Eton sits on the ground.

"Find anything useful?" he says sarcastically.

"Yeah, we did. A tourist office is just down the street, and there was a map of where the Goyar is. We're going to the tourist office and then the Goyar," Morren says firmly.

I don't think Morren cares much for Eton either. It doesn't matter since we're stuck with him.

We're nearly jogging down the street trying to reach the tourist office before it closes. All we need is something on the Goyar that will help us visualize it. Then we can jump to it. Morren runs up to the door and pulls at it. I exhale loudly as it gives and pulls open for him.

Inside, the cheery office is painted in pastels accented by greens and blues. It seems they like these colors here.

"Hello! Welcome to the Sentursyd Tourist Center, where the history and future of Sentursyd, the center of Anfar, come together. What can I help you with?" The cheery greeting comes from an older Anfarian female approaching us.

Her head has small nodules on it, in different shades of brown. The back of her hands have the same odd nodules, which I notice when she hands us each a tourist map. She picks up something with her long fingers that boast sharply pointed violet nails. She then gives us each a small piece of chocolate wrapped in a shimmery green wrapper made to look like a coin.

"Thank you. Do you have any info on the Sovereign Goyar?"

"Oh. Of course," she says, fluttering by us to pick up something from a table. "It's one of our most popular destinations. People come from all over Anfar for the Goyar. And I'm sure you know, tonight's a special night. There were some unexpected additions, and Director Jable Narp himself is going to be there. We don't get him personally at every Goyar. Like I said, tonight is…special." She swoons noticeably as she mentions the Goyar and Director Narp.

"We might try to go," Morren says.

"I'm closing soon so that I can get there myself. I wouldn't want to miss it! The Goyar only happens once a week, but I think for what these people do and the backlog, it should be done more often."

I think the confusion in my eyes is misunderstood. I have no idea what this thing must be, but after what she says, it doesn't sound like what I thought.

"Well, I don't mean it quite like that. That may have come out the wrong way. I simply mean, that you know, those people who do those things shouldn't have to wait for their fate to be decided. A week can be too long, that's all."

"Ohhhh." My nodding barely conceals the fact I don't know what she's really talking about.

"Well, if you're going you might want to go ahead. General seating is first come-first serve. I've got reserved seating but as a tourist, you won't."

She hands us a pamphlet of the Sovereign Goyar. On the front is a picture of what looks like a circus ring with seats around the outside. Several large gates are around the center. It looks festive, with a brightly colored tent covering.

"Oh, and that cover is removable. Sometimes when the weather is nice, we have a wonderful view of the night sky. Maybe tonight it'll be open," she says gleefully.

"How long of a walk is it there?" Morren asks.

The more I look at the picture and listen to her speak, the less sure I am about the whole plan.

"You may want to take Sentursyd transit or the shuttle from here. Walking would be nearly an hour. There is a shuttle that will take you straight to the Goyar today. It runs right past here and drops you off right in front. It's only two folls, but they only take coins. And that's two folls for each of you.

We have no folls, whatever that is, and no real coins. An hour is far if we have to walk, but we have no intention of doing that either.

"Thanks for the info. We're gonna try and head over there."

"It'll be a night you won't forget! Take care." She's as bubbly as she was when we came in, though clearly in a hurry. She's packing up her things even as we walk toward the door.

Morren is the first to leave, his head shaking. Reyn and Eton follow. I linger for a moment before turning back to the polished and chipper Anfarian.

"What do they do at the Goyar?"

She looks at me with a sweet smile. "Oh, that's right. You are still young and haven't needed to be concerned with the Goyar. The Goyar allows the administration of justice. Tonight, those who've been captured for crimes against Labor and Welfare will face justice. It is always fair. The Goyar does not err."

"So they have court tonight?"

"Yes, they are judged in a court based on Anfarian law. If they are guilty, their punishment will be immediate. If they are innocent, they must simply show it at the Sovereign Goyar and will be free."

I nod uncomfortably as I think about the female from the woods captured for leaving work an hour early and stealing labor from her employer.

Opening the door, I join the others on the sidewalk.

"What took you so long?" Eton asks.

"I asked her what the Goyar is."

"And?" Eton asks.

"It's like a court where justice is administered on the spot."

"Wow. Now that's something I might like to see." For the first time Eton sounds interested in something other than himself.

"Well, it sounds interesting at least," Reyn says.

"It sounds scary," Morren says.

"It sounds fair," Eton says. "Let's go."

"Hold on. Morren, we need to look at this map and the building so we can jump there. Let's get inside but not on that center floor."

Morren and I study the pamphlet and I know he can feel how nervous I am. This planet makes me antsy, and it's more than the fast turning. There's something about the people, and I can't place my finger on it, but they make me feel a tiny bit…slimy, despite how pleasant and orderly they seem.

"You guys ready?" I ask Reyn and Eton.

"Yeah," Reyn says.

She seems more energized. Maybe it's being off of Baselonica. Eton is working my patience to its end, moping and attitudinal over everything except the Goyar. I know he's not thinking about what we're trying to do. Two things to do are on his mind, but neither of them are what we're trying to do on Anfar.

I take Reyn's hand and Morren's hand and face Eton. Here we go again.

"Three. Two. One."

Chapter Nineteen

That was our best entry yet, thanks to Morren. We're still holding hands, although awkwardly in the restroom. I guess I had to use it more than I thought.

"Hey, you aren't allowed in this restroom." What appears to be a female, points to Eton and Morren.

"I'm sorry, we were confused. We're leaving."

"I'm calling security. The law is perfectly clear about this. You know it's illegal and you are old enough to know the law." She reaches for a black screen on the wall and presses and swipes it, while eyeing us with disdain.

We rush out of the restroom and try to blend in with the others coming for the Goyar. A man with a fuzzy hat passes us, eating what looks like popcorn. The counters serving food and drink have lines several people deep as they prepare for whatever is about to happen. I wonder if I'm wrong about how

I was feeling about this. It looks like people have come to have fun at a sporting event, like I'd done when I was a kid.

"Where do you think we'd find Director Narp?" I ask Morren.

"I'm guessing he's somewhere with important people, not up here."

I walk over to the rails that separate the seats from the food level. There are areas set back with seating, their own bars, and servers. They line a level just above the floor level. Box seats. Of course.

"Down there," I point.

"How are we gonna get down there. We don't have tickets," Reyn asks

She's right. We don't have anything. My stomach makes a loud growling sound. I hungrily eye an unidentifiable collection of food on a plate an Anfarian holds as she passes by. I realize we haven't eaten since leaving Baselonica Xuna.

"We can wait until it's over, then catch him on his way out," Morren suggests.

"We'll watch from back here. They are really uptight about their laws here," I suggest.

The sound of drums brings a roaring cheer in the Goyar theatre. A band follows the drummer, wearing colors much like those on the tent. The striped blue, green, purple, and red tops are a contrast to the gray everyone else is wearing. The crowds stand up and become quiet as the band finishes what I have to assume is an anthem.

"In our land, we consider law and order to be the utmost representation of a civilized society. While we are respectful and helpful, most importantly, we are lawful. Who agrees?"

A tall woman with a headpiece made of a stiff purple fabric speaks. The headpiece plumes on top of her head like an ostrich feathered mohawk. It waves as she moves her head to address her audience. She's not dressed in the drab gray, but rather a matching purple suit that is a cross between pants and a skirt. Around her neck is a thick gold necklace with a pendant shaped like an S.

The crowd of Anfarians are going wild. She smiles for a moment as she waits for them to enjoy their cheering. She raises one hand to the height of her shoulder and the crowd immediately falls into a hush.

"As you are well aware, we have high expectations of our people and the behavior of each of our citizens. We generally frown upon sudden emotional outbursts, arguments, and behavior that disturbs or threatens a peaceful existence."

Yelling and cheering erupts again throughout the theatre.

"But tonight, we put that aside for what is one of the most important activities in our cultured society. The Sovereign Goyar!"

"Yeah!!!!" shouts someone behind us before the chanting begins.

"Goyar! Goyar! Goyar! Goyar!" they repeat to the beating of drums.

"This week the Goyar is hosted by the Agency on Monetary Value of Labor and Welfare. There are three cases being brought forth tonight. We believe the Sovereign Goyar is indeed that – sovereign, above all else and it reflects the highest law of the Goyar. There is no escaping the Goyar. It is everywhere and sees everything. The Goyar knows if the accused jarosos and jarasas are innocent or guilty, and is never wrong."

"Never wrong! Never wrong! Never wrong!"

"As you know, it is always fair. The Goyar does not err," she encourages them again.

"Always fair, does not err! Always fair, does not err!"

She silences the crowd with her hand again before looking to her left where a man is seated.

"Tonight is a special night at the Sovereign Goyar. The esteemed Director Jable Narp will introduce this evening's Goyar participants and will oversee the administration of justice. We always respect the outcome of the Sovereign Goyar as final. Family may mourn for the following week, if needed, but following this period, we expect all affected to honorably accept the outcome and resume normal activities. Continuing to grieve belittles our system of justice, Anfarian morale, and the ability to be productive. These are three things we hold in high regard. Now, let us welcome Director Jable Narp!"

The drums sound again as Director Narp stands and comes to the microphone dangling from the ceiling. He waves to the crowd and fixes his fuchsia suit.

"Tonight, we hold the Sovereign Goyar to determine justice for three individuals in fact, not just two, as we'd originally planned. I will give their names and the crimes they have been charged with. All of these crimes are Level Two crimes and are punishable by expulsion to one of the ally penal colonies. If you want to live with lawlessness, you can do it somewhere else!"

"Am I right, law-abiding citizens of Anfar!?" he cries out.

Again, the crowd cheers.

"Yes. At least you can live. In fact, we may be sending back a transfer from Baselonica Xuna who tried to bring that unwelcomed lawlessness here. We took a risk and allowed her into our peaceful home and this is what came of it."

The crowd erupts, laughing and cheering. My eyes go wide and mouth drops. Could there possibly be Anfarians on Base X and we just didn't notice?

A man runs onto the center of the ring juggling two balls before adding a third one and smiling. He walks back and forth across the open theater before throwing all the balls in the air. He catches one and bows.

Morren's eyes are as wide as mine. "What is this?" he asks.

"I have no idea, but it doesn't look good. Why were we brought here?" I ask.

Reyn shakes her head as if she understands something now that she hadn't before.

"There are some on Base X who've mentioned the transfers to Base X, and also from Base X to other places."

"And now, the first participant. This jarosa, Carsa, is a teacher who felt it was okay to not grade her students' papers within the required timeline of three days. In fact, she was two full days over when reported, justly, by several parents of her students. She failed to remedy this situation by immediately producing the graded work and in fact chose instead to miss a full day of work, causing Anfar citizens to have to pay for a replacement. She did not produce, and she did not request an adjustment in earnings. She is accused of accepting welfare from the Land of Anfar as evidenced by her continuing to earn a salary without meeting her obligations and for doing this without meeting the qualifications of being in need. She is participant A," Narp announces.

"Welfare Queen! Welfare Queen! Welfare Queen!" the crowd shouts as a scared woman is pushed out one of the gates lining the theater and into the center.

"My child was sick! I'm sorry. I'm sorry!" she cries.

Her words are drowned out by the chanting.

Next, we have a jaroso, Mirk, who is accused of charging his customers different prices for wake-up juice. We have laws that set prices to ensure consistency; however, his prices fluctuated daily. He is guilty of manipulating the value of money for gain, and cheating people out of their money. He is participant B."

"Cheater! Cheater! Cheater!"

"And last, our third participant, Willa, is a very recent transfer from Baselonica Xuna," he begins with a look that says, "I told you so."

"Boooooo! Send her back! Send her back! Send her back!" they chant.

"Now, now. Everyone deserves a chance to go through our justice system to determine guilt or innocence. It is never wrong. We accepted this Baselonican because of skills she has in technology and separating the elements of the natural resources we receive from Base X. It is a critical skill that is in high demand here. We had lofty expectations of this foreign immigrant. But she has already been accused of cheating her employer out of labor. When she came here, she was already on probation as a transfer from Baselonica, who didn't want her…"

"Booooo!!!!" the crowd yells.

"And we still gave her a chance."

"Send her back!!! Send her back!!!"

"And yet, she left work a full hour early and expected us to pay her and Baselonica for that time! We DON'T pay for unworked labor," he booms.

She stumbles out beside the other two. I recognize her from the woods. I think about the girl from the Base X cell. I hadn't gotten to see her at all, but she'd seen me. It had been as a Baselonican, not an Anfarian, but perhaps she would recognize me.

I try to figure out how long ago that would have been in Anfar days, but my angst makes it difficult to make the calculation right now. We'll have a hard time doing what we came to do, if at every turn we risk breaking a law.

The drums beat again, this time slow and steady, as the juggler walks over and leads them to the center of the theater floor. The sound of raucous cheering is deafening. I don't hear the female behind us until she's standing mere feet away with an officer.

"That's them. Right there. Those two jarosos were in the jarosas's restroom,"

I turn to Eton, Morren, and Reyn. We're gonna have to blow our cover or risk Morren and Reyn being caught. Knowing now that they'd be sent right here for the ridiculous Goyar. If the ridiculous crimes the three out there are accused of could mean banishment from Anfar, what would being in the wrong bathroom mean?

"Is this true? Were you two jarosos in the jarosas's restroom?"

"I'm sorry. We were confused," Morren says, sounding apologetic.

"An apology does not expunge you. It does not serve as a remedy for breaking the law. Being confused is no excuse. It is your responsibility as a law-abiding citizen of Anfar and the city of Sentursyd to be fastidious in the knowledge of our laws and living in accordance with them. Do you agree?"

Morren and Eton look at the officer, and the female who stands with her green, chameleon-like arms folded over her chest, awaiting justice.

"Yes. But, we were just…"

"You either agree or you do not agree. There is no 'but'. Do you agree?" the officer asks again.

"Yes," Morren says, mortified.

"Yeah," Eton says, clearly pissed.

"And you seem to not be so sure if you agree." A scaly finger points at Eton.

"I'm sure. I agree." Eton bites his lip, drawing drops of blood.

"How old are you two?"

"Sixteen," Morren answers cautiously.

"And you?"

"Nineteen." Eton's shaky voice is barely audible.

"Sixteen and nineteen?" The officer rubs his chin. "I'll need to verify that. Cards?"

I reach over and grab Reyn's hand. She takes Eton's who grabs Morren's. I look at Morren and mouth, "Three."

"Cards. Why are you holding hands? It is an unnecessary display of affection. Are you couples? That is also against the law. Only couples approved by the Sentursyd

Relationship and Continuity Force are allowed. And no couple is more than two years in age difference. That is a more severe crime."

"Two."

"I need your cards. All of you, now. And I need to know if you are holding hands because you are a couple."

"One."

Chapter Twenty

I land against Eton, all of us squished together in some kind of box made of a hard sterile material that reminds of me plastic. I lean back away from him, but there isn't anywhere to go.

"Yuck! I stepped in something wet!" Eton mutters.

"Okay. Where are we now?" I ask.

The sound of flushing answers the question.

"Another bathroom?" I whisper.

I realize I hadn't actually used the restroom, and it was becoming a pressing matter.

We are in a large stall, waiting for the footsteps we hear to silence.

"I'll meet you out there. Figure out where we are," I order them and push them out the stall.

Eton's left foot squishes and squeezes out red water onto the floor as he goes.

I look at what I assume is a toilet, trying to get my bearings. I carefully balance myself over the seat that looks like a conveyer belt that connects to the wall. I refuse to sit, certain it'll start moving. A green light in the wall flashes as I stand up. The light turns red and seconds later the conveyer belt begins to turn, revealing the unused side of the toilet seat. The space behind the wall rattles and then there is what sounds like pressurized gas being released.

I hope we are still at the Goyar. It will set us back at least a day if we aren't.

"We're still at the Goyar," Morren says clearly. "I think we're close to the box office where Narp was."

"Great. We just need to find someplace safe to wait til this thing is over," I say.

"You still think he's the answer?" Reyn asks, unbelievingly.

"He has to be. Someone has to be willing to listen to us about what's happening on Baselonica Xuna," I say.

I'm trying to convince myself as much as Reyn. After what we'd just seen, I'm not so sure he's the right one to help, or that this is even the right place.

"Hurry up, Karana, before we get caught in the restroom again," Eton says as I dry my hands.

"I am. I say we go out and find a good place to watch the Goyar and keep our eye on Director Narp."

Morren opens the door and peeks out before pulling it the rest of the way. This level is nearly vacant. Only a few Anfarians who appear to be servers are walking in and out of what I assume are the boxes.

The four of us look out of place. We draw too much attention, and our mysterious escape won't help.

"I have an idea."

"I hope it's good, since I'm sure by standing here we're breaking some law," Morren says.

"And now for the first judgment of justice!" we hear in the hall.

Morren runs over to a door down the hall and pulls at the handle. Locked. He gives us a thumbs-up sign and a smile. We hurry to join him in front of the locked door.

Okay. Everyone ready?

"Morren, they have no idea what you're talking about. They can't hear your thoughts."

"Oh yeah. So this is the plan," Morren smiles sneakily.

***

"This uniform is too tight," Reyn complains.

She tugs the black pants with white stripes on the sides. I notice they're also too short. Mine aren't much better. Both of the females serving down here were petite.

I shrug as I move my hips, but trying to loosen them up is futile. "I guess they never heard of spandex."

"Stop complaining," Eton says.

I try to stifle my laugh at the pants that barely reach his ankles.

"Yeah. At least we fit in down here," Morren says.

It had taken four trips. By the last one, the storage closet was getting cramped, but it had worked. We'd taken a server one by one to the closet, jumping in to avoid the locked door. I

153

wished it wasn't necessary to jump with all four of us each time, but the first time Morren had tried with the first male, they'd wound up standing right beside us.

I look at the trays in front of us. "If you want to eat, now's the time."

"What is it?" Eton says, his face twisted in disgust.

"Nutrients. Calories. Energy. Food," Reyn says as she picks up what looks like some form of bread and takes a bite.

Eton shakes his head, searching for something that looks safe.

We eat from the trays until we've had enough to fill us for now. There's no guarantee when the next meal will be.

Eton and Reyn walk behind, as Morren and I push trays in front of us. We smile politely at two guards passing the other way who only stare back, not returning the gesture.

"Hey, we need our drinks refreshed," a voice calls from inside one of the doorways.

Morren wheels his tray over and walks in, keeping his head down. A minute later he's back out and we continue walking down the hall, looking for Director Narp's room.

"Snack refill," calls a male from another doorway.

I look down at my tray. *My turn.* I walk ahead to the room and disappear inside. I come back out and smile.

"That's the one we want."

"Okay, stay close. At least we know where to find him even if we have to wait," Morren says.

"What is that noise?" I ask, nearly tripping on Eton's foot.

"Watch it," he says, rolling his strange eyes.

"It sounds like howling," Reyn answers.

"More like high-pitched screaming."

This isn't making sense.

"We need to get moving and out of this hall," Eton warns.

"The first judgment has been made! For her crimes against the City of Sentursyd, in the Land of Anfar, for illegally receiving payment for work not done and for failing to perform her duties, the Land of Anfar releases Carsa of Sentursyd to an associate penal colony. Do you have any final words before you depart Anfar?"

I wait, frozen, in disbelief. She's being banished.

"There are no words that can be spoken to remedy this. I am sorry to my family, my son, my students, and my great Land of Anfar for failing to uphold my lawful duty to meet my obligations. For that, I accept my punishment. The Sovereign Goyar is always just and right."

I hear the pain in her trembling voice and wonder if she believes the words she just said. She can't really be okay with being banished from her home and taken from her child.

The noisy eruption of applause is quickly replaced by Director Narp's voice.

"It is time for us to say goodbye to Carsa. Teacher, mother, wife."

The silence of the crowd was broken only by a chuckle from one of the nearby doors. I put my finger up to my lips.

"Fools. They think they're going to live out their days on a penal colony. They're worth much more being rented out until they expire."

"Ha! I know. I got a great fee for her. Young and healthy with the heart of a servant, she's got a lot of years in her to work."

"Where's she going?"

"Cuupton is the first stop, as usual."

"I should've known. They've got the best market. And our new contact has been giving us a better split lately."

I can hear the smug smiles in their voices as my stomach knots.

Don't even think about it, Morren sends me.

But it's too late. I'm already pissed.

What the fidgets and gumdrops, Morren? They don't even know what's really gonna happen to them. I bet none of those people out there screaming and cheering for justice know. Shirt. Hanger. Iron. Table!

Calm down, Karana, he sends. *We have something to do here and then we get back to Base X and then home. That's the plan and we can't waste time.*

I look at my brother. He's got a point. We're losing more time here than we were on Base X. We don't owe these people anything. It isn't our problem. It isn't our fight. We have problems of our own.

Still.

"Karana. We can't do anything about this. We have to wait and speak to Director Narp," Morren continues to argue, his words intruding on the thoughts I'm already having.

"He's not gonna do anything, Morren. You already know that. What do you think's gonna happen? He's gonna care about what's happening on Base X? What have you seen here so far that makes you think that?"

Morren slides along the wall to the opening of an empty box suite, and inside the open doorway. We scoot along, shoulder to shoulder, until it opens up into the room. Crouching against the festively painted wall in turquoise, yellow, oranges, reds, and purples, I feel as if I've gone to a carnival and not court. All of the décor and interior colors, except for the sterile bathrooms, are obscenely bright and cheerful.

A small figurine bearing a strong resemblance to Director Narp smiles at me from a side table. It's wearing an audacious purple and green suit.

We strain to watch what's happening in the Goyar. Carsa stands in the center of the floor, where the ring was spinning earlier. Three Anfarians roll over a clear, egg-shaped tube with a seat. They open the door and Carsa steps inside the tube. One of the attendants straps her in, places a mask over her face, and watches her fall asleep. She never even struggled.

The men step out of the circle that spins, leaving Carsa and the tube in the middle. One of the men presses a button on a controller he's carrying. The floor underneath the tube turns around slowly for everyone in the audience to get a view. It completes the rotation and the floor opens like a camera shutter. The egg drops down and disappears.

Again the crowd breaks into thunderous applause and screams.

Director Narp steps forward again, avoiding the center of the theater that is now closing. As he comes out, he puts his hands in the air. I can't tell if he's trying to calm them or excite them.

"And now for Participant B, Mirk. Mirk has been accused of price-fixing. For this he receives the same punishment if found guilty by our incorruptible justice system."

"Are you ready to face the Sovereign Goyar?" Narp asks.

He turns to Mirk, who stands near the circle. Mirk's hands are twitching uncontrollably.

"I am ready to face justice," he says, his words trembling as much as he is.

"Step into the circle of truth and justice."

Chapter Twenty-One

I peek over the edge of the rails to see into the theatre as Mirk walks into the circle. One of the men who'd rolled out the tube for Carsa places a large device with goggle-like glasses and earphones over Mirk's head. His ears and eyes are completely covered as he stands in the center of the circle.

The attendant leaves the circle and returns to stand with his associates.

"And now, let the Sovereign Goyar determine the innocence or guilt of Mirk, and administer justice."

Narp walks over to a panel on the side of the theater and presses something I can't see. Whatever he's pressed clearly turns on the contraption the male wears.

He throws his head back and puts his hands up as if trying to stop something. He moves to the side again and stumbles slightly. The fighting against something we can't see continues for what feels like several minutes, his screams now joining his physical desperation. "Noooo! Stop! It burns! Please. I didn't...I didn't...Make it stop! I'm sorry!"

Narp presses something on the panel and Mirk, breathing heavy and crying, stands near the edge of the circle.

The device on his head is removed and I can see what looks like discolored skin on his face. Burns? I wonder. But that's not possible. It must've been some virtual reality confession test.

Narp steps forward. "The second judgment has been made! For his crimes against the Land of Anfar and for price-fixing through illegally changing prices, the Land of Anfar releases Mirk of Sentursyd to an associate penal colony. Do you have any final words before you depart Anfar?"

Mirk pats his eyes tenderly and looks around the theater. He says nothing.

"Do you have any words before you depart. Our system is just and has determined justice for you. What do you have to say?"

Mirk looks at Narp with disdain.

Narp walks closer to Mirk and away from the microphone that dangles in front of him. He leans in, covers his mouth, and says something to Mirk. Mirk glances over into the first row of the theatre. Two children sit on either side of what may be an older Anfarian female. The female covers the children's eyes. Mirk becomes even angrier and he looks down at the floor of the arena and then at the smirking Director Narp. Mirk takes a deep breath and speaks.

"I accept the judgment against me in our fair and incorruptible system of justice," he says struggling, "and I apologize to anyone I've hurt." His gaze settles back on the three Anfarians who must be his family.

The raucous clapping annoys me.

You know this is bull, right Morren?

"Very well. It is time for us to say goodbye to Mirk. Entrepreneur, son, widowed father. Mirk has chosen to honor our just system and we will repay that honor in our acknowledgment of the difficulties to be faced by his mother. May this serve as a lesson to all Anfarians that our actions impact not only ourselves, but generations to come; as well as those that come before us."

The silence permeates the space as another clear tube is brought to the center of the spinning ring. The men do the same thing to Mirk as they did to Carsa. He struggles against the men more than Carsa until one of the handlers whispers something into his ear and eyes his family menacingly.

I watch as Mirk falls asleep inside the tube chamber and the ground beneath him slowly opens. The tube disappears into the hole.

Remember why we're here, Karana, Morren warns me.

To help the Baselonicans. And that's what we're going to do.

Don't do anything stupid.

Too late. We passed stupid long ago. Now we're at the intersection of crazy and insane.

You know what I mean, Karana.

You're right, I do, Morren. It's obvious Narp and these people won't do anything to help Base X. They might be just as bad, if not worse. At least on Base X they know they're screwed up.

You're impossible. What is it you're trying to do?

"Are you two doing that thing again? Talking to yourselves again?" Eton nudges Morren to get his attention.

"Sorry," Morren says.

"Cut it out. I don't know what you two are scheming but we came here to get help for the Baselonicans and get back. I'm already late for work, I'm sure. I don't know since I don't know what time it is on Base X, but I bet I'm late and I blame you for that. I don't know what the two of you are saying to each other with your mind talk, but it better be about how we're leaving this messed up place, and fast!"

"We have to get help, but it may not be as easy as we thought," I admit.

"What are you talking about?" Reyn is now curious.

"Narp's not gonna be any help. If we want to help Baselonica, we're gonna have to help Baselonica help themselves."

"How? No one there is gonna go against the Zo clan willingly."

"They just need a leader. A reason. Maybe even some support of others who feel wronged."

"I don't think I like where this is going." Eton settles back from us as if those few inches will distance him from whatever is going to happen.

"Now for the third and final judgment for this week's Sovereign Goyar. Willa faces the charge of withholding labor while on probation as a transfer. This charge does not carry the same punishment as those from Anfar. If the Goyar finds Willa guilty, she will be returned to her home of Baselonica Xuna."

"Willa?" I say louder than I should. "That's the girl I met in that cell on Base X. That's her!"

"Are you ready to face the Sovereign Goyar?" Narp turns to face a pissed-off Willa.

"Your system sucks. It's incorruptible cuz no one can win."

"Not true. People don't always receive guilty judgments. All you have to do to is remain in that circle for three minutes without apologizing for your wrong or confessing. If you do that, then the judgment from the Goyar will be in your favor. See, it's completely in your power. The innocent will be judged as they are, the guilty will be judged as they are," he smiles. "Now, I'll ask again. Are you ready to face the Sovereign Goyar?"

"You just want to send me back. I'll tell you this. I'm the best they've got at what I do and if you send me back, anyone else is gonna be second rate. I promise your pompous ass that."

Director Narp smiles as he walks toward Willa and away from the dangling microphone. "We shall see. I don't know why we bothered accepting you anyway. We heard you were trouble," he hisses into Willa's ear.

He backs away and returns to his microphone. "Step into the circle of truth and justice."

Willa doesn't move.

"Take her to the circle of truth and justice," Narp orders the attendants.

Two walk over and carry Willa, kicking and scratching at their faces to the circle. The third man places the contraption on her head.

I look over to the panel where Director Narp now stands. He looks at a tablet in his hand and then presses something on the panel. If I'm not mistaken, that's a sly smile.

"You guys ready?"

"For what?"

"To get Willa and get outta here."

"We don't know where we'll go," Morren says.

"Only if it means getting back to Base X," Eton says.

Reyn shakes her head and takes a deep breath. Her nose flares.

I think of Tezzi and wonder if she thinks we've forgotten about them. I wonder if she's still in the compound, and if she and Dad are okay.

"This is why we can't waste time, Karana. We have people waiting on us, on all of us," Morren sends me.

"We're gonna get Willa and get off of Anfar. We can figure it out from there,"

"You can count me out after this," Eton says. "I happen to like my life on Base X and I don't need you ruining it for me."

"Everyone hold hands. Three. Two. One."

"Oh crap!" I yell as we tumble onto Willa. The headpiece falls from her head as she screams.

"You're the one from the cell. How'd you get here? What are you?! Watch out!" she yells.

I turn to find one of the attendants coming behind me. Before I can get my body in position, Willa's foot is at his chin, sending him spinning back. The other two are coming and I hear Director Narp calling other guards in.

"We don't have time to fight," I say as we watch an attendant running toward us.

Morren looks back at Narp, uncertain.

Narp points toward us and the attendant continues.

He's about to reach us.

Morren and I clasp hands.

Before he can react, we clothesline him.

He's still standing, though obviously caught off guard.

Reyn comes around and behind, her elbow landing square in the back of his neck.

I look for Eton. We need him before we can jump.

He's got his arms around the other attendant's neck. The attendant has him locked with an arm and they pummel each other in the stomach and face.

Willa steps over and slams the headgear viciously into the attendants head, just missing Eton.

She swipes her foot under the attendant's feet.

He stumbles.

Eton's knee hits his gut and he falls back.

Willa runs and Eton limps over to where I stand with Reyn and Morren. The guards are running toward us. They seem only to act out of duty. A peculiar thing.

"We better hurry," Reyn says. "I'm not a fighter."

"Neither are they," Willa says.

We hold hands, in a circle, our backs to each other. I hope we end up someplace safe.

"Three."

One attending guard holds up what looks like a gun and points it at us. "Two."

He hesitates a moment and opens his mouth to speak at the same time I count down to one. The explosive sound muffles my voice.

Chapter Twenty-Two

"One."

"God damn, son of a Baselonican baby-maker!" Willa cries out. "That SOB got me!"

We can't see anything in the pitch black. I can't tell if what I feel under my fingers is a floor inside or hard ground outside. I have to assume we're inside since I can't hear any normal outside sounds or see any sky.

"I can't see a thing," Morren vents.

"We need to get outta here and get Willa help. Wherever here is," I say.

"Hopefully we're back home. Base X, I mean," Eton winces.

"Are you hurt too?" Reyn asks Eton.

"My ribs are killing me."

"See, Karana, this thing you seem to be obsessed with almost got us killed. We better hope we're closer to help like we promised Lari, so we can get back home." Morren is justified in his frustration but that won't speed anything up.

There's nothing I can say that would make any of it better. Our only option is to find a way out of wherever we are and hope there is help nearby. Light would be good too.

"Where are you hit, Willa?" I ask nervously.

"My side. Hip. I think I can make it outta here. It's bleeding, but it feels like it probably grazed me. Still hurts. I'll be damned if they think they're gonna kill me after what I've been through."

I nod, realizing she can't see me.

"Someone find the door," Eton orders.

The sound of irritation and impatience is thick in his voice. I'm certain he's over all of this, since he'd never been into it to begin with. He only has one reason for being here.

We were supposed to have a simple reason, too. Get whoever the Immune is on Base X and bring them home. But it's two Immunes and now a can of worms has been opened. I want desperately to be okay with just going home, killing the bastards who have Tezzi and Dad, and finding the other Immunes.

You want to be okay with that because that's what we're supposed to be doing, Morren says.

"I don't need you in here right now," I say back.

"Who're you talking to?" Eton snarls.

I'm not answering him. I feel around for a flat surface and perhaps a switch.

It's your stubbornness that has us in here, so you don't get that privilege of privacy, sis.

He's rarely mad at me, but I hear it in the tone of voice he sends to me. I'm not gonna pretend I'm exactly where I want to be, or that this is what I was hoping for. This is especially true since I have no idea where this is and what I want is now complicated.

Something has changed. Before our planet was destroyed by Eli's people I... *Eli!*

"We need to call Eli for help. She can help us!" I say excitedly. "Eli! I don't know where we are, but I'm sending out a call for help."

"We still need to find a door," Eton says.

I crawl along the surface we're on and feel for the wall. My fingers touch it, and I begin to let them find their way up. Now for a door, I think.

I close my eyes at the brightness coming from above us. Someone found the light.

"That helps," Reyn says.

She stands to her feet and rushes over to Willa.

"Where are you hit?" Reyn asks.

Willa leans against the wall, hunched to the right. Her bloodied hand moves from where she holds the wound.

"Let me take a look at it," Reyn says.

"Do you even know what you're looking at?" Willa asks suspiciously.

"Yes. I used to help my mother back home with those who were sick and wounded from the virus and from fighting," Reyn says softly.

I look at Morren and Eton. She's seen more than I would've suspected.

"Eli?"

"Ahhh. There you are." Eli stands near Morren. "I could hear you, but I was on the other side of the door."

She turns to where Reyn is trying to tear Willa's shirt to expose the wound.

"What happened?" she asks.

"We went off mission," Morren answers.

"What do you mean?"

"We just came here from Anfar. We went there for help, but only got trouble," I answer.

For some reason, having her ask makes me feel guilty. It isn't my fault we're in this situation. If anything, it's hers.

"Where were you? What about that connection? Couldn't you tell we needed help?" I walk closer so I can glare at her as I grill her.

"I got here as soon as you called for me. None of us thought this was going to be easy. We have to trust that you would get through some trials without me being right here. You knew if you needed help to call. That's what you did."

"So you just leave us out here flailing until we call out for help? That's messed up. If it weren't for you, Eli, none of this would've happened. We'd be home, not already, but still. Reyn and Eton wouldn't have ever gone to Baselonica Xuna, and Willa wouldn't be lying against a concrete wall bleeding."

Eli says nothing, but instead continues to study Willa's situation. She feels the back of Willa for the exit wound and nods.

"Perhaps this will help," she says and places her tentacle-like fingers over the wound.

"Aaaaahhhhh. That burns like a…"

"Healing? Cauterizing? Yes. You'll be sore and you'll need to take it easy, but you'll be fine."

Eton watches her. "Can you fix my ribs?

Eli walks over to Eton and gently places her hands on his ribs.

"There's nothing broken. Bruised maybe, but not broken."

"But you can take away the bruising?"

"I possibly could, but that bruising likely serves as a physical reminder of some lesson you're meant to learn. I wouldn't want to take that away from you."

Eton rolls his eyes.

"Any idea where we are? If we walk out that door, what are we walking into?" Morren asks.

"I know where you are. My curiosity is in how you arrived here," Eli responds.

I bite my lip, wondering if I should try to answer. I don't have a good answer of exactly how. I just know we needed to help and it seems we're drawn to where we need to be for some reason.

"So, you think you need to be here?" Eli asks, turning to face me.

"I don't know. I had to help Willa and we needed to get off of Anfar. They were gonna send her to someplace called Cuupta or Cuppa, or something."

"You mean Cuupton." Eli nods her head and tentacles knowingly. "I wasn't sure when I landed outside that door, but it makes sense. Why here?"

"Cuz this stupid girl suddenly wants to save everyone for some reason. She doesn't save her beloved sister, but she's traipsing across sun systems to rescue people she doesn't even know. Meanwhile we're getting our asses kicked and shot at," Eton growls. "I wanna get back to Base X. I happen to like it fine there."

"That's cuz you're a male, Eton," Reyn says meekly.

"What?" Eton asks.

"You heard me. Don't act like you don't know, never noticed. You enjoy it there. You like it there, because you are a male." Her voice is louder this time.

"That's not true. Everyone has the same rules, and the rules are for the good and preservation of the Baselonican people."

"If you say so. You're too blind to see anything else. Anything that doesn't go along with what you want to see."

"Wait. What did I do? Nothing. I didn't have to come, and if I hadn't, none of you would've been here. I only came because you promised me something." He glowers at Reyn.

"Go screw yourself!"

"That isn't the way our deal's supposed to work. I see why they have to keep you in your place on Base X. You can't follow through and can't follow reason. We're safe there."

Reyn walks over to Eton, more sexily than I expected. "I know we have certain qualities you do appreciate, right?"

"Of course. Many qualities we appreciate. I'm glad you can see that we do value you."

She stands in front of him one hand on the wall, her body pressing up against his. He smiles. She continues to press against him, putting her weight into it.

"Don't hurt the ribs, baby."

"Oh. Which side hurts?" she asks sweetly.

"The left side."

Reyn smiles. "You mean right here?" She takes her other hand and pushes into his bruised and sore ribs.

"Owww. Reyn. Geez, I just told you."

"I know. I'm not your baby. I'm older than you and from all I've seen, a lot smarter too. You just have something swinging between your legs. Only in Anfar and in your head is that enough to make you the boss. So, get over yourself, that stupid mind-numbing job, and the idea of screwing me. The third thing will never happen. You're just not my kind of guy."

"But you promised," he says angrily.

"No, Eton. I didn't. That's just what you wanted to hear, so I let you."

"Well…now that that's outta the way, maybe we should figure out what do next," Willa says with a whistle.

"We don't want to leave this room without a plan," Eli says. "The Cuuptons are leery of outsiders. They've got a lot at stake, being a penal colony."

"More than Anfar sends their criminals here?" I ask.

"Yeah, they come from around the three nearest sun systems. It's been years since any of our people visited here. Perhaps things have changed, but if they were sending you here, I doubt they have."

"The male we overheard said he got a good deal for the teacher they sent here," I add.

"Hmmm. That might mean that the Cuuptons are paying them slightly higher than before for some reason," Eli reasons.

"What do we do? If this is a penal labor colony that means they're gonna be heavily guarded." I lean against the wall, pretty certain we're screwed unless there's some miracle.

"Yes, they will be," Eli nods. "Outside of these walls are more walls. It's almost a nicer version of the place we left on Earth. You must've been drawn here because this is where they send the new transfers." Eli's tentacles sway around her.

We're going down a spiraling hole and the only way back up is through the bottom.

I just wanted to help. Lari, and then Willa. It's all unfair. They're just as captive as us. Different kinds of prisons, but the same thing.

"What's your plan, Karana? Since you seem to be making decisions for all of us."

Morren looks at me expectantly, waiting for an answer. The lines around his eyes are much more pronounced. The narrowed gaze of disapproval always irks me, as I'm the oldest. I don't have a good answer for him, or for any of them, yet they are all waiting. They deserve an answer, having been thrown into another place, complete with its own perplexities, and that is still far from home.

"Well?" Eton asks. "Apparently, none of us can leave without the others. Except them." Eton tilts his head toward Eli and Willa.

I stand taller and look at the five of them in the room with me. This wasn't supposed to be our fight, but it is now.

"Reyn, you're here because you want to go home and you don't like how Base X treats you. I can say the same about you, Willa, right?" I ask.

Reyn and Willa both nod.

"Those people on Base X have been living under the Zo for so long, they've forgotten what it's like to even be free or even kind. After all those years, they are angry, and it comes out in ugly ways. We can't just go back to Earth and leave it like that. People like Lari will never be able to be who they want to be. And in Lari's case, who she's *supposed* to be." I need them all.

Willa looks around the room, letting her eyes rest a moment on Eton. "I can't go back to living like that. I can't. I lived there my whole life. It's taken everything I have not to be like them. If I go back and nothing has changed, they'll make me a permanent slave until I can't work anymore. Then they'll just kill me."

"We can't let that happen."

"What about me? You all dragged me away from the only place I had a decent life so you could take me back to Earth where there's nothing for me."

"Eton, I know you don't want to be here, but whether you like it or not, you're stuck with us, and we need you. We need you here. We need you to help us make Base X better for everyone. We need you back on Earth. There aren't many of us left."

"Morren, I can't do this without you. You've always been my anchor and the one to push me. I need you." Morren's eyes glimmer with a hint of optimism. "I don't have all the answers. I just know we can't leave here with all these people, from who knows where, working as slaves. I have to do something."

Eli takes us all in. I know she's thinking of something, but I hesitate to ask. I wonder if she knew what would happen to us when we made that first jump from Earth. I wonder if we're still going down the rabbit hole.

Chapter Twenty-Three

Eli's tentacles shimmer in a grayish blue with specks of gold. "Cuupton isn't all bad. No place is completely bad. When we were last here, there was a small resistance growing. They were in hiding but you could see some of the results of their actions. If we can find them, they may be willing to help us. From what you said about the teacher, maybe they've become more powerful."

"It's worth a try. How do we find them?" I ask.

"They don't have a formal place. They move about, like everyone else. They hide in the open. At least last time we were here. A lot might have changed since then."

"A lot has changed everywhere. So how do we know if they are the good guys?" Morren asks.

"The best place to go is the market. You can see the new transfers and the merchants looking for buyers."

"What?" I ask incredulously.

"You heard me right, Karana." Eli's black eyes don't blink.

"So, do they stay here?" Willa asks, concerned.

"Sometimes. Or they may go to another home planet, depending on the buyer."

"Why? Who would do that?" Reyn asks.

"You'll get to see who very soon. The market isn't quite what you might think, but if you pay attention, you'll see it. We need to watch for the most aggressive buyers, willing to pay higher prices. Those are likely the Comrades of Liberation."

"Comrades of Liberation?" It sounds like another group that's going to want more than we can give.

"They're the ones trying to end this way of life and free the people of Cuupton. They want to end Cuupton as the go-to place for slave labor. But the aggressors are from everywhere. Baselonica Xuna," Eli says with a turn of her head to Willa, "is one of the worst offenders. They have a lot to lose if the liberators are successful."

From all over, I think to myself. No doubt, if those mines on Base X weren't all free, they would need labor too, and there wasn't enough of a natural labor force to meet demand. They had to be supplementing the penance mine somehow.

"Peoples from all over come to Cuupton, and Base X is a big player?" Willa asks nervously.

"Yeah. Why?" Eli answers.

"No reason. They're the ones who transferred me directly to Anfar. Then that sleezeball Narp lied on me. I didn't leave an hour early and steal pay. I wasn't getting paid to begin with, the Chapis was. And that wasn't the deal," Willa says.

The anger shows clearly as she bares her teeth.

"So how do these Comrades of Liberation hope to win?" Morren says.

I hear him say he's not so sure about this plan. "We already have Chapis Kun Zo looking for us and don't forget we're losing time," he sends me.

"They've been saturating the market. They add labor into the markets, bid up the prices, and buy their people – who aren't slaves to begin with. With this, they've made it so people want to bring their slaves here and it becomes more expensive for the buyers. The sellers are making out well, but it means the liberators have to buy their own people as well as others out of slavery. It costs a lot and it's risky. It's like taking out a constellation when you're talking about a galaxy. It's not enough."

"That's why those guys on Anfar said they were getting a better split. They'd gotten a better deal because of this," Reyn reasons.

"Most likely. It's a short-term solution, just a step in the plan. That's what they were just starting when we came before. If they've done this like they'd hoped, they should have amassed a sizable force," Eli says.

There is a hint of optimism in her voice, and I want to grab onto it.

"Wouldn't they know? Suspect them?" Morren asks.

"Not necessarily. They have to bide their time. From where I stand, this is probably the time," Eli answers.

"How do we blend into this market? Do they let non-buyers in?" I ask.

"It's a closed and secret event, but getting in won't be the problem for us," Eli says.

"Getting out?" I ask nervously.

"Not just getting out. I'm guessing the goal is getting out with enough information to do something about it." Morren crosses his arms over his chest. I know he's feeling the same thing I am – a need to help.

"We need to disrupt their system, somehow," Willa says.

"We need a disturbance, create some chaos," Reyn adds with a smile.

"What do you have in mind?" I ask Reyn.

I laugh in disbelief at Reyn's idea, before realizing she's not joking.

"They are gonna be looking for Willa at the market. She was supposed to arrive, so it's expected that she'll be there."

"No. It's too risky. Someone else might actually win the bid. And then what do we do?" I argue.

"We rescue her if that happens. But that's not gonna happen because their entire system is gonna crash before they can do anything like that," Reyn reassures us.

"And you're gonna crash it?" Eton snorts.

Reyn shifts her weight, one hip jutting out as if in a dare to Eton, "I'm gonna crash it all."

Eton stares at Reyn as if he doesn't recognize her.

I let out a chuckle and Eton turns to glare at me. I know it's not funny, but the whole thing is unreal. Perhaps laughing is my way of coping. I don't know though, since we haven't gotten through anything yet. Only deeper.

"Who's gonna be the buyer?" Willa asks, wanting to get back to details.

"It'll be most believable if Eton does it. He has more of the demeanor," Eli suggests.

"What do you mean by demeanor?" Eton asks, defensively.

"Calm down. No one's attacking you. We're just trying to figure out the best one in the group to handle what needs to be done," I say.

"And what about you? I haven't heard anything about what you'll be doing, or your brother."

"You're right, Eton. We'll be watching what's going on and ready to pull everyone out at the right time. I'll try to stay close to you and Willa. Morren will need to stay close to Reyn, wherever she'll be, so we can jump out."

"Where? We need a meeting spot," Morren says.

"We don't know yet. We'll have to follow the liberators," I answer.

"Then it is settled. We'll go to the market, figure out who the liberators are, and follow them. If anyone is going to overthrow their system, it has to be them. We can't come in and try to take over and do it for them. That's a recipe for disaster," Eli says.

"Maybe getting rid of Cuupton's system will hurt the Zo Clan in the one thing they care about – money," Reyn snarls.

"If they operate a mine without paid labor, you can bet their buying it here," Morren says.

"Are you okay with this plan, Willa?" I ask.

It's my fault we're here, and everyone else has more at risk than me.

"Yeah. If it means destroying Chapis Zo, I'm in."

"Then we better get going. These things can go all day, but we have no idea what time it is or exactly where we are," Eli says.

We grab hold of each other's hands, and this time Eli counts.

"Three. Two. One."

Chapter Twenty-Four

We land hard enough to draw someone's attention. The footsteps are definitely coming this way.

"Find a place to hide. Quick," Morren whispers.

We scuttle into the nooks and crannies of what must be a warehouse. I find a spot behind an empty wooden pallet.

"I know I heard something in here," a voice says.

"Check the doors. Sometimes we have the transfers trying to hide in here," another voice says.

"Better not today, or we'll have some very angry members."

"I know. I'll check over here. You get that side."

We must be close, I send to Morren and Eli.

We need to get over to where they just came from. Morren, Eli, who's closest to you? Willa and Reyn are close to me. I can get them.

Eton's behind the next pallet over, Morren sends.

I'm on the other side of Reyn," Eli answers.

Okay. We have to do this fast. As soon as they get past you, jump. I'll get Willa. Eli, you grab Reyn, and Morren you grab Eton and don't waste time, I order.

I watch for the guards to walk past. There is something about them that we hadn't seen on Base X or Anfar. They are each a different type of being. I don't recognize either of them. I need to see myself. I wonder if we're going in as humans and if Eli is going in as an Eliatar.

Stop daydreaming, Karana! Come on. Go! Morren yells.

I run over to Willa and grab her hand. She has no idea what I'm doing as I look at her, then the hall the guards had come through. Large crates made of a wood-like composite are scattered about the warehouse. We are hiding behind one as I count down to myself.

In less than a second we're standing in the dimly lit hallway with Morren, Eton, Eli, and Reyn.

"Did you hear that?" one of guards asks.

"Yeah. I think they somehow got past us. Come on."

"Shirt. Hangar. Iron. Table!" I whisper. "We need to move. Get on the other side of that door."

"We don't know what's on the other side of that door," Eton panics.

Morren agrees. "We could land right in the middle of trouble."

"Or we stay here and have trouble run into us," I argue back.

Morren starts running down the short hallway and cracks the door open slightly, peeking inside. Light shines through, and voices filter past us.

"We can't jump in there. We need another way in."

"Down this way," the guard says. His flashlight hits the wall as they approach. If we don't do something soon, it'll be shining directly on us.

"We don't have a choice," I say.

We run toward the door and I look through quickly.

"See the door on the other side? We'll land on that side of the room," I say quickly.

"Three. Two."

***

"One"

I stand to my feet and slowly turn around. The room is full of people, beings, and aliens. They're staring at us, and I have no idea what they're seeing. There is only silence. I don't know what to call them. Eli was right. They are from all over, each of them looks different.

A young girl standing near me opens her mouth. "No. Don't yell. We're here to help." I hope she understands me.

The others don't move. There's a look of detached acceptance in their eyes. The teacher from Anfar, Carsa, is near the back and studying Willa. We can't stay, not in here. The warmth is already making me damp and I can see I'm not the only one uncomfortable in the small room where they're being held.

The girl looks at me suspiciously before letting out an ear-piercing scream.

Now we really must go.

"Where now?" Eton asks, frustrated.

"I don't know."

There are no windows in the white room. Even if there were, I'm not certain I could see out of them with all the people packed inside. I scan over their heads. There is one door. I push past several people including the screaming tattler and yank open the door. It's not a closet. It's a passage or tunnel.

"This way," I say.

I start running down the hall and my new friends follow. Our chances of escape are becoming slim. If the guards don't catch us before we get to the other side, whatever is on the other side might do us in.

"Why don't we just jump where we're going?" Eton asks.

"Because, we don't know where that is," Morren says back.

"We could try," I say back. "Grab the person in front of you." I wait a moment and then begin to count down. "Three. Two. One."

Nothing.

Everyone is irritated and frustrated.

"I guess we're all together and there isn't anything stronger to pull us away from this spot," I reason in frustration.

I stop running for a moment to listen. The narrow tunnel splits. The guards are behind us, and this passage is ridiculously long. I can hear something.

"To the right," I send Morren and Eli.

I begin running again toward what sounds like a train starting or stopping. There are engines going on and off. It's getting louder, which means we are getting closer. I stop short of a steel door with a window that looks onto what appears to be a bay for small spaceships. The others bump into me, nearly causing me to push the door open. Those walking around and getting out of the spaceships are like the people we left in the room. All types.

I scan the large area. Most of the activity is on the level below, where the ships are docking. I notice two guards monitoring the upper level where this door leads. On the far end of the bay is a stand where those who exit the ships appear to be checking in. I smile.

"They're using some kind of card to check in," I whisper behind me.

"We don't have a card," Morren says with frustration.

"Not yet. We're gonna have to get one."

I consider the others behind me. Unfortunately, it's all or none. *Eli.* She can jump alone. She'll have to be the one to do this.

"Eli, we need you to get one of those cards so that Eton can get into the market."

"I can do that."

"Good," I say before pausing.

I pull away from the window. It can't be. Now the sound of voices and jogging feet are close. I hope they go left. "Not good."

"What?" Morren asks.

"They're close. And…he's here. He's got Lari."

I peek out through the window once more, with Willa and Morren looking too. I'm not seeing things. He's dressed in his finest, much nicer than the ruddy leather. He almost looks clean. Brute and another man have Lari, pushing her forward toward the check-in.

I listen as the footsteps fade in the opposite direction. We're safe, at least for the moment.

"What do we do now?" I send to Morren.

He says nothing.

The large bay below has gray concrete walls, and the rails are on this level. The ships are parked on either side and the space is filling up. If we get them now, it'll blow everything else. But now we have a chance none of us had truly foreseen. Chapis Zo out of his own element, only two guards.

"Take me down there, and I'll take care of this nice and quick," Willa offers.

"Thanks, Willa. But Chapis is just one fish. We take him down and everyone else gets left behind, still trapped," I say.

"He's not just one fish, Karana. He's one of the big fish. You take him out and you'll be taking out one of the intergalactic leaders of the slave labor market."

"How do you know?" I ask.

"When I worked on Base X, I had to go between all the mines. I saw the people he ran through there. I heard them talking. I saw the work they did in the Institute to increase the labor population – and not just through the Baselonicans. It's why I refused to be a part of that system. I tried to speak out. I actually believed the bastard when they said I was being transferred and would work. I figured what I can do is pretty valuable. But it isn't valuable enough for me to be paid for it. I didn't really understand until I was sent to Anfar."

"What didn't you understand? What did you learn?" I ask cautiously.

"When I got to Anfar, I was brought to Sentursyd and the factory, like they said. Only thing is, that's where I was going to live, sleep, eat, work. I wasn't going to leave. That crooked Director Narp was in there talking to Chapis. He told Chapis, 'She's worth more alive than dead, but we can't afford people like her on our planet. You keep her and use her. Just send me the rent. I have more like her. Good workers.' That's what he said about me."

"So Director Narp and Chapis Zo are in this together."

"Definitely. And I know there are more. This," Willa says with a wave of her hand, "doesn't happen without some serious support."

I consider what Willa's said. If she's right, then I'm willing to bet Chapis Zo isn't the only one here and won't be the only one looking for her.

"As soon as the arrivals slow down, Eli, grab a card and come right back. Eton, you need to be ready to go. Willa, you have to get back to the room with the others. We'll have to walk back. Those guards will come this way looking for us."

"So when they start coming close, we all jump back to the main passage," Morren says.

Eton is looking at Reyn and Willa. There's something in his eyes that makes me nervous.

"What are you thinking, Eton?" I ask.

"Why? Why are we doing this? You really think you, pretty much a bunch of girls, are going to bring down an intergalactic lord like Chapis Zo? Really? With what? Your looks and charm?"

"We have more than looks and charm, but we'll use those too, if we need to. I always believe in using all of my assets. I suggest you do the same. Perhaps starting with your brain. Stop being a donkey's rear and think about how you can help us."

Eton's eyes become narrow slits. He walks up to within an inch of my face. "I *am* helping you. Helping you not make a mistake that will cost everyone here their lives. Don't you see? I'm here giving you the warning no one else will cuz everyone else is looking through hope goggles, and I'm being real. This mission is as screwed up as you are. I've told you why you shouldn't bother with all this extra stuff. Just do what it was you came to Base X for and go home. But no. You're stubborn. You persist. So, when this all goes to the bottom of a barrel of mud, and it will, don't come asking me for favors. I'll do my part so I can get home. Then that's it. I'm done."

"And we'll be glad to see you go. Don't try to intimidate my sister, punk. I'd take fighting through an endless universe with her any day than existing in Baselonica with you."

"Thanks, Morren. He's a class A bully."

"That's what family's for."

"I think you might want to watch yourself." Reyn smirks at Eton as she takes his hand.

I'm trying not to let his ignorance bother me but don't avoid stepping on Eton's foot as I turn to face everyone and get ourselves in a circle to jump.

"That's my foot!" he yelps.

"Sorry. I was just trying to keep it on the floor, so you don't keep sticking it in your mouth."

I don't even bother to look at his snarl. Eli has popped out already and with the sound of the guards, it's our turn.

"Three. Two. One."

Chapter Twenty-Five

We're in the hall outside the holding room where Willa must go. I can see she's nervous, even if she's being brave.

"I'll be in the main hall. Just stay quiet and when you come out, Eton will make a play for you. Right, Eton?" I ask.

"Right." His tone doesn't inspire confidence.

"Eton?" Reyn asks again.

"I said right. Yes. I will, if it gets me off this stupid mission you're on faster."

"Good. The rest of us have to get out there."

"I've returned with the card. I'm pretty sure he'll notice it's missing once he comes out of the restroom, so go fast. I'll take you down."

Eton holds Eli's hand and they disappear. Willa is gone too. We'll have to wait to see both of them on the other side.

"Our turn," I say to Morren and Reyn.

"I'm going back to that door we were at," Reyn says. "When everyone goes in, I'll sneak down to their system. I saw a computer panel of some kind, and it looks like they have their administrative offices down there.

"Okay," I say. "Morren and I are going to be in the market hall. If I jump, I can't come to you first. I'd jump first to Morren, then we could come to you. But we'll come."

"I know how to stay hidden and out of the way," she says.

I understand her. We spent years living the same way. "When the guards are coming back this way, we'll jump together back to that door to drop you off."

We hear the sound of their footsteps again. They're getting closer, but no longer in chase. I think of Tezzi and Dad and how we jumped into their room in time to beat the oncoming boots. We hadn't saved them.

"I bet someone else caught them. They couldn't have gotten too far," one of the guards says.

"Yeah. They'll turn up. They always do."

They pass the cut-in that we thought was a closet and keep going out another door.

"Time to go. Hands?" I say and grab Reyn and Morren.

"Three. Two. One."

We land in the same spot, this time I am careful with the door.

"Good luck, Reyn."

"You too." Reyn reaches out and hugs me. I hug her back, knowing she hasn't had anyone who cares about her in what might be years.

She doesn't have a brother like I do. She isn't trying to get home to her family. They are already gone. She's been stuck with Eton.

I drop my arms. "Morren and I need to get to the market."

"Okay. I'll see you after." Reyn peers through the window into the bay. "I'll sneak in when there's a lull."

"See you soon," Morren and I say in unison.

Morren, let's try to land in the back. Hopefully we won't be seen.

Right. I didn't see any humans here, so hopefully being human won't get us immediately kicked out.

I hadn't thought of this, but there is no sense worrying about it now.

Let's go find us some liberators, Morren. You count.

Let's. Three. Two.

"One more minute before the market opens and you may confirm your initial bids submitted prior to arrival."

Eton is leaning up against a wall in the back. He looks nervous, unnatural. From where we are, I don't see Chapis Zo or Director Narp.

"Esteemed colleagues, welcome to the Market. I am Haunir, your announcer for this evening's affair. If you haven't already submitted an opening bid, do it now. You can review your options on the tablet you were given at check in. If you submitted an opening bid and there are no other competing bids, you will win your labor."

I look down at myself. I wish I had a mirror. All this time here, and I had no idea what others might see me as, and those who knew me couldn't tell me. My hands look like mine, but I'm seeing myself and if I've learned nothing else, I know that doesn't matter.

"I haven't seen you two before at the market. I didn't know the Earthlings participated in the market. Is this something new?" a man who seems to have a lot in common with a yellow tang says. His lips pucker with each syllable and I can't stop staring.

"Yes. We're exploring new resources."

"I'd imagine you'd finally get on board, what with the decimation of your planet's people. Without labor, it's completely unsustainable."

I smile sweetly.

"Is this your partner? Business partner?" the tang says flirtatiously.

"Umm, yes. He is."

"Wonderful. And might I say, that dress is absolutely smashing on you. I love the color gold. It's one of my absolute favorites."

"Thank you."

"Might I ask, how long will you two be at market?"

"What do you mean?"

"Well are you staying for the…after affair?" the tang asks.

I laugh nervously. I don't want to stay a minute longer than necessary.

"Well, we weren't invited."

"Nonsense. All buyers are invited. I certainly hope to see you there."

"Okay. Well good luck today."

"Yes. And until this evening, good luck to you too."

I nearly snatch my hand back, catching myself before it's too late, as he plants a wet fish kiss on my palm.

"Bye bye." I wave the wet palm back at him.

Morren laughs.

"Ha ha. Very funny."

I wipe my hand on the back of Morren's sleeve.

"There's a party after this? The gall," I whisper.

"That's actually good – for us. It gives us a chance to chat with anyone that might be part of the Comrades of Liberation," Morren sends me.

"And now, for labor item number one this evening; she comes from Lansavar in the fourth system. She is young, skilled with tools, and still fertile. She is on market due to the inability of her family to pay debts. She is a permanent labor placement. Please review your tablets for the current highest bids which have now been updated. If you would like to bid higher, you may do so now," Haunir instructs.

Haunir waits, allowing the buyers to consider the young girl. Two walk over to the platform where she stands and check her teeth, hair, and hands. The other squeezes her shoulders and hips, before waving his hand in disinterest.

"Are there any other interested bidders?" Haunir asks. She looks around the room to see who may be active on their tablets. "Going once." There is a brief pause. "Going twice." Haunir's pause is extended this time before she smiles broadly. "Excellent. Going to one of our favorite and esteemed buyers, Chapis Kun Zo. Congratulations, Chapis, on another fine purchase."

Chapis Zo is sitting down at a front table. But he raises his hand, holding up a half-empty glass that sloshes back and forth.

Eton shoots me a worried look. I know he's thinking the same thing. I wonder if Chapis Zo will see us as he did on Base X or as humans. Only time will tell.

Twenty-eight additional males, females, and children are sold for either permanent or temporary placement, with Chapis Zo securing another three. Finally, Willa appears on stage.

I can see Chapis Zo's back straighten. He casts a look across the front row to someone else. I strain my neck to see who the recipient of his gaze is. Director Narp. They are both surprised. The Chapis smiles as he picks up his tablet.

"Oh no. The Chapis is gonna run up the bid." I'm getting nervous.

"That's fine. We just need to pay attention to who else is willing to pay more than what it seems market price is," Morren sends me back.

"So far, only two people have tried to run up the bid. If Chapis Zo wins, what happens to Willa?"

"We rescue her," Morren assures me.

"We seem to have a slight bidding war going on, with this one. It's funny since we were certain we'd lost her. So be warned, she's kind of a wild one. You might need to tame her," the announcer Haunir laughs.

Willa glares across the stage, her eyes seething, forehead pulsing.

Eton raises his hand and punches something into the tablet again.

Across the room, another hand goes up. It's the same one who was bidding up before.

Chapis Zo raises his hand slowly.

"A three-way. This is gonna be good," Haunir smiles hungrily.

Eton bids again.

Chapis Zo is now looking around for the other bidders. Eton has found a seat and is trying to remain unnoticed. If this goes on any longer, it will be impossible to not draw the full attention of the audience, Zo, and Narp.

If Narp sees him, he'll know. Then we're screwed.

Narp stands up and steps to the side of the room. He's looking for something or someone. Possibly us.

I signal to Eton to stop bidding. He looks at me and shakes his head no. I mouth at him to wait and nod my head in the direction Chapis Zo is sitting. Eton shrugs his shoulders. He's indignant, refusing to listen.

"You tell him to stop, Morren. He's not listening to me."

Morren looks at Eton and mouths, "Stop." Eton ignores him, too, as he looks around the room and presses a button.

"Is he trying to get us caught?" I send Morren.

"Seems like he might be."

"Final bids? Final bids?" Haunir asks.

Chapis Zo stands and walks to the other side of the room near the front. If Eton doesn't stop, he's gonna get caught.

I lock eyes with Eton. "Stop bidding. They're watching you."

Eton notices Zo standing now. I don't know what he's thinking. But I think I'm right. He's acting like he wants to be caught.

I mouth, "If he catches you, he'll kill you."

This seems to get his attention. He puts the tablet down and lowers his head.

Idiot, I think. He might get us all killed.

Chapter Twenty-Six

Willa's eyes are panicked. She sees that Eton has stopped and that Chapis Zo is holding his tablet, just like the other bidder.

"And lock in your final bid," Haunir instructs.

Haunir looks at her tablet and smiles. "Congratulations again to Chapis Kun Zo on another successful purchase. And for resecuring one of your own! A very unusual thing, but very appreciated. We always appreciate your business."

Chapis Zo smirks from where he stands in the corner and then sits back down, satisfied.

"What just happened?" Morren asks.

"I think we just screwed up. But that man, I'm pretty sure he's one of the good guys. He hasn't won tonight, but he's raising the bids."

"We have one final labor items before we get to celebrate this evening. She is from Chapis Zo's home of Baselonica Xuna and he's offering her today at a discounted rate. This young lady is a skilled companion, adept in providing relaxation and pleasure."

Several buyers pick up their tablets from where they sit on the tables.

"As usual, the bids you see now are the highest starting bids. We will begin bidding immediately on this deal. If you would like to add a bid or bid higher, you may do so now," Haunir smiles.

Nearly a dozen hands shoot up across the room, including my suspected freedom fighter. This girl is popular. There's no way he's gonna get them.

"If you've already placed a bid, you may come up to inspect these items."

Suddenly, the tablets are being pulled back.

"Ugh!" one man exclaims.

"Take my bid off the table!" another calls out.

"What do you take us for? Fools! We don't want used up and diseased goods!" someone else yells.

"Yeah. She shouldn't be sold. You couldn't give her away." It's fish-face.

"What's happening?" I whisper to Morren.

"I don't know. Something must be in the system about Lari."

"What do you have to say for yourself, Chapis?"

"Nothing. She is fine. The information in there isn't true. It just isn't." Chapis fidgets while tapping at his tablet in frustration.

"If it's not true, how's it in there?"

"I don't know. I submitted the data like I always do. I wouldn't bring her if she wasn't clean."

"Hmmm. Now I know why you're offering her up for so low." Haunir casts Zo a disappointed look.

"Ladies and gentlemen, those are all the labor items on market at this time. I apologize for the lack of consideration, business-sense, and decency of the Chapis of Baselonica Xuna. We make it our business to run a reputable market and I can assure you this won't happen again. You may collect your purchases at the end of the evening or when you are ready to leave. Thank you all."

Haunir walks off the stage and immediately toward Chapis Zo. Despite only coming up to his chest, she says something that clearly irritates him, before she walks away. Zo whispers something to the man sitting beside him - Brute.

A woman leads Lari back into the room with the others.

"This is it, Morren. We need to get Eton, Willa, and now, Lari. Then we need to get the man over there." I tilt my head to the man I suspect to be one of the Comrades of Liberation.

I wave Eton over.

He begins to walk toward us. Director Narp starts walking toward him from the front of the room.

Zo takes notice of Narp, and his eyes follow him to meet Eton. I wait, holding my breath. He doesn't recognize him. It's likely Eton never met Zo, but he'd made a very recent and marked impression on Director Narp.

Zo grabs Brute and walks on stage. I watch to see if they come back out.

I look at Morren. *What if they go the other way? Out the back?*

That's problem number two. Problem number one is heading over here now. If Eton doesn't stop, he'll lead Narp right to all three of us.

I'm going to walk over and talk to the man over there before Narp notices me. Even if he does see us, this fiasco can't be for nothing.

I try to walk discreetly to the man furiously pushing into some device in his hand. He looks serious, his single brow twisted in concentration over deep violet eyes. He stands taller than most of the others in the room, and his broad shoulders fill out the long navy colored lightweight coat he wears. Despite being dressed like the others, there is a slight hint of discomfort. My approach startles him, and he shoves the device into his pocket.

"Hi," I smile.

"Hello."

"I noticed you were interested in some really good, ummm, buys."

"Yes. However, none were secured."

"I see. I hope that doesn't disappoint you too much," I prod.

"The time for disappointment has long passed."

"Oh?"

"Yes."

"This is my first time here, at the market. It's not something I'm used to. Very…different…the way this works."

"Well. It remains what it is, until it's not."

"Interesting." I try to read his stoic demeanor.

"What?" He continues to look forward; not letting me distract him.

"What you said."

I pause and wait for some explanation, but instead he looks toward the stage and where those sold are now held.

"Will you be staying for the party?" I ask.

"I have no interest in after parties. I have other business to which I must attend."

"Of course. Yeah, I understand. I probably won't stay either. I'm pretty busy too. Can I at least ask your name?"

"Doc. This is the name my friends call me."

"Alright, Doc. Nice to meet you."

"As I said, that is the name my friends call me. You and I are not even acquaintances."

"Well what do your *not* friends call you?" I laugh teasingly.

"They don't. Now, if you'll excuse me." With nothing else he turns and walks away, focused.

"Wait… I really wanted to talk to you about something important."

He doesn't bother to turn all the way to look at me. "Important how?"

I hesitate. If I'm wrong about him, I'm exposed. If I'm right, I can't say it here.

"I think we have some mutual interests. A friend of mine said there were some who were very interested in this market, but for perhaps… different reasons."

"Yes?"

"Yeah."

"And who is this friend of which you speak?"

"She is an Eliatar. We know her by Eli."

"An Eliatar. They are a people I once came across. It has been a long time."

"I'm here with one."

"Oh, does she plan on leaving again when things become messy and difficult?"

I don't know what he's talking about, but there is clearly something going on that Eli didn't bother to share with us.

"I don't know about that. What I know is that I believe you are the person I'm supposed to talk to."

He looks at me with suspicion as thick as his eyebrows.

"How would talking to you be of any use to me?"

"Because I think we have a common interest."

His violet eyes turn to me now and search my own. There is something unsettling about them, as if by simply looking at me he can see me deeper than I'm comfortable with.

"Excuse me, there is something that I must do now."

He turns again to walk away. I reach for his arm, and he looks at my hand on his coat. His broad shoulder pulls back and away from me, as if he's disgusted.

"Sorry. I was just wondering if we can talk. After?"

"No strange hands touch me. Not ever...again." He comes back to stand close to me.

He leans down and whispers in my ear, a scowl on his face. "I see you for who you are. I know you have come to help. We cannot be seen here in any positive fashion that may raise suspicion. An Earthling's presence at events like this is always suspicious, since your kind withdrew their secretive involvement. But that was after they'd already put their undesirables into this trade."

"I think you're mistaken. We've never participated in this."

He looks at me now as if he's trying to determine if I'm serious, kidding, or just stupid.

"Your kind are scattered amongst the stars. Those humans who were considered too much of a threat to the power of your dynasties have been relegated to new masters."

I shake my head.

"No. You've got it wrong. Our planet has been destroyed." I can only assume his mistake is an honest one.

"That's because you sent some of your brightest away."

He looks down at me with pity, before his hypnotic eyes focus on my wrist. He lifts it up. "What's this?"

"What?" I'm confused now.

"The mark here on your wrist. Where did you get it?"

I look down at where he's pointing.

"It's just a scar."

"Where did it come from?"

"I don't know. I've had it for as far back as I can remember."

He wipes his brow and drops my hand, resuming his cold and detached stance.

"Who'd you come here with?" Once again, he doesn't bother to look at me while he speaks; choosing to study the room instead.

"My brother, Eli, and well, a few others."

"You are not safe here. If the wrong eyes fall on that scar, you will not be returning to your precious Earth or rescuing your sister."

"Wait. How'd you know?"

"I see. Clearly."

"Then you know why I'm here."

"Yes. And why you cannot remain here. It is too dangerous."

He pauses and turns before stopping once more.

"Meet me at the start of the first song in the corridor behind the keeping room, where those in the trade are being kept. Keep that scar hidden. I must go now."

"But," I call after him.

This time he does not turn back around and walks quickly toward the stage.

I turn around in search of Morren and Eton. My eyes scan the room but I can't see either of them, anywhere.

"Over here," someone says.

I look toward the source of the sound, the floor.

"Under the table."

It's Morren. He and Eli are crouched under the large round table. His fingers come from under the tablecloth. By now, most people have a drink in their hands while the final business is being taken care of near the stage. Zo is up there standing to the side, clearly upset.

Director Narp is with him as they scan the room together, no doubt searching for my brother and Eton. We must leave now. We've found who we needed to find and there was nothing else in that room for us. I back toward the table, trying not to draw any extra attention to myself. Choosing a spot in the back of the room was a good idea. I now understood the glances that I was drawing. I thought I just looked that nice, as fish-face had thought.

I sit down in the chair beside Morren's hand. Zo and Brute strain to find me.

"We have no time. We gotta get outta here now," I whisper.

I grab Morren's hand. *Three*.

Zo spots me again and is charging this way.

Two.

Not again. Narp has pulled out some gun and a laser is pointed at my chest.

One.

Too late suckers. The thought comes out before I can catch it and I suddenly feel ridiculous.

Chapter Twenty-Seven

I slam into someone, Reyn, knocking her to the floor.

"Of course," I mutter.

Reyn looks at me as if she's annoyed. I'm sure I've interrupted her.

"Excuse me." She stands back up.

Another room. There are only two computers but there are monitors along the wall showing the hall we'd been in and the holding room. A third monitor has the spaceship bay. Both sides are filled with strange markings on the outside. I'm sure they mean something to whoever arrived in them, but to me, they're just markings.

"I talked to him. I talked to the man who must be a liberator." I stand and try to smooth down my dress.

"Why are you smoothing down skin tight pants? Why are you wearing a skin tight outfit anyway?" Morren asks.

I look down, embarrassed. This place is utterly frustrating.

"Never mind that. Point is, I made contact, and thankfully Eton didn't blow it and get us all killed." I turn my attention to him.

"She's right, Eton. You put all of us at risk. We could've been captured and neither Narp or Zo are fans. They'd just as soon kill us as sell us."

"Look, I never asked to come here. I didn't sign up for this. This is your crazy mission, and it really doesn't have anything to do with me. I just want to go home."

"Maybe not before, but you're in it now. We all are," Reyn says quietly from her seat in front of the computer.

I turn to look at Reyn, wondering what's going on with her.

"While you were gone, I found a map. It's not anything I've ever seen before. It's simple, but it can help us get rid of Zo."

"We can't look at it now. We have to get Willa and Lari; then meet Doc in the corridor by the keeping room. We need to hurry. He's expecting me when the first song plays."

Out of the corner of my eye I see Eton, arms folded, standing in the corner of the twelve-foot by twelve-foot white room. I grab Morren's hand and then Reyn's hand.

"It's time to go, Eton."

"I think I'll stay. Say I was kidnapped and forced to participate."

"You know you can't do that, Eton. We all go, or none of us do."

"Maybe you should've thought about that before," he smacks back.

"Eton, come on. You gotta come with us. We're losing time," Morren says calmly.

"We've already lost time. Wasted time. Jumped time. You care about all these people you don't even know, more than you care about yourselves or even your family. What would your sister think if she knew you could've gone home to save her, and instead you were out saving someone else?"

Morren closes his eyes for a brief moment, his nostrils filling with a deep breath. *He says one more thing, Karana, I swear, I'll break his nose.* His jaw is clenched just like mine. I try to breathe my anger down, but I'm not Morren.

My chest is hot and my neck constricted. My instinct is to run and kick him between the legs, but I stand where I am. I let go of Morren's hand and put up one single finger. "You don't know the first thing about sacrifice. Now get your sorry excuse for a human being over here so we can go."

Morren looks at me, waiting for me do something else. I know I can't take him and I don't have time to fight.

"Now," I growl.

I clasp Morren's hand again and tighten my grip on Reyn's.

"You aren't in charge of anything, you know. You may think you've got some kind of power, but you don't. None of us do. We're all just pawns." Eton takes a step over and lets his fingers graze Morren's hand.

"I don't want to stay a pawn. If there's even a small chance I don't have to be or that someone like me doesn't have to be, well then, I'm ready to do what I can." Reyn doesn't bother to look at Eton; choosing instead to focus on where our hands are joined together.

"Let's go," I say.

Morren nods. "Three. Two. One."

***

One of the best landings of the day.

"You have made it. I was concerned you wouldn't." Doc moves from against the slate corridor wall.

"Yeah. We still have to get our friends from the keeping room."

"And how will you manage that? It is well guarded."

The darkness of the corridor seems to stretch on without end as I consider this. My eyes adjust to the dark, and I know Morren's do as well. There is little in the hall that would help us escape if chased. Morren and I have to jump together and I'm hoping we don't get pulled to Reyn and Eton. Not now. I have to trust that the pull of prana as Lari would call it, would be stronger first for the captives then to the Immunes. At least right now. Bringing everyone along each time would mean an excruciating number of jumps. We are inextricably tied to them. Our freedom being their freedom.

Eli. I send out a silent request for her. If she is good for anything, it's this. She still has a long way to go to make up for the mess she and her people made.

"What is your plan for entering the keeping room and securing your friends?" Doc asks again.

"It's handled. She'll be here soon."

I trust Eli this much. She'll do it, I'm sure.

"When she arrives, through whatever unusual means you all have for moving, we will need to hasten. I know you all have questions and desire to be helpful; however, we cannot afford any liabilities or anyone who is uncertain about what we are trying to do," Doc locks in on Eton.

Eton crosses his arms defiantly but says nothing. I hear a slight commotion behind the door leading to the keeping room before Willa, Lari, and Eli stumble into the corridor.

"We'd better hurry." Eli urges.

"They weren't too happy." Willa looks a bit shocked.

I turn to Doc. "So, where are we going?"

"The Capellan."

"But, I thought she…," Eli begins before becoming silent.

"She did. You will see, if you are successful in getting us there."

"Will you let me in to see what you see?" I ask and immediately sense Doc's distrust.

"Just for a moment. I need to see where you want to go."

"This happens only once. You see what you must see and then you exit. Is this understood?

"Yeah. Understood."

Morren and I pause for a moment, seeing the one image he's allowing to be projected. "Got it," we say.

"Okay. Let's do this." Morren grabs the hands on either side of him.

I look around to make sure everyone is connected.

"You do it, Morren. Your landings are better." I smile at my brother.

"Okay."

Morren takes a deep breath.

"Well find them, useless idiot! What do you think I'm paying you for?" It's Haunir's squeaky voice.

"Three."

"Two"

As Morren continues counting down, we hear, "They escaped some way! They can't just vanish into thin air!"

But we have.

Chapter Twenty-Eight

The Capellan is in female form today, using one of its two primary hosts, Selvedon. I study the floral wreath pattern on her head; the only marks where hair might be. She is the beautiful wife of Trevius who was killed in a much earlier uprising. Her whole life since then has been lived in secret.

The Capellan is intense, always. She has gathered Morren, me, and the others for today's practice and mission preparation. She looks different today. Her normal radiance seems faded. She catches my eyes, and squints as if considering what I might be thinking. Embarrassed, I turn away and study the dirt beneath my chipped nails.

"Today, Comrades of Liberation," she begins as she always does, refusing to call us fighters, "we are seeing the prana grid of our universe. You will gather images, and I will receive them from you. I will put these images together in a map which will be used later."

I can't help but roll my eyes slightly. I hate astronomy. A star is a star is a star. At least that was my view until I'd touched my feet onto one of those distant stars.

Today is like so many other days. It feels impossible; impossible until we do it.

As usual, Morren and I must sit in the center of the circle, allowing our energy, our prana, to be the focus and starting point. When we first began a few months ago, we would be drained for the rest of the day. The Capellan came to us after the third day of this and told us we weren't doing it right. It was that day that we'd learned that it wasn't about us.

***

"You are trying to give prana from your own storage. You need your prana," she'd said. "You must give through you, not from you. You must allow yourself to simply be a conductor, the channel that the prana flows through. It is utterly ridiculous to think you can be the source that will give prana to all of these people who will carry the strength and power required for the liberation."

"So, where's it coming from?" I asked on that day.

"Everywhere. The prana is everywhere. In you, outside of you, in me, in Morren, the ocean, the trees, the air, the sun, the universe. It cannot be contained, but you can focus some of it."

She handed me a small clear prism.

"Hold it up to the fire," she'd instructed.

I'd done as the Capellan asked and held it up. The light refracted, spilling out and against the walls, multiplying.

"Is that light you see from the prism?" she'd asked.

"No. It's from the fire."

"But would you see it hitting all these other spots without the prism?"

"No."

"Be like the prism."

"Can I keep this? I can feel the prana more with it."

"If you wish."

I'd held it in my fingers, turning it and shifting the reflections of light.

"Do I get something like that to help me too?" Morren had asked.

"Do you need something?"

"Yeah. I want to boost my prana too."

"I have something special for you then. Give me one moment to return."

I recall how Morren smiled as he waited for the Capellan. "That's really nice, Karana. I can't wait to see what she has for me."

The Capellan returned, her hands behind her back.

"Now, close your eyes and open your hands."

Morren closed his eyes and stretched his hands out, cupped together. The Capellan placed a single stone in his hand. It didn't look much different than the ones we saw near the water. One side was nearly smooth and the other still rough.

"You may open your eyes now."

Morren opened his eyes and looked at the stone in his hand, confused.

"I don't understand."

"You wanted something to boost your prana. Here it is," she'd said.

"Yeah. But this is a rock."

"And?"

"Karana gets this pretty, clear, crystal-like prism. I get a rock."

"They are both stones."

"What am I supposed to do with this?"

"What would you like to do with it?" she'd asked with her head eschewed.

Morren looked at the Capellan with frustration. He'd shoved the gray rock into his pocket, shaking his head as he did.

"You can use it for whatever you will," the Capellan said.

Then she turned to both of us and brought her hands up. One palm she placed on my forehead and the other on Morren's forehead, letting them linger for several moments. I could feel my forehead pulsing under her fingertips.

"See."

She then placed one hand over one of my ears and a hand over one of Morren's ears. She held them in place and my ears began to buzz.

"Hear."

Her hands moved down to our necks, and she gently placed her hands on our throats, and I could feel a tickle beneath my skin.

"Speak."

She dropped her hands from our necks and held them palm up before taking one of my hands and one of Morren's.

"You have power untapped. You must see, hear, and speak from here," she said and placed our hands on our hearts. But you must always use your mind. It is your most powerful tool. All else is just matter, eventually falling away and changing form into another thing."

"What are we supposed to do here, Selvedon?"

"You must inspire the will of the people, bring them together, and help them free themselves."

"How?" Morren asked.

"Why us? I asked.

"You will do it with practice and intention because it is your purpose. Now I must rest this body. Good night, Karana and Morren. I will see you in the morning."

The Capellan let Selvedon have her body back to rest, but the energy lingered, hovering near my side – warm and welcoming. Morren and I had sat up talking about what she'd told us, and how much of it could be real.

We settled on the idea that it doesn't really even matter how much was real. But, from what I can tell, it's all real and we're expected to use the prana.

Chapter Twenty-Nine

I swipe my hair from my eyes and as I pull my hand away; the scar mocks me again. I wish I could scratch it off, dig it out, make it go away somehow, so I can be like the others. But it's there, permanent. It's a constant reminder that my life was never mine, but that somehow before I ever knew I was a part of this great universe, I was marked. And so was Morren. His mark is on his heel.

The Capellan recognized it when we met at the Market. Doc had been hosting. I don't know why we never noticed it before. Perhaps trying to survive made paying attention to details like that a luxury we couldn't afford. It was also the Capellan who spotted Morren's. The Capellan made the connection that our scars bear a striking resemblance to the yin yang symbol, and when held side by side, seem to fit.

She told us the story that went further than the one Lari was told as a child. When I'd left Earth, I was a human being just trying to help my family. But I now know that Morren and I aren't that, or at the very least, we aren't just that.

We Immunes have deviant DNA, but that isn't what makes Morren and I different. The Capellan says it was likely our mother's people, through generations who bore the mark. She said sometimes it skips a generation, sometimes it splits, but she must have been one of many lines who bore those like us.

The Capellan told us that we, Morren and I, have a special force that when activated, compels us to act on behalf of freedom and justice. It's why I couldn't just leave Base X, or Anfar or now, Cuupton. It's why, despite Morren's sometimes resistance, he couldn't leave either. It was him that got us going on this journey in the first place.

We are now in the seat of the Comrades of Liberation, and everyone is looking to us for answers that neither of us have. My only confidante is Doc. He allows me to call him that now that I've earned his trust.

We've been working for months at gathering intel, identifying the key players, and training the liberators. Willa, Reyn, and Lari are all here doing their part with me and Morren. Eton is around, though I don't know how he spends most of his time. He trains and then disappears. Perhaps he's still sulking. No, I'm sure he is.

Down here in the cave, it can be depressing. There is always something important to do, but we do have our breaks when we can laugh, joke, and pretend for just a short while that the balance of the universe doesn't rely on our success.

Morren and I must train more and continue to use that training. My mind and body feel an exhaustion that even the years of hiding and running can't compare to. I've never been in a place like this; a place where I understand as much as I do about what I hold inside. I'm still heavy with the weight of what we hold on our shoulders. The weight of a universe in crisis, and an expectation that feels too great to live up to.

But here, in this dark corner of this cramped cave, no one else expects anything of me. I can just be my miserable self, failing and flailing all alone. I know Morren has his moments too, but he won't talk about it. At least not with me. Perhaps he talks to Lari about it, but I know he thinks that talking to me about it will somehow make it real. *News flash, brother, it's already real. Everything is real.*

I heard that. Where are you?

I need to be more careful. He seems to be so sensitive to my thoughts, and the same is true for me with him. I don't want him to find me, not yet, so I try to block any more intrusions.

Chapter Thirty

"We are near the end of our lessons. Today, you will channel your prana."

I can't help but smile a bit. "It's still early and that's what we do *every* day."

"True, but we must reassure some. There are some liberators right here who are uncertain whether you are the key to unlock the binds. You must show them that you can break the chains of the masses."

"How do we do that?" Morren asks.

"First, you will call them out with the goal of eventually having them join us," the Capellan says.

"That's easy." Morren jumps up and starts heading toward the cave.

"You cannot use your mouth or any other part of your body."

The looks on our faces mimic each other - confusion.

"You speak to each other in your mind quite often, yes? And to Eli as well?" The Capellan asks.

"Yeah," we answer in unison.

"Do you believe you are limited to this small circle?"

I suddenly felt trivial and petty for not thinking beyond my brother and Eli.

"Before you do that, you need to know the remaining tasks that will prepare us for tomorrow." The Capellan walks around us in a tight circle. I watch as he clasps his hands behind his back and am reminded that Doc is still in there. He's been holding the Capellan more often than Selvedon lately.

"What are they?" I try to not allow my nervousness show.

"This is where only a few of us reside. The Comrades of Liberation are many, and while you have been contacting them and raising them up, we must now draw them here."

"Okay?" the hesitation in my voice is clear.

My hands feel warm again, as they have begun doing often since studying with the Capellan.

"Our comrades must be drawn here to Cuupton."

"We've been talking about this for the next market. Do you think they'll get here in time?" Morren asks logically.

"You've been working on several things that will allow it to happen."

"You can get them here and to the market, and anywhere else required for what must be done."

"Are you speaking of the portals?"

"Yes."

"But we've only done it on Cuupton."

"Is it not all the same? Space?"

"We can bring comrades from anywhere?"

"You must make sure your energy matches and that you know the destination."

"That's kinda like our jumping," Morren says.

"Yes, very much so. However, it does not require you taking an entourage each time. It doesn't require you leaving or moving yourself at all. All may be drawn to you, or to where they need to be."

"So, can I try to draw out Selvedon?" I laugh.

The Capellan looks at me and then shrugs. Everyone knows that when she's not hosting the Capellan, Selvedon can be testy in the morning or if she hasn't gotten enough sleep.

"You may try. Just know she can be quite…resistant."

I sit on the hard ground letting the sunlight warm my skin. I put my hands up toward the cave door and feel them begin to tingle. I imagine myself walking into Selvedon's quarters and whispering in her ear. She shakes her head and rolls over. I move to the other side and whisper, "Selvedon? Time to wake up and come outside."

"Go away."

"Selvedon, I need your help. Please come outside."

"What for?"

I pause. *What for?*

"To make my new morning boost drink."

Morren shoots me a disappointing look as does the Capellan.

"Sorry, no drink. I just need your help to prove something important. Mission critical."

"I am trying to sleep. I'm tired."

"But you're mostly up now. You might as well come out."

"You don't understand. I am tired."

"Please, Selvedon. Come for just a minute and then you can go back."

"Fine. Just a minute."

"Fine? You're coming?"

"Yes. Now get out of my head, Karana. And I'm getting your biscuit this morning."

She's coming. I am almost giddy at the thought of how this will work. If I could get her out, could I get Tezzi and Dad too?

"So, Selvedon only has to come from the cave. No portal needed. How do we get those who have to come through space?" I feel myself deflate.

"Excellent question. And today you will begin with one of your contacts that has been prepped the longest. Planet Jarra is not a large planet, but of its population of one billion people, there are over one million living and working as slaves. You must give the call to the portal heads that we must open Jarra."

"Then?" I ask.

"Then you must give the call to Jarra that it is time."

"Wait. Now? We don't have room for a million people here."

"Not all will come but many will, and we always have exactly what we need."

"Where will they go?" Morren asks.

"The portals are set up in safe places around Cuupton. They will go to these different locations. We must surround Cuupton with the comrades. Our battle will be waged on all levels, and we need the forces here to ensure that no one, particularly Zo, Narp, and Haunir, can escape or call in for aid. We must isolate them."

"Got it." Morren and I say in unison.

"Good. You will repeat this for each of the planets."

"Alright. What was the mission critical reason for dragging me out of my sleep?"

I can hardly believe Selvedon's appearance and now feel guilty for doing this to her. Her golden glimmer is almost gone, faded like her energy.

"Are you okay, Sel?" I ask.

"Is that why you asked me out here?"

"No, it was a test to see if I could get you out using telepathy."

"I see," she smiles weakly. "You did it." Selvedon nods toward Doc. "They are progressing so well. You are doing such a good job. But you can't do it alone."

Doc says nothing, letting his eyes fall toward her feet before he raises them to her eyes. "Thank you. You should get your rest Sel. You still have a job to do, too."

They were speaking in some code Morren, and I weren't meant to understand.

"Karana?"

"Yes, Sel?"

"You can stop trying to listen because I'm not saying anything."

Chapter Thirty-One

Eli. I can't believe I'm saying it, but I miss her moody blue tentacles and calm demeanor. She's gone back to Earth once again to help prepare it for our return. Part of me wonders if after all this time, there will be a place for us.

"Good morning, Karana."

Morren comes into my area and leans against the wall. He's different in ways I only wish he could see. If either of us had been who we are now while we were still on Earth, we probably wouldn't have left.

"Good morning, little brother," I smile.

"Ready for another day on Cuupton?"

"I guess so. Not that I really have a choice."

"We're getting close. Soon we'll be done." His smile is comforting.

I smile back. How he does it - staying calm and steady in all of this, I still don't know.

"Hey, did Eli say anything to you about Dad and Tezzi before she left again?"

"Not enough to know what's going on for certain."

"Do you think she's not telling us on purpose? Like she doesn't want us to know?"

"I don't know, Karana. I don't want to try and guess, and it won't do us any good either way. We're here."

"Why can't we get through to them? We're able to connect with beings we don't know. Before we left Earth, we didn't even know they existed - but can't connect to Tezzi and Dad?" I shake my head, bewildered. "It doesn't make sense."

"I know. But before coming here, we didn't know how to connect with anyone besides ourselves and Eli. It's possible that we just haven't figured out Tezzi and Dad?"

I pull at the mismatch materials on my blanket. Old scratchy towels, shirts, and pants cut into large strips and hand-stitched together. More function than comfort, like everything here.

"Maybe in the compound they're blocked." I know he's trying to calm me.

"After all we've learned and done since coming here, you really believe that?"

I get up, checking the floor first out of habit. I'm still no fan of the little mice like rodents that skitter about in the shadows. A cat would be nice.

"There's gotta be a reason. We're getting good at this, and it seems that we should be able to reach them too." Morren finally acknowledges my concern. That's a start. I know I'm not being unreasonable.

"What if something's happened?"

"Karana, I can't even give that idea my thoughts."

"I know. But one of the things we've been taught is that the truth can withstand questions while the false, under scrutiny, falls away."

"The Capellan was talking about big truths, Karana."

"No. A truth is a truth is a truth. What's false is false is false. Size doesn't matter...at least not in this case."

Morren sits back on my bed, which is more of a raised cot wedged into a small sleeping nook. Everything is sparse. The only beauty and escape is in the mind, or outside the mouth of the cave.

"I don't like to think of it because there is a part of me that may not be ready for all the possible reasons we can't reach them. All I can do, all we can do, Karana, is keep trying."

Unfortunately, he's right. Maybe Eli will come back next time with news. Or perhaps, soon enough, we'll be back ourselves and can get answers.

"Karana, right now we must focus on what's going on here. If we do this, things will begin to balance again. It is what this universe is always seeking. I read that once in a book called *Crossed: The Karma Crusades*. There are things working that we don't always see."

"I know this – in my head at least. I really do know it. I just don't know it in my heart, and maybe that's where I'm disconnected."

"Do you remember when Laisa was pregnant with Tezzi?"

"How could I forget?" I chuckle at the memory.

"She was so sick, but every day while Dad was trying to figure out how to get her better she would just rub her belly and talk to Tezzi. She'd have us do the same thing. Remember?"

"Yeah. We'd sit in front of her and put our hands on her big belly, and Tezzi would kick your hand when you pressed down."

"Then, she'd kick your hand," he laughs.

"We'd play that game for an hour until Laisa finally needed a break from being poked and kicked."

I think about how much we did together with her. Our interactions with Tezzi had so often been together - and even with Dad, especially after Mom died.

"Morren, what if we need to contact her together?"

"Why would that matter?"

"I don't know why. We always played with her together."

Morren's chin wrinkles a bit as he thinks. "It's worth a try."

We walk in the room with the single, old, beat-up computer. Reyn turns and faces us. The frown Reyn has when she's upset or disappointed turns her lips as she speaks.

"You two have to get this right. I can only tell you where to focus based on where we know the market trades. The rest is up to you."

"I know, Reyn. We're trying." I shake my head and Morren nods in agreement.

We are trying, but all of this is new to us. Reaching out with only our prana and our minds to beings light years away isn't easy.

Selvedon walks in. I can't tell whether she's hosting the Capellan today. She moves slowly into the room and then rests against the wall.

"You are doing fine and making progress. I understand the frustration that Reyn holds, but you are close. Soon you will have contacted all those aligned with us on the twelve planets active in the trade," Selvedon says.

"Sel? Why did Earth stop participating? Doc said we once did." I need to finally know the answer to this. Maybe it will help me in some way.

"It was not because Earth chose not to. They were forced out because of the virus killing your people. No one knew how it was spread, or who could be infected. The announcer, Haunir, and the trade cooperative don't take those kinds of risks. They chose to quarantine Earth. The quarantine impacted more than the slave trade. No one could come or go - at least not by any normal means. So, to see an Earthling at the market is unusual and can be suspect."

"If that's the case, what's that mean for the next market?" Morren asks.

"It means all of you Earthlings will need to remain out of sight as much as possible. It also means you and Karana must continue issuing the call for the recruits."

"You're saying we can't help with the market? We just sit around, literally, until then, just connecting with these other beings?" I ask Selvedon as she stands in front of me.

In its natural state, the Capellan no longer holds a physical form. Having risen to the level of prana, its physical hosts, Selvedon and Doc, are mostly willing. Selvedon's eyes focus intently as she looks at me, and then past me to answer.

231

"It is not just a *just*. It is absolutely imperative that you focus on bringing your awareness to them so they can understand your purpose and prepare themselves and those on their respective planets. At this point, we do not know how long we have, so we cannot squander time."

Reyn turns from the computer and looks at Morren and me. "And I am not going back to Baselonica Xuna. We need to get it right. Morren, today you are reaching out to Zanthar Six. Karana, you need to contact Pejakot. They are one of the more populous planets and were active in the last market - several buyers."

I listen to Reyn and understand her lack of patience. None of us can afford to return to Base X before destroying the market.

"Got it," Morren says back to Reyn.

With no more words, he walks out of Reyn's work room.

"I guess I better get busy too."

"I will come to check on you in a couple hours and give you your cycles for the day," Selvedon tells me.

"How many are we up to now?"

I see Morren's head peak back around the corner. He's as anxious as I am.

"Today you received nine and ten. Once you confirm contact, you will receive the last two."

Light, finally. Some contacts have taken just a day or two and others a week. We know from the intergalactic chatter Reyn and Doc monitor that the next market is being planned, but when it will happen is always reserved to the last moment possible. Only those cleared receive the information. Our contact from Baselonica Xuna, one of the women working as a pola who was left behind, will let us know.

"Let's get to it, Karana. Why don't you come with me today? It'll get you out of your routine," Morren smiles.

"Wait, Sel. Where are you going?" I wonder if she'll finally tell me what I suspect.

"Don't worry, I'll be back with your cycles."

I can only nod as she leaves the room. I feel the Capellan's presence still, and it answers my question of whether Selvedon had been its host. Why was it lingering so close?

Its warmth surrounds me. I can sense the question it has wanted to ask for weeks. The question that answers the question I have about Selvedon. It is less words and more a feeling of whether I will allow myself to be a willing host for it. To be the feminine balance to Doc.

My body tenses as I consider what it means. I wonder what will happen to me if I agree. I relax with the awareness that I remain intact and in control of myself, even while hosting the Capellan. The Capellan would simply speak through me when needed, allowing me to be fully myself at other times.

The look on Morren's face lets me know he isn't so certain. The Capellan moves to him and surrounds him in the same warmth that had enveloped me. Morren's grimaced look softens and acquiesces into a look of resignation.

I guess it's okay, he sends me.

I give the Capellan permission to use me as its host and wait for whatever is supposed to happen. It moves back to me and fills my space with the intense warmth and prana. Now it was with me. Simply with me, peaceful and loving. It will be speaking through me today, and I wonder if I'll be able to resist when it wants us to do something I don't want to do.

The Capellan is sending Eton with us as recorder.

For crying out loud. I know that's not you for sure. It must be the Capellan.

I know. I'd think we'd be getting a reward for me accepting this. Eton's a punishment.

I immediately feel a twinge in my side, instantly knowing why the Capellan did it. I would still rather have nearly anyone else. But I have to admit that he makes me stronger, since whatever he puts off forces me to raise my own frequency to go above it.

"Are you two talking to yourselves again?" Reyn interrupts, and I wonder how long she'd been watching us.

"Oh. Sorry. We're getting ready to go."

"No, it's okay. You two are just over there doing strange things and making faces. I figured you were having a conversation."

"We're going now."

I consider whether or not to tell Reyn about being one of the hosts, and then think better of it. Doc should know before anyone else. I certainly don't plan on telling Eton. I cringe again at the idea that we have to go work with the one person who seems bent on seeing us all fail.

You know, not everyone gets what we're doing or why, Morren says.

You were listening again, Morren.

I can't help it. You're practically screaming. Even still, it's true.

I know. I just think he's eventually gonna hold us back, or worse.

Hopefully not. Gotta appreciate him for now. You always have to kick it up a notch when the Capellan assigns him. Ha! And since the Capellan is with you; in a way you kind of chose him."

I shoot back a look that says 'Really?'

"And why does she give me Eton more than she gives him to you?"

Morren shrugs. He's got Lari today. It doesn't matter what else happens, he'll be happy.

"You two aren't talking about me, are you?" Reyn asks over her shoulder.

"No. We're just planning how we're going to work." I hadn't told the full truth, but it isn't a lie either. "We'll see you later, Reyn."

We walk into the main room. Everyone gets up early here. Surek, the cook, spots me from where he stands near a makeshift table. He's got biscuits baking, and he's passing out ones from the tray already done. He gives me his big bright smile and a nod. His ears remind me of our fairy tale elves, but I think his golden speckled skin is the most fun, especially when light from the fire or sun hit it.

I know it's not fair, but I hope he put aside a big biscuit for me. Morren and I get in line behind the others. Eton is several feet ahead of us. I don't see Lari.

"Hey, you two," Lari's voice calls out from behind us.

"Hey," Morren's gushing smile almost makes my eyes roll.

"Hey, Lari," I say back.

"Morren," Lari smiles. "I get to work with you again today."

This time I do roll my eyes, while giving Surek the look we've gotten familiar with.

"Who do you have today?" Lari asks me.

I tighten my lips and look over at Eton, giving a nod toward him.

"Oh." She drags out the 'o'. "Sorry. I was hoping you might get Reyn or even Doc. That is Doc without the Capellan."

"Yeah, me too. Reyn is too busy. But I guess the Capellan thinks he's good for me."

"The Capellan is probably right."

"I know. What is everyone else working on today?"

"The rest are doing skills. Doc and Selvedon want to make sure everyone's on the same page with this and help bring them here." Lari says this while eyeing Morren and then me. "And it's not nearly as easy as they made it seem when we came."

"Well finding the high vibration prana spots isn't easy," I add.

"And then the whole prepping for battle. It's not like those in control are gonna turn over their empires without a fight," Lari says.

"Thankfully, they don't have to. We just have to turn over some minds; the rest will follow," I say with feigned certainty.

Lari looks at me skeptically.

"It's true. It better be true."

"Otherwise, this is a waste of time, and we can't have that. At least you two are getting better at this." I know Lari's words are barely masking the worry she and everyone else here is feeling.

"Yeah. We can usually make contact within a day or two. But I'm still working on the first planetary contact, and getting him ready while trying to reach number nine today."

"Is that why Reyn and Willa are frustrated?" Lari asks.

"Willa too?" I am surprised. I knew Reyn was, but Willa?

"Yeah. You can't blame Willa. Or even me, for that matter. We've got Chapis Zo looking for us."

"It's gonna be okay. Get your biscuit, Karana. We have more than enough to think about today, rather than worry about who's frustrated. We're doing the best we can." Morren stands beside me and nudges me forward.

I grab my extra big biscuit. "Thank you, Surek. You are the best."

"You're welcome. You need your strength."

I wonder if he knows I'm hosting the Capellan or whether I'm reading more into his words and smile than what's there.

I lean against the wall with Morren and Lari and eat my biscuit. Surek has baked some kind of nutty-buttery substance into them, making the biscuit melt on my tongue.

Eton spots us and walks over. I'll have to try and be nice to him today. If not nice, I'll go for cordial.

I don't see Willa anywhere. Knowing her, she's putting her skills to use here. She can do what others can't and none of us can explain. I guess some call it alchemy, but she can pull the essence out of a fricking rock to harness it or transfer it. Or out of any natural substance. It's why Zo could rent her to the

Anfarians, and why he wants her back. She's gotten stronger, applying it to more than just the mines. I've seen her do it once with some of the rocks near the water. She's changed their essence so they can be used to help power the cave. If she can understand how a thing works, she can figure out how to use it or change it. Now, she's changing the natural elements here into gunpowder and bullets. For some reason, she's all excited about it. I've never seen her work so hard.

"I hear I'm with you today, Karana." Eton smiles smugly, as if he knows his mere presence still irritates me.

"Yeah," I smile. "We're gonna be busy."

Bastard won't get to me today. I'm hosting the freaking Capellan – the epitome of prana and love. Try that one on for size, prick.

Morren glances at me and then Eton. I guess hosting the Capellan doesn't solve my Eton attitude issue or that Morren has to hear about it too.

Chapter Thirty-Two

This hasn't been anything like I'd expected, but then, I don't know what I'd expected. Nothing has happened in any way I could have anticipated since the moment Eli, Morren, and I left Earth. I don't even know how long it's been now. I've lost track of time.

Everything is different, including me. I barely recognize the person I've become since this all began. I'm constantly tormented by guilt. My sister was only eight, and too young to know for sure if she was an Immune. By now, they know what we in our hearts already know. By now, she and Dad were no doubt being tortured for the answers and secrets that live inside of them.

We're doing things differently today. Lari sits between Morren and I on one side, and Eton between us on the other. Morren suggested we go close to the water and I think he's right. The water seems to boost us. And maybe in this circle with our recorders, Lari and Eton, we will not only make contact with the ninth and tenth planets, but with Dad and Tezzi.

I reach out and grab Morren's hands before beginning the process of forgetting my body and where I am. For us, it's not about becoming blank, but rather of becoming mindful and aware. Morren and I both call to Tezzi. As if it were as natural as our childhood, we take turns tapping in. We recall the womb, helping feed her, the hide and seek games that we played to save our lives, the lullabies we'd take turns singing as we lay on the pallet our dad had put together for us in the basement of an old abandoned warehouse.

Tears stream down my eyes, but I barely feel them. The water lapping against the rocks mockingly mimics my up and down emotions.

I squeeze Morren's fingers and remind myself he's here with me. Morren tightens his grip on mine. His hands are warm, almost hot. The prana flowing through us together is stronger than I'd imagined.

Where are you? I send out.

There's no answer.

Where are you? Morren sends out.

After waiting a few moments, I try again.

Where are you?

Tezzi, Dad, where are you? Can you hear me? Morren tries.

For what feels like hours we call out to them, until Eton gently clears his throat. I know. We've spent too much time trying to reach them. We haven't even begun what we came out here to do.

Tezzi? Dad? Where are you? We're alive. We're coming back! I yell out from within one last time.

Karana? Karana?

"Tezzi!" Morren and I both say aloud.

Morren? Karana? I'm here. I'm here.

Tezzi! Where are you? I ask.

I'm...I'm still in the compound. Maybe a different one. Please come and get me. Please, hurry.

A pang shoots through my heart at the sound of her pleading.

Are you there? Karana? Morren?

We are coming back. Soon, I answer.

Soon? You've been gone for years! Please don't leave me here. I've been waiting. Are you on your way now? I can't do it much longer.

Hang on, Tezzi. Don't give up, Morren says.

We've finally been able to reach you. But we can't get you out without you, I tell her.

What do you mean? I'm trapped here in a cell unless they let me out for testing or to use the bathroom. I haven't seen or heard from Dad...in I don't know how long. I can't get out, Karana.

The distress in her voice, and knowing what they are doing to her, brings another round of tears to my eyes.

You can, and I will help you. We will help you.

You don't understand. I'm certain the minute I leave this bathroom, you'll be gone again. They're watching me right now as I wash my hands. They'll turn the water off, Karana, and you'll be gone, she cries.

I thought about it - the water.

Tezzi, the water raises your consciousness to hear us. You are over seventy-percent water. You already have the water inside you. Everything is inside you. When you get back, use that water to tap back in. Morren and I will be waiting. We're working on a way to free people, including you.

What? I know Tezzi is confused.

We're working on a way to free people like you, Morren repeats for me.

You left me here so you can free other people? I was eight when you left us in here. I don't know how long you've been gone, but I've gone through puberty since you left. I know that was delayed, so it's gotta be at least seven or eight years. And you are helping free other people?

I swallow hard. Seven or eight years. I don't understand how that is even possible.

I'm sorry, Tezzi. We didn't know how long it's been. Where we are, we've been gone a few months, maybe more. I'm so sorry.

Tezzi, we will help you get out of there, Morren says matter-of-factly. I can tell he is choking back his own tears.

My heart aches at the anguish in our little sister's voice. We really messed up. But there is no going back; we could only try to make it better from here. I wonder about Dad, but am afraid to know the truth. I don't want to question it now. Tezzi doesn't know. I don't want to break the connection, but the entire mission requires that we connect with the twelve planets, and with Rache on Baselonica Xuna to see if there is an update on the market.

Tezzi, we have to go now. We're outta time. But we'll be back in touch as soon as possible, Morren says.

I can barely speak.

Wait! No, she says, but I think it's more to the guards. *No, Morren. No, Karana. Don't go. They're taking me. No. no. no. Karen, stop them.*

Another voice breaks in that sounds vaguely familiar, but I can't fully place.

I'm sorry, Tezzi, but we must go now. Let's hope they come back. But if they don't, we'll be okay.

Tezzi's gone.

My eyes snap open and look at Morren. "Karen?"

"Who's Karen?" he asks back.

"She was talking to someone."

"Maybe she's being held with someone else," Morren wonders.

"And we could hear her like that?" It wasn't normal.

"Maybe because we're hearing what she's hearing?" Morren reasons.

"We didn't hear the guards, Morren. That was strange. We have to get back to her."

"Not now," Lari says. "I'm sorry, but the sun is high above us, and you haven't even started what we're out here to do."

"And as much as I'm glad you found your sister; trust me the only reason I'm out here is for my health. If I don't do this today, I don't get dinner, so let's get to it," Eton adds.

"You're not helping." Lari shoots Eton a glare that bounces off him like he's made of rubber, unfazed.

I'm shaken. I don't know that I can focus on anything else. Maybe it was a mistake trying to reach Tezzi and Dad.

Seven or eight years? I'm a full-grown adult back on Earth, and so is Morren.

"We've screwed this up bad, Morren."

He's silent.

"We left her for years, locked up, tortured, in that compound."

He's still silent.

"We abandoned them, Morren. Damnit! And it was you who did this! You wanted to follow Eli and leave!"

I jump to my feet and push Morren down, standing over him. I kick him once in the side before walking off. They can have this. All of this. I'd come to save Tezzi and Dad and hadn't done it. Instead, trying to help everyone else, I'd left her and Dad behind to rot in a concrete cell.

I look back, hearing footsteps. It's Lari. It's her that kept us from returning home when we were on Base X.

"Don't talk to me. If it weren't for you, I wouldn't have started on this insane journey and left my family behind. Your people will probably be just fine."

"I'm sorry about your sister and dad, Karana. You couldn't have known. None of us could have. We're all in territory that we didn't even know about. It's new to all of us."

"Is that the best you got? Ignorance? And that's supposed to make it okay that my little sister is being held and tortured on a dying planet because we chose you and all these other aliens over our own blood?"

Lari looks at me, with an expression of sympathy or pity. I don't know which, and I don't care.

"She said seven or eight years, Lari. She was only eight when we left. She's lived another lifetime and I can't even

244

imagine what she's been through. The torture. Feeling abandoned. Not knowing what happened or what's happening..."

Lari tries to reach for me, but I continue walking, leaving her where she stands, looking after me. I hear the Capellan trying to speak to me, comfort me, but even that doesn't work. I don't want to hear any of its well-intentioned wisdom. I want to go home, and none of this will matter once I'm back. Earth isn't even a part of this sick game anymore, and it's none of my business.

Where are you going, Karana?

Get out of my head, Morren.

We still have work to do.

It doesn't matter. None of this does if we've left our sister and dad to die.

"I think she needs some time to herself," Morren whispers behind me.

Chapter Thirty-Three

"Would you like to talk, Karana?" The Capellan asks.

The deep voice is usually calming. I'm grateful Doc is hosting as I couldn't put up with the Capellan, not right now. Maybe it figured I'd listen if it weren't inside my own head. It's also smart, knowing I find Doc intriguing.

"No. I don't want to."

"It has been two days since you have come out."

I don't care how long it's been or even that Doc has come for me.

"Morren has told me about your sister and father. That you reached your sister and have learned of her situation and the years that have passed. For this, I am sorry. I realize it must be difficult."

"Difficult? Ha! What would you know about that? You're a piece of energy that just pops in and out of Doc or me as you please. My sister is stuck on Earth. They are experimenting on her. Whoever's left is doing crap to her and I'm here helping everyone else, while my own family wastes away. So, tell me how you realize the difficulty?"

"I haven't always been the Capellan. I have not always been in my form of prana. I was once a person, many persons, over many lifetimes. I have suffered and hurt in most of those lives. I have loved and watched those I have loved be killed, die, or just walk away from me. I've had to walk away from some of them as well."

"You've been a person, or a being before?"

"Yes. Many beings. Many types. They all have the same issues. All trying to connect, relate, and as Lari calls it, have more prana."

"How did you do it? When you see the people you love being destroyed and hurt?"

"I let myself hurt too, for a while. I let myself be angry for a while. I let myself feel what beings feel – for a while. But I never forgot why I was there, or what I was doing. In fact, all that pain and hurt and anger all came from the same place. It existed for the same reason. I made it my goal to rise above so I could focus on why I was there, and what I needed to do."

"I guess you must've done it."

"Generally. Yes."

"But I'm in it, still."

"Yes. You are. You have many beings relying on something you have to offer. That includes your family on Earth. They are part of the many that need you. You can no easier separate them out, than separate yourself from the intricate web of this vast universe. You are a part of it, whether you are from Earth, or Cuupton, or Anfar, or Baselonica Xuna. It is all the same. The same prana."

"Then why do I feel so far away? Why do I feel so helpless when it comes to Tezzi and my dad?"

"Because you see the disconnect, when you need to see the connection."

"Where is all this going, Doc?"

Doc looks at me, just as he did the day I met him at the market. He looks into my eyes and then past them, seeing me in ways that still make me uncomfortable.

"This is bigger than any one person, any one being. You must be willing to be bigger as well. The sacrifices each of us must make are for a greater cause. One that cannot be measured in individual beings because it impacts every single being."

"Doc? Not the Capellan. I need you to be real with me. I need to know if I'm gonna get out of this place and be able to get my sister and dad."

"I do not have the answer to that question. I know that it is possible; but your family must be in agreement. You cannot pull them out if they are not ready."

"Not from here. But if I go back to Earth, I can. I can jump into the compound, get them, and jump back out."

"So why did you not bring them before?"

"Because they were too weak to jump."

"And what if they are weak in body still?"

"We'll try anyway."

"I see."

"Do you wish to save their body, or their being?"

"What?" I asked. The Capellan is back in full again. I sigh.

"What is it that you wish to save?"

"Them!" I say frustrated.

"What part of them?"

"All of them! All of them." The Capellan is frustrating me. Does it not understand?

"Then you must first save the mind. And that is what you are doing with and for each and every one of the contacts you have been working with. You and Morren are contacting them, to help them free their minds so that they can make the cross to Cuupton from wherever they are. But if you don't believe it, Karana, you won't be a part of it."

"That makes no sense, Doc."

"The beauty is that whether you fully believe it for yourself or not, you do understand it and that understanding is being shared and those you share it with, they do believe."

"Are you saying that even though I'm the messenger, I might get left behind?"

"I am saying that you do not have to believe for yourself in order for others to get and hold onto the message you give. It would be better for you, if you do, but it is not necessary."

"What kind of crap deal is this?"

"It is not a deal. It is just the way it is. You can lead them and your sister out of their bondage, even if you refuse to set yourself free from yours."

"You're making no sense."

I immediately know that I'm lying. The Capellan is making sense, but it's not what I want to hear right now. I'm not like Morren. I question and doubt. And I'm angrier than I've been in what must be seven or eight Earth years. At least since we hit that red sand on Baselonica Xuna.

I rub the scar that looks like a tadpole swimming head down or a tear drop. I wish that I could be content leaving this all, grabbing Morren, Reyn, and Eton, and jumping home, but I wouldn't be. And, I can't. The draw to this place is too strong, not allowing us to leave together. I've already tried it twice.

"I will do what I must, Doc. But in the end, Tezzi and Dad have to be part of those who are freed."

"I understand your desire. Karana, no one can guarantee anything with this."

"I know. I'm just making it clear to this big universe what I want. We will do what we must. We will bring together the Comrades of Liberation and we're gonna break this ring apart. Then I'm getting home."

Chapter Thirty-Four

I have never had to spend so much time with only myself, learning to listen. I have never before had to trust others like I am now. I've never had to let go of so much control. Between those we are trying to contact off of Cuupton and the Capellan who comes to me in spurts as I grow as a host, being in my own head is becoming exhausting.

"Karana, you cannot control it all or do it all," that's what the Capellan told me.

"Of course, I can't," I'd said.

"Understand that all of those here are here because we too are compelled by something greater than ourselves to be here. You and Morren may have the mark on your bodies, but many of us bear the mark on our hearts. We are here because we believe in the movement of the prana. It is freedom itself and it cannot be bound. Our battle is not against those restraints that hold the feet and hands of the enslaved. Our battle is against the restraints that hold their mind."

"But how do we battle that? They gotta be free to even be able to get free, it seems. It's a catch twenty-two."

"I do not know what catching twenty-two is. But it is difficult, I admit, to free people who have been taught to not be free, or even worse, who believe they already are."

"I think I've been set up to lead a mission doomed to fail," I'd said sadly.

"If that is what you think, then you have."

"What kind of pep talk is this?"

"You, Karana, are the one who said it. You are the one who thinks it. I neither thought nor said" it."

"Technically, I'm not one hundred percent sure you didn't think it. You are in my head."

"Why do you not believe in you? In us?"

I didn't have a good answer for the Capellan, not then. Maybe because I'd seen only death and darkness. There was very little telling me that something different existed anywhere in this universe. Maybe because I wasn't convinced I could do it - that I could bring up the prana in me that the Capellan speaks of. Perhaps because I didn't have a reason to believe.

But that was months ago, at least. Time feels so fluid now that I'm no longer sure how long I've been gone. What I know is that I'm not the girl who walked into this cave with Doc, Morren, Reyn, Eton, Willa, Lari, and Eli. No. And I never will be again.

I get my legs under me, stand, and head out of the corner I've grown so fond of. The corner that asks no questions, expects nothing, and gives only peace. The large cavern where everyone gathers in the group meal around a fire opens in front of me. This is my favorite time here, when we let ourselves eat, drink, and laugh just a little before the gaining of knowledge and practice continues.

As I approach, a smile crosses my lips.

"Come on over, Karana. We have been waiting for you. Your place is here." Doc pats a pillow on the floor beside him.

I walk over to the large pot being tended to over a second fire by Surek, and he pours me a bowl.

"Thanks, Surek. You make the best soup."

"I know I do," he smiles.

"Sitting by Doc, again?" Willa comes and stands beside me.

"What do you mean 'again'?" I pretend not to understand her inference.

"You know what I mean. How can you like him? He's so...stiff."

"I don't like him. I like that he's focused and smart, that's all."

"Sure. Whatever. Have you heard about Chapis Zo?"

"No. What is it?"

I check the faces of Lari, Reyn, and Morren as they wait too, bowls in hand. It's like they know they need to hear whatever Willa's gonna say to me.

"Chapis Zo has sent out a search team for me and Lari. He says we were stolen from him and Narp. But from what he sent out, he doesn't know where we are. Right now I don't think he has a clue, but who knows how long that will last."

"We're gonna need to do something soon to end this; or risk the Zo Clan combing the last place we were seen – right here on Cuupton," Lari warns.

"He can't win. If he does, we know where Base X is headed," Willa says.

"And if they aren't stopped, the trading won't either." I sit and the others follow.

"Does the Capellan or Doc know about Chapis Zo?" Morren asks.

"They do. It's accelerated the plan, apparently," Willa answers. "Sorry, Doc was hosting when this came up, not you."

"It's okay. Thankfully, I don't host all the time. What can we do about it?"

"We've got one computer system here and it sucks, a lot, but I can at least get into some of the communications that are sent to or from Cuupton about the market," Reyn chimes in.

"What are you hearing?" Morren asks.

"There's another market planned but the date hasn't been set. Chapis Zo and Narp are both on the invite list."

"Good. That means we'll have a chance to stop them and the whole operation if they come." The look on Willa's face shows more optimism than it has in weeks.

"They'll be here. It's like a drug to them. Power and control – they can't resist it," Lari says.

"That means we need to be ready. Once we get them, we still have to deal with all those below them that are still under the control of the system." I look at my adopted family through the bouncing light of the fire.

"I'll be able to give a window of time it's planned but we have to have the liberators here and ready. Once they set the exact date, we need to be able to act," Reyn adds.

There aren't enough people in this place to really take it down. Without those we're trying to get to Cuupton, we'll never do it.

My soup is nearly cold now. I drink it quickly and put the bowl down.

Chapter Thirty-Five

Morren taps my shoulder gently. "It's a new day, Karana. We better get up and practice."

It's always on now. He's always charged. He says the same is true about me, but I can't tell.

"Is Doc waiting for us?"

"No. Just you and me right now, sis. Unless the Capellan is with you."

"I'm hosting. Why are we up so early then?"

"Because we don't have many more solar rises to catch here, so let's see it while we still can. There's not much else to enjoy."

"Why don't you just call it a sunrise?"

"I don't know. Maybe because that's what we call it back home, and we're not home."

I throw back the thin blanket and the cool air hits my exposed arms. I pull my long sleeve shirt over my head and put on my boots. Morren and I walk out of the cave into the quiet of the early morning. The moons are high. Both are full tonight. Apparently, that only happens once every two years. Soon they'll fade until they resemble circular clouds against a green-tinted sky.

Now I understand that green isn't just for greed. It can be the color of love, like pink. Something I hadn't known before Cuupton. This place, perhaps, didn't know it held both meanings.

Morren and I sit outside the mouth of the cave and look out at the water as Cuupton's sun begins to color the gentle waves in flecks of golds, reds, oranges, and pinks.

"You ready for this?" I ask Morren.

"I have to be. We don't really have much choice."

"We always have a choice. I just don't want to choose wrong and then wind up having to redo this."

Morren smiles before opening a pouch and passing me a piece of bread from last night's meal.

"Do you ever wonder if we're too late?" I ask him.

"Late for what?"

"For Dad and Tezzi?"

"What kind of question is that? And right now? Of course, I wonder. What we started all this for was them, and now we don't know where they are or even how much time has passed for them."

I nod. I know he thinks about it too, but I need to hear him say it so I'm not alone with my apprehension of what comes after this.

"Morren, they are all expecting us to lead beside Doc and with the Capellan tomorrow. They believe these stupid scars mean we're special. Do you believe it?"

"Wow, Karana. After all this time, after all you've seen, and even being chosen to host the Capellan, you still don't believe it?"

"I didn't say that. I'm asking you what you think."

"And I know you well enough to know why you're asking."

"Fine. I get it. I do."

"I don't know if you do. Karana, it was you that pulled us along to keep going on what is a certifiably crazy and unbelievable mission. You got us all psyched up to save these people. That was you. You didn't allow yourself to think yourself out of what you were doing."

"That's cuz I wasn't thinking. Now I am."

"Right. You were feeling. You were acting from the place we all need to act from, and letting that fuel your mind. Not the other way around."

"And how many times did I almost get us killed or captured?" I roll my eyes.

"More times than I want to remember. And don't forget, once we did get captured. But we got out because you've got both heart and mind. They work together, but you were driven by the prana in your heart. It's why the Capellan came to you."

"Since when did you get so philosophical, little brother?"

He snickers. We don't get to do that much anymore.

The sun is beautiful over the water and soon it will light the mouth of the cave, reflecting on the metal plate at the entrance. The plate will warm just slightly, causing it to vibrate and ring a bell that wakes those we've lived with. There is no time for extra rest. Then it begins again, for one last time.

I take another bite of my bread. Somehow Surek can make anything taste good. The Capellan says it's because he puts his prana in it. Since no one has ever clearly defined prana for me, it still makes me a little hesitant.

The sun hits Morren's chin. He has changed, too. He's stronger and even more confident than when we left Earth. This trip has made a man out of my younger brother, and I wonder if it will eventually let me see a woman in me. Out here we aren't a couple of teens. Our Earth years aren't a match to our years here and don't seem to matter as much.

"Come on. Let's grab our supplies." I stand up and help Morren to his feet.

"Your prana is so strong, Karana."

I look at my hands. They look just the same as they ever did. Nothing special, but it wasn't about what I could see with my eyes that only see the physical.

"Yours too, Morren. I think you've drawn energy from every place we've been and somehow kept it, stored it." I smile at him.

We turn to walk back inside. Doc is already at the cave's entrance. Today, the Capellan is with Doc. He stands, hands clasped in front of him, looking toward the glowing fire in the sky.

"I see you have chosen to rise early. The morning is young. Have you already had nourishment?"

"Morren got us some bread from last night."

"Good. I would hope that you are ready to begin then."

I take a deep breath. I know the Capellan has great expectations of us.

"Ready as ever," I say.

"Always ready," Morren says with a smirk.

"Good then. We will stay out here."

"But we don't have our stuff."

"You have everything you need."

"But our supplies are in the cave."

"Are they?"

"Why are you being so cryptic this morning? It's too early for that and since you guys don't have coffee, you're gonna need to be a little bit clearer for me."

Neither Doc nor the Capellan say anything, and instead look out from the cave.

"Do you see the grasses growing out there, Karana?"

"Yeah."

"They are tall and straight, are they not?"

"Yes, they are."

"Except for when they bend a little with the wind, yes?"

"Yes. Otherwise they'd break."

"Yes, Karana. They are flexible or they'd break."

"And do you see the waves of the water that hit against the rocks down there, Karana?"

He's picking on me now.

"Yes. I see them, Doc." I turn my head so he doesn't see me sigh in frustration.

"They are strong, and over time they change the surface of the rocks. Where the water hits them daily, they become smooth. Without the water, they would remain jagged."

"Yeah. I've seen that."

I thought of the rocks I'd seen along the beaches in upstate New York and Maine during the rare childhood trips.

Doc casts his eyes toward the sky again.

"Do you see the sun there, Karana?"

"Yes, of course, Doc."

"It's very powerful, and strong, and consistent; is it not?"

"Yes, it is."

"It provides our light, our warmth, and gives us hope that there will be a new day and new chances for everything we dream for ourselves and those we work for."

"And it's beautiful," I whisper.

"Yes. It is also beautiful. What does it use to be those things? What tools does the sun have?"

"It's the sun. It doesn't need any tools."

"And the grass there?"

"It has soil, dirt."

"Therefore, it comes out of the dirt but it uses no tools, it has no supplies besides what is already there."

"And what of the water?"

I sigh.

"It doesn't have any tools or supplies either. But it does move, driven by the pull of the moons and winds." I feel justified.

"And did it need to go and get the wind or the moon?"

For heaven's sake! I think.

"No. The water just is."

"Correct. It already has the connection with that which is around it. All these things, the grasses and plants, the water and rocks, and even the sun, pull on the prana that exists all around us and within us to do what they do without the need of some supply or tool. What makes you different? What makes either of you different?"

Finally…he's not just picking on me. I look to Morren to answer this one.

"Nothing. Except that we are sentient and aware that the prana exists and that we can use it."

"I was gonna say that too. We know."

Doc looks at me and raises one suspicious eyebrow.

"I was. I just wanted to give Morren a chance to answer something since you were asking me all those questions."

"You do not need to substantiate yourself with me. You only need to understand these things for yourself. And what makes you think the grass has no awareness?"

We didn't bother trying to answer that. The Capellan is especially smug today. I suppose everyone else would call it being wise, but at this time of day, it just feels smug. I let my eyes fall on the grass, realizing that I love the Capellan anyway. And even more confusing, I'm uncertain if that love was for it or Doc, whose form it holds now.

Morren's eyes meet mine. He heard my thoughts. I look away, embarrassed. I must remain focused.

The Capellan looks at both of us. "So, as I said, we'll begin now."

Chapter Thirty-Six

I'm feeling better today than I have for the past week. Perhaps it's from seeing some success for our work at last. Or maybe it's knowing that saving Dad and Tezzi is a part of the plan. Morren and I can do this. We have to. We will.

"Ready?" I ask Morren.

"As ever."

I smile at Surek and wave my oversized biscuit in thanks.

In a few Cuupton days the result of everything we've done will be real.

Morren and I walk out of the main room toward the computer room. Lari and Eton are already there with Reyn.

We walk in and stand behind Reyn's shoulder. She wiggles in her seat, slightly uncomfortable. I step back and look at Morren, to do the same. The time she spends alone in the cave has changed her, too.

She pulls up another screen with a list of buyers and home planets.

"This is from the last market. Everyone who came had to log into the system. It registered their home planet. Every person who was being sold on the market is also registered and their home planet is listed. Both show on this map."

"That means even the people being sold have two registrations," Morren confirms.

"Exactly. The buyer's home planet is applied to anyone they purchased at the market. Until they reach the planet the buyer's from, everyone sold has two registered planets," Reyn explains.

"I'm sorry. I don't get it. How does that help us?"

"Some of these planets appear to be pretty far away. Many light years, maybe decades away. They are able to travel faster than we ever thought possible from Earth, but it may still take them weeks or months for hyper-jumps, and then the remaining travel. For example, one of the people Zo bought is from out here. It's where she's registered, but if she went back, she'd be going back to a time when everyone she knew would be decades older, maybe dead."

"They must have taken her young," Morren drops his head. I know he's thinking of Tezzi.

"Not necessarily. Their time works differently," Reyn clarifies.

"That really sucks, but what does that do for us?" I ask.

"Yeah, it does suck. It also means that if he makes another purchase like that, we can crosslink his registration, or at least I can. That link will allow me to send him back to that planet; if and when he finds his way back, he'll lose a lot of time."

"Right, because in spite of hyper-jumping and traveling faster, time is still moving. We've learned that painful lesson," I run my hands over my poufy, dirty hair.

"What about the others? Narp and Haunir?" Morren asks.

"It will work for Narp, too. Haunir doesn't always make purchases. She sometimes will buy and then rent out the person to someone else. If she does that, we can do the same to her."

Is there another option in case she doesn't make a purchase? One that makes it so she can't get back?"

"It would take longer and be trickier, but I can hack the system if you all buy me time. I know that I can confuse this system by using someone else on the market already in the system. I don't think I can just make something up without it getting flagged," Reyn explains.

"Maybe Doc, liberator version and not the Capellan version, can help us. We need to talk to him and see what they've been working on."

"Right. Zo and Narp are just two people, but what we need to do is bigger than them," Morren nods.

"We need to get Haunir. She runs the whole thing. Where is her home planet?" I ask Reyn.

"It lists Cuupton as her home planet, but there doesn't seem to be any more info than that on her."

"We need to get Willa and then find Doc. Willa needs to alter some of the chemicals and Doc needs to share his plan of attack," Morren says.

"And you two," Lari says pointing at Morren and me, "need to keep gathering the forces, or else none of this is gonna matter."

"What about you?" I ask Lari.

"When Chapis Zo gets here for the market, Eli is supposed to jump us back to Base X. He's coming to find us and whoever changed the data," Lari looks to Reyn.

"Okay. It's getting so close. Morren and I have a lot to do, but so far, we have eight planets participating with well over seven-hundred thousand beings." I don't bother to shield my excitement.

"I thought it would be more." Lari begins pacing back and forth, tapping her fingers together.

"Seven-hundred thousand individuals is good. Really good. We got all these people here without any physical communication. That means every one of these beings is here cuz they tuned in, and we got them up to a level that literally drew them here. I'm not short-changing that." I didn't mean to sound defensive, but we'd worked hard to amass an army of this size.

"You really think that's gonna be enough?" Eton asks.

"We'll have more by the time we're done, and whoever we have will be enough. There are four billion beings on Cuupton. They are spread out, and most don't even know what's going on with the market. The reality of a system like this is that one third of the people are apathetic, doing nothing while another third suffers by the hand of the offending third. We really only have to deal with a third of Cuupton and even then, it's just the ones who will defend this slave market at any cost."

"She's right," Morren says. "It's the ones in the city that'll be the problem. If we reach our goal of one million Comrades of Liberation here and on the ground, we'll easily take the guard around the perimeter, and all of the market apologists and sympathizers."

"We'll be able to get in without trying to hide and then take them down," Reyn says.

"But they have real weapons." Eton's lip turns and he raises one eyebrow.

"True. But we have Willa and her team. She can turn a stick and stone into a gun," Lari says, smugly shutting down Eton.

I smile. The end is in sight, finally.

Chapter Thirty-Seven

I can feel them all as I sit in stillness with Morren, Selvedon, and Doc. Selvedon leans against Doc, and I wonder how much time she has and why she holds on. I am hosting the Capellan this morning. The butterflies in my stomach won't go away, but that's okay. I'm not the only one nervous.

Morren's eyes are open, strangely focused at something beyond me. All the preparation has led us to this moment. We are ready.

No one in this small circle is speaking through our lips. The chatter going on between our minds is enough. We need to get a count of our numbers. Once we do, we can organize them into the different locations around the city before Doc and the other leaders meet them to lead them toward the city. Selvedon will stay behind. She says there is more she can do from here when her body can rest and her spirit can be free.

I can feel over a million comrades have joined us, I say.

Same. It feels like one million plus another three thousand, Morren says.

Excellent. This will be enough to create a barrier of protection around the city, Selvedon nods. Where her golden shimmery skin once extended around her head, I can no longer see it, as if it had all been muted.

We will need the strongest minds to help lead their people and to remain connected with you during the mission, Doc says.

All of my primary contacts are ready, I say.

So are mine, Morren adds.

Good. Doc considers something silently before continuing. *We will have one comrade force to form the barrier around the city as the Capellan said. This will be the largest force. I will assign the majority, 800,000 to this purpose. The next seven forces will surround the city near its borders and will enter to eliminate threats before the final forces take the market. The comrade groups taking the market will be the smallest, but the other forces will serve as back up.*

What if they try to get away? I ask.

Several of the Comrades of Liberation are very adept at flying. When the market's active, it's full of ships, and they're all equipped for battle - just in case there's trouble during travels. Don't worry, we've prepared for that possibility, Doc says with certainty.

You must confirm with those twelve comrades who'll lead forces that they are clear on the expectations for this specific service. We must know that no minds have changed. Once confirmed, show them where they must assemble when the skies become dark, Selvedon says.

We've received confirmation that the market starts tomorrow morning. All the comrades need to be in position, where they'll be expected to wait for our signal. That includes you two, Doc addresses Morren and me.

Does that mean we get to go? I ask hopefully.

"That hasn't changed. We can't risk something happening to you. You'll work from here, but you must be ready just like everyone else."

I think about what Doc has just said. We'll be in the middle of it all – just not physically.

Our people here are nearly done taking the supplies to the outposts where the comrades will gather. They've been doing this for many days, but tonight's the last night. The city will be on a higher guard come tomorrow, Doc says.

One of the liberators working here in the cave walks by the door and peaks in. I'm sure she, like many others, is curious why we spend so much time looking at each other and what else is going on. Despite these people being part of the larger group, we can't risk certain information getting out ahead of time. Only those who need to know are part of conversations like this. She continues on to wherever she is going and Selvedon returns her attention to our conversation.

Once you ensure the locations of the comrades, you will draw them to the energy portals for those areas. That's what they are expecting – your guidance. You two must rest. Tomorrow will be a very busy day.

Will you be there? I wonder if her position had changed.

No, I will be here with you, as I am right now. I can be most helpful that way.

Doc will be leading the group at the market, as we'd suspected.

Is Willa still leading a group? Morren asks.

No, her skills are better used helping maintain supplies. Besides, she's too recognizable. Narp, Zo, and Haunir are all looking for her, Doc answers.

Who's taking her place? I ask.

Sitav, Doc answers.

Good. She's strong. I realize I'm nervous, or perhaps anxious or excited. I hadn't spent much time with Sitav, but I've felt her. I take a deep breath. I can't tell what the precise feeling is, as they all feel similar.

She is strong. In many ways, Selvedon says. *You two must begin now. Doc and I will leave you until this initial task is complete.*

Thank you, Morren and I respond.

They get up and leave us near the water, my favorite place. Morren remains quiet. His eyes glaze over and I ponder where he is this time.

Morren?

Morren?

"Morren?"

"Yes? What?" he answers with a start.

"Where were you?"

"I was…here. I was listening. I know what we must do."

"Are you sure?"

"Yes, Karana. I'm sure."

Something else is going on, but he's shielding his thoughts from me.

"This isn't the time to be keeping things from each other, Morren."

"Karana, we have a lot to do. We need to get to it."

"You're acting strange. Everything we've given up either has meaning or not because of this moment. I need you all the way in this with me, Morren."

"When have I ever not been all the way in with you?"

He's right. "I think it's my nerves. We can't mess this up."

"I know that just like you. Let's get to work."

This time he closes his eyes, and then I close mine.

***

Sleep and rest elude me. My mind is busy with the filtered chatter of hundreds of thousands of beings. In between listening to the restless thoughts of others, I think of Tezzi, as I often do. I've only gotten through to her once more, again on her bathroom break.

I can't tell if she's alone. Karren, not Karen, as she's corrected me, seems to be with her. She must be older since Tezzi listens to her. She's a little bossy, considering neither of them have any power there. I think about that, realizing I no longer thought that was true. They do have power, even if they don't know it.

I couldn't get Tezzi long enough to really talk to her without Karren interrupting or the guards ending her bathroom break. I just hope she heard me tell her I'm sorry and that I love her.

"Are you awake?"

I turn my head around to see Eli. It still surprises me that I can be happy to see Eli, after what she started. But even with the part of me that still holds a grudge, I am.

"I'm awake. I can't sleep, even though I know I'm supposed to."

"I'm sure your mind is quite busy."

I nod but say nothing else.

"We've been quite busy on Earth as well. Karana, when you return, things will be much different. It is ready for you."

"Eli, do you have any news about Tezzi or my dad?"

She looks down and her tentacles go darker; the shimmer diminishes noticeably.

"Eli? You know something."

"Yes, Karana. But new things to think about at this time do not seem wise."

"You don't get to decide that, Eli. You don't get to decide if it is wise for me or if I can handle it. I've been in touch with Tezzi, Eli." I try to be firm without getting angry.

"This I know. Much has changed, Karana."

"Eli?" Morren smiles as he walks in. "I thought I heard you."

"She was just about to tell me about Tezzi and Dad, right?"

"You may want to sit down, Morren."

Morren sits on the edge of my bed. "What's going on?"

"They've moved all of the survivors they consider to be Immune. Tezzi is one of those they've moved. They're not in the same compound you were."

"Where'd they take them?"

"That's the thing. We aren't sure. My people haven't been able to find them. We believe they took them deeper underground to get further away from any one still alive and infected."

"But they are still on Earth?" I ask. It was a question I wouldn't have even considered a year ago.

"We believe so."

"Who would still be alive that wasn't an Immune? Who could do this?" Morren asks.

"There are those like you who were completely immune and then there are those whose bodies fought the virus. They became ill. Some lost their hearing, eyesight, or both; but the virus didn't completely break down their neurological systems. It may have slowed them but it didn't kill them. It is those people who are still alive."

"What? They have neurological damage, but they are still functional and experimenting on Immunes?"

"Yes. They were able to manufacture a vaccine that slows the rate of neurological damage. It inhibits it to an extent but cannot reverse it and requires regular booster shots. They still hope the Immunes will provide a way to permanently cure the effect and reverse the damage."

"And until then? What are they doing with the Immunes?"

Eli averts her eyes again. "They manufacture the vaccine from the Immunes."

"What?!" I yell.

"You're saying that our sister is being used as a living drug?" Morren asks.

"To an extent; yes, she is. I'm sorry."

I don't know what to say as I think about the time that's passed and my promise to her.

"That's ridiculous. How many Earth years has it been, Eli? Tezzi thinks it's been seven or eight?" Morren asks.

Eli looks at me curiously.

"How many years, Eli?" I repeat Morren's question, afraid of what her hesitation means.

"It's been nine years."

"Nine Earth years?" I ask, hopeful the unit is somehow different.

"Yes."

"We've lost nine Earth years!?" Morren stands to his feet and begins to pace.

"Tezzi was seven when we left. That makes her sixteen. That's how old Morren is now."

Eli takes a deep breath, and her tentacles rise slightly around her head. I don't know what to say. I'm past anger.

"Eli, how many humans are left?" I look at her expectantly.

"We've only been able to count the ones we can find, so there may be more hidden, deeper down in the earth."

"How many, Eli?" Morren repeats for me.

"We've counted eleven-hundred and seventy."

Morren plops back on the bed.

"That includes the Immunes," she clarifies.

"How many Immunes?" I look at her hopefully.

"We have identified one hundred and forty not including you two, Reyn, and Eton. But that does assume your sister is an Immune."

"They wouldn't have kept her this long if she wasn't," Morren says.

I nod my head. There are enough of us to start over, but there are ten times as many who would want what we have.

"We will get back there. We will find Tezzi and her friend Karren. We will find out what happened to Dad," I say stubbornly.

It was the thing Morren and I would not speak about. Dad. We both knew.

"Eli?"

We all look toward the shadow standing in the doorway. It's Doc.

"Yes, I'm coming."

"Thanks. Besides, you two are supposed to be resting, right?"

He lets his eyes linger on us for a few seconds

"You okay?"

"Yeah, thanks," Morren says quickly.

"We'll try and get some rest," I smile weakly.

"Alright. You can come with me, Eli."

I watch Eli follow Doc out, my thoughts now on the planet I call home.

Morren studies me. He won't let me in, but I can feel what he's feeling. He's afraid. He's afraid for me and Tezzi.

"We're gonna do this, Morren. We're gonna get home."

Chapter Thirty-Eight

The breakfast line has a different air this morning. It is noticeably quieter and even Surek isn't in his normal cheerful mood. His eyes are somber and he's moving more slowly, taking a moment longer with each person he serves. My stomach growls at the smell of soup to go with our normal biscuit.

Surek sees Morren and me coming up and tries to smile for us.

"I put aside two extra big biscuits for you two today."

"Oh, I get one too?"

Surek smirks at Morren.

"Today's a special day. It means a lot to me what you and everyone else are doing. My people have been used by these people and sold on the market for centuries. I was rescued by the Comrades of Liberation from the market when I was a kid. They saved me. Every day when I cook and feed the people here and live in this family, it is my way of saying thank you. It is my contribution as part of the liberators. Thank you, Karana. Thank you, Morren. I honor you today. I wish you well on this mission."

I look at Surek, unsure of how to respond.

I go around his table and hug him. "I didn't know, Surek. Thank you."

We'd been working so hard, I hardly ever got a chance to think about what it meant personally for everyone living in this cave, seeking refuge and freedom.

"Thanks, Surek. And you're welcome," Morren takes the biscuit that is nearly too big for the soup bowl.

Morren and I find our friends gathered on the floor near the usual wall. After today, the usual ends and we'll never be as we are right now.

I don't want to spoil the moment with words. I mash the biscuit into the soup, making it soggy and the soup thick. Thrown together out of necessity, here we are, eating biscuits and soup out of worn metal shaped by hammers.

Willa looks around the group and nods her head, "So you guys ready to go out there and kick the turd out of the slime balls not worthy of using our poop pots today?"

I laugh, nearly spitting out my soup. I love that girl. She's wild and funny, and somehow makes me remember I'm human and a sentient being, even if we're from different worlds.

"I'm ready," I say.

"Ready and absolutely willing!" Morren says.

Lari is oddly playing with her bowl and avoiding looking up.

"What's going on with you?" I ask. "This is what we've been waiting for."

The spoon stops its irritating grind against the inside of bowl. Lari looks at Morren and then me. "I'm leaving today for Base X."

I knew it was coming, but wasn't expecting it today.

"What? When did you find out?" Morren exclaims.

"We're taking it back from the Zo Clan. It's our best chance of catching them with defenses down since Chapis Zo will be here. I found out this morning." Lari looks back to Morren, guilt clouds her eyes.

"That's a good thing, right? It's what you wanted," I ask.

"That means we won't be battling here on Cuupton today. Eli is taking us and about a few hundred liberators back home."

It'll be the biggest group Eli's ever jumped, even if she breaks it into multiple trips; but that's not what's bothering Lari. Morren looks over at her and takes her hand before looking up at the voice coming from behind them.

"You're fighting for freedom too. That makes you one of the Comrades of Liberation. Don't think that what happens here doesn't have a ripple. Or that what happens on your planet doesn't ripple, Doc says as he towers over our circle.

"I know. It just feels so different. After all this time, rather than helping you fight, I'm going back home. No one else gets to just go back home today," Lari says.

"No. You don't get to feel guilty. You've been through more than your fair share of crap and now you're going back to make it better for everybody. This is your day, too. You get to be a hero today for your people." I look at Lari and realize my statement is as much for her sake as mine.

"Thanks, Karana. I guess I just wish I could be with you all, too."

"Well you will. At least up until we know Chapis Zo and his crew are here and you can safely jump to Baselonica Xuna," Doc says with a smile and a shrug. For such a large man, he moves with such grace. Or maybe we were just distracted and didn't see him coming.

He's in a good mood today. Or else he's faking it. Either way, it's working. I already feel a little bit more confident.

"Where's Selvedon?" Morren asks.

Doc looks away. "She's resting up, preparing herself. She wants to give all she has today, too."

His words mean much more, as I understand from the Capellan whispering within me. A wave of sadness rushes over me, but Doc looks at me as if there is no time for that.

"When you guys finish, we need to meet once more to go over today's plans, and make sure everyone's clear on how this is going down. Because, it is going down." Doc waves to someone across the main gathering area coming through the line and then walks away.

I know he's glad he won't be hosting the Capellan today. He's ready to finally take the battle to them. So am I.

***

The cave feels empty without the other liberators. They've already gone, and Eli has taken Lari back to Baselonica Xuna.

Everything is in motion, and we know Chapis Zo and Director Narp are almost on Cuupton.

For hours, we've been in here, with Reyn and Eton beside us. Two guards keep watch at the mouth of the cavern that will soon no longer be our home. My mind is vibrating so much it almost feels numb and I touch the ground to keep away the feeling of floating away. But we can't stop. They are all relying on us to serve as communicators and connectors with the forces that have surrounded the city. I silently thank the Capellan for the extra prana. Then I send Selvedon, who is in her bed as she so often is these days, a thank you as well. I know it is the combination of both of them being with me, giving me their prana that is making me so strong.

Confirm comrade force one position, Doc says in my head.

Comrade force one. Are you in position? I send out.

Confirmed. We are in position, waiting for confirmation on the surrounding forces.

Comrade force one position confirmed. Need confirmation on seven surrounding forces. Are they ready?" I ask.

Confirmed. All comrade forces are ready. Communicate that when the sun crosses the second moon on the west, we will begin the attack with comrade force one, Doc responds.

I communicate this information to comrade forces one through eight. There is nothing left to do now, except wait for the shadows to form and the sky to darken as the sun begins to take respite. When it wakes again, Cuupton will be free.

I relax my mind for a moment from the intense concentration to speak with Doc and the others.

Are you there? a voice calls out.

It sounds like a young girl.

I'm here?

Are you coming soon? she asks, in a whispering whine.

I look over at Morren. Is he getting this? The look of confusion on his face, tells me he is.

Tezzi? he asks.

Morren? Are you coming? I'm scared, she says.

Then we hear the voice of the other girl, Karren, who's been with Tezzi.

Come on, Tez, I've got you. You don't need to be scared. I'll take care of you, like always.

Tezzi? I call out.

Tezzi? Morren and I both try again.

I'm taking her somewhere safe. I have to protect her. I'm the only one who can.

Where are you from, Karren? I ask.

I don't remember. But she needs me. I have to be here for her. Be strong for her, just like you and Morren used to be.

Karren?

Yeah?

Thank you, I whisper and my tears well up and choke my vocal chords even as I speak silently through my mind.

We do what we have to. We must survive. The guards are coming back. We have to go.

Wait, I-,

Bye.

Morren wrings his hands. "Something's wrong. I don't know exactly what it is, but something is definitely wrong."

"Yeah, something's wrong. We abandoned her. We can't expect her to just be okay. We need to get back so we can help her."

"Maybe. I guess. She sounded different today. Like she did when we left. Last time we talked she didn't sound so much like a kid."

"She's probably stressed. Not probably. Of course she's stressed. Who knows how long she was by herself before Karren showed up there."

I can't talk about it anymore. She was stressed and alone because of us. I can't let myself get distracted and blow the mission, and our chance to get back to her.

Leaning back against the cool cave wall I cup my head with my hands. My fingers are dry and nails chipped. I can fix that in no time once I have some basic supplies like lotion and a finger nail file. But everything else…Tezzi…Earth…that may take a while.

"I'm gonna go lay down, Morren. Everyone is in place and by morning we'll be ready to start."

"Good idea. I'll do the same. I'll see you in the morning."

We both have a lot on our minds. Added to the mission we're responsible for orchestrating, is our sister. Someone else had to come fill the space we'd left when we'd abandoned her more than nine years ago."

**

"Karana?!" Morren calls impatiently.

"What?"

"It's time. You were sleeping hard."

"Time? Oh! It's time!" I say and sit up hurriedly from the sleep that had stolen me.

Morren and I hurry out to where we are set up near Reyn.

Karana? Morren? Doc says.

We're here, Morren answers.

"Karana, I need you to send the command to the surrounding forces that they will take up position and begin infiltrating the city. They have their orders and weapons. Make sure they understand that this is non-negotiable. They must seize control. Do you understand? Doc orders.

I understand. I mentally step away and begin contacting the seven leads. In the background, I hear Doc speaking to Morren.

Give the command for comrade force one to approach the city and form the barrier. Inform them that they are to use all available means to hold the perimeter from any Cuupton agents. Understood?

Understood, Morren responds before going silent.

My team is already in the city, near the market. When the city is secure we will take it. Then, you'll join us here.

The leader of comrade force five isn't coming in. *Sitav?* I say for the third time. There is still no response.

Doc? I can't get comrade force five, Sitav?

Have you gotten the others?

Well one to four. Should I keep on with six and seven and then try again? I ask nervously.

Yes. Get everyone else ready and then try Sitav again. Maybe she fell asleep.

284

Funny. Not.

Morren chuckles at Doc's poke at me.

Hey, you only had to get one group. I've got seven.

Well you have the Capellan and Selvedon helping you. I only have me. I think you better get going.

I'm already gone though. Six and seven are both accounted for.

We've got something happening here, Sitav finally comes in.

Good, you're there. What's happening?

There are armored vehicles blocking the streets on our side.

One or two?

From what we can see, there are at least two dozen. Someone must've seen us and called it in.

Shirt. Hanger. Iron. Table. I tap into Doc again; he'll know what to do.

Doc. Comrade force five is compromised. Sitav is reporting two dozen armored vehicles blocking their entry. They are still in hiding but someone tipped them off.

I wait for Doc to respond. After several moments, he says, *Copy.*

Copy what?

We can use that. All the other groups are still clear?

Yeah. No other reports of trouble.

Tell Sitav they will approach, but to delay their approach until you give word.

What do you mean?

Someone tipped them off, so they are going to be looking for trouble. We want them to keep looking right where they are.

But that means comrade force five would be specifically under attack when they do come out.

It means the other six comrade groups will have an easier chance surrounding the city and entering it to secure it, Doc says matter-of-factly.

But what about comrade force five?

Doc says nothing.

"Do you have to ask that question?" Morren asks.

Finally Doc responds. *Karana, you are here because you care about this mission and what it means not just for Cuupton but for the other worlds out there, including your own. Am I right?*

Yes, of course I care.

Every single Comrade of Liberation out there by the city cares just as much as you, if not more. They are willing to fight for their liberty, for all our liberty. They are willing to make the ultimate sacrifice for that liberty, especially if it means giving the mission a better chance for success.

So, you're saying they are willing to die, and we're gonna let them make that sacrifice?

I'm saying we are all willing to die. We must also be willing to let each other make those sacrifices.

Sitav breaks through our conversation. *What should I do, Karana?*

I pause, considering Doc's response, and the feeling I have that Selvedon and the Capellan agree with him. I understand the concept, but this was real.

Karana? What should I do?

Hold your position, Sitav. We will let you know when to move. Are you prepared to defend?

We are.

Thank you. Thank you.

No. Thank you. We are all in this together. We are one.

Her unwavering sentiment and purpose move me. It's contagious, and just what I need.

Chapter Thirty-Nine

Comrade forces surround the city. They are an intergalactic mix of beings willing to die for each other. I can feel their heightened energy as I tune in to what is happening.

Forming a second ring around them, about fifty meters from the surrounding forces are the first group charged with keeping a barrier. More Cuupton agents have come to the side of the city where the Sitav's group, comrade force five, is. Groups four to six are forced to shorten their perimeter to avoid detection.

Morren is intently guiding several of the surrounding comrade forces while I focus on groups four through six. I'm thankful for the support. Doc waits, his team divided into several abandoned and empty buildings and warehouses near the market. It is a desolate area, where regular Cuupton citizens wouldn't willingly venture. An undesirable and seedy area, perfectly suited for this business.

There's a lot of them, Karana. We're never gonna make it through them, Sitav says.

Don't give up, Sitav. I try to mimic her earlier confidence.

They've brought out cannons and have a row of soldiers lined up with machine guns. Our weapons aren't a match for theirs. They're fanning out. Six and four are gonna have to pull back some more.

Thanks, Sitav. Don't do anything yet.

I'm getting good at masking my guilt. Better than I'd like to be.

One, two, and three are ready. That whole side is surrounded. Willa and her tech team are ready with the tools Eli brought back. They'll take down any air strikes, I tell Doc and Morren.

Is it just four to six now?, I ask Doc.

Yes, Karana. We need to send in one through three, and groups four and six.

Here I am in the safety of a cave, while more than a million liberators are out there prepared to fight and die. And I'm supposed to get them on to it.

"We're just as much a part of this as anyone, Karana," Morren says.

"I know."

And I do know.

I send the command Doc told me to give to four and six with an extra warning. I then set comrade forces one through three in motion. It won't be long before they fill the city.

What's going on? Sitav asks.

What do you mean? I say back.

There's something going on down there.

We've sent in the other comrade forces. Everyone except those on your side.

No. The agents are starting to pull back.

Doc, Sitav says the agents are pulling back. Do we send five in?

Do it.

Sitav, you have to come out now with your group.

Sitav is quiet.

Sitav? Did you hear me? I ask.

Yes. I heard you. I understand. Give me a moment to talk to my team.

I can pick up the sadness mixed with conviction in her voice. There is nothing I can do about it. I know that even without an order or command, Sitav would do this and so would the others in her group.

Thank you, Sitav. Thank you and all of comrade force five for your bravery.

Sitav says nothing else to me, but I sense it. Morren does too. I know, because I can feel him.

I hear screaming, like that of a battle cry, sounding loudly in my head. The screams of war quickly turn into screams of pain. A sharp pain shoots through my side, and then my shoulder, my neck. The sting on my skin doesn't compare to the holes that must be ripping through them as they continue to charge the forces meant to stop us.

I can feel the drop of consciousness, as one by one, the Cuupton agents bring down our comrades in force five. They charge on, nearing the machine guns and the cannon topped vehicles. Many remain.

I send my thoughts to the others. *Keep moving. Keep moving. Take the city. Make the sacrifices worth it!*

I call the barrier group to move closer to the perimeter of the city and maintain the borders.

The six active groups have almost made it to the market. The few Cuupton agents they encounter are no match for the hundreds of thousands of liberators who've besieged the city. Another pang rocks me in the back.

Sitav? I call out.

Can't talk. Busy. Keep going.

Doc?

Here.

Sitav and comrade force five are holding the agents as best they can so everyone gets in. They're close. You should see the first liberators in the next minute or two.

Got it. We're looking out.

I open my eyes and look up. Selvedon has come to sit beside me. She is so weak, but I know she isn't going anywhere, not yet.

She doesn't say anything, choosing instead to place her long, thin, golden fingers on my shoulder and Morren's shoulder. I can feel it. Strong and unmistakable; the prana the Capellan and others speak of. It hits me like a shock, amplifying everything around me. She removes her hands and steps back.

"Thank you, Morren. Thank you, Karana. You will always have a place with us. She nods once and slowly returns to her place, where she is sending prana to the forces as well.

They are here. We are heading to the market, Doc says.

I check in on comrade force five. They are still in battle.

We've taken control of the weapons, Sitav says.

I nearly fall back at the bone crushing pain on my arm. An armored vehicle tracking right over someone. Some of the large vehicles are leaving the area.

Morren sends a command to the barrier group to keep the trucks from entering the city.

I send commands to the forces within the city to take down any armored vehicles that may come.

They have tanks with cannons, I warn.

My body tingles. The surge of prana from Selvedon is running through me as I try to process the emotions and commands coming from Doc.

Get ready, Karana and Morren. We'll be inside the market soon and you need to get to the holding room and command room.

What about Zo and Narp? I ask.

My team will be searching for them, Doc answers. *You have to get Reyn to the systems. Otherwise, everything else turns out to be just a battle rather than the war we need.*

I turn to Reyn and Eton. "This is it guys."

"Finally," Eton yawns.

Reyn cuts her eyes at Eton. "Don't do anything Etonish today, okay?"

"Whatever. I want outta here as much as you. Besides, you better be nice. You can't leave without me."

"Enough. We need to go," Morren gives them both the eye.

I grab Reyn's hand and then Eton's. Morren does the same.

"Wait. Wait."

I open my eyes to see Surek. He's holding four biscuits wrapped in towels.

"For your travels. In case you get hungry," he smiles.

He hands us the biscuits and I grab him for a hug. Then I plant a kiss on his cheek. "Thank you, Surek. I'll miss you, my friend."

He nods and steps back. "Thank you."

Morren closes his eyes again and mouths, "Three. Two. One."

***

I can hear the commotion with my human ears this time. It's just outside the room we're in. There is the unmistakable dull thud of bullets following the sharp pitch of guns firing. Those are Willa's stick guns. Regular guns, taken from the agents who tried to attack our forces, are fired too.

All clear and secure, Doc sends to us.

He doesn't mess around.

Find them, he orders.

I finally look around the room we're in at the stunned people who are staring at the four of us. It's packed, too crowded to see everyone.

Is it safe for the people in here to come out? I ask Doc.

No. We haven't found Zo, Narp, or Haunir.

We can find them, I offer.

You need to get Reyn to the command room. Immediately.

And then what? Sit around and twiddle my fingers?

If that keeps you out of trouble and alive so you can be the voice you need to be, yes.

"Morren? Eton? We aren't gonna just sit around, are we? Not after what they've done. We've come too far."

"I don't plan on sitting around," Morren agrees.

"I don't plan on getting killed this close to getting home," Eton says smartly. "I'll wait here."

"Well, you can't. You need to come with us so we can get Reyn in place. Then you can sit on your ass all you want." My hand finds its way to my hip like my mother used to do.

I see Morren stifle a laugh. I realize how awkward this is. Four people mysteriously appearing in the holding room.

"We're here to rescue you all. But you need to stay here until we make sure it's safe to come out," Morren says.

"Where will we go?" a young child says, pushing through the arms and shoulders of taller people. His eyes are shaped like large lavender almonds and his ears, rounded bulbs on the side of his head.

"Someplace safe," I say. "We're trying to make it safe to live where you came from or live here – free. And please, don't anyone scream. We're the good ones."

"Free?" A girl who looks my age asks.

"Yes. Free. You can do what you want with your life. No owner."

"So, it's true. We've been getting messages, but we didn't know if it was true. But it's true. It is true, isn't it?"

"Yes. It's true."

"Then we want to help. We want to be liberators too," she says.

Heads nod all around the room; even the young boy who couldn't be any older than Tezzi. I take a deep breath. They deserve to fight for their own freedom as much as anyone else.

Doc? We have people here who want to help. What can they do?

I don't know, Karana. I'm trying to find these guys. You'll need to lead them yourself. Figure out what you need and who can do it.

I look at Morren and then around the room. "Together?" I ask him.

"Together."

"Who here can fly?" Morren asks.

What? I send him. *Fly?*

Trust me. Doc says they have enough, but I know they don't.

Several hands shoot up and Morren calls them over. I try to think about what is needed, before a smile crosses my face.

I take a group to the side and whisper to them as Morren talks to his pilots.

"Wait. What are you doing? We can't take all these people with us to the command center!" Eton exclaims.

"We can. And we will," I say back. "If you don't want to help, I suggest you keep doing what you're doing."

"But I'm not doing anything!"

"Exactly."

Morren and I form a connected web with his six pilots and the four people who will help me. Eton and Reyn gather round as well.

The door bursts open.

It's Willa.

"I found you!" She whispers loudly. She's out of breath. "Willa!"

"I figured you'd be in here. I thought I might be too late. Not that I want to be back in this room again…ever."

"Well you just caught us. We're about to go to the command center. Come in, right here." I look at the spot beside me and wait for Willa to step in.

The odd crew of volunteers gives me a sense of hope. We are all in this together. "Everyone get ready. First stop, the command center."

Chapter Forty

I found her. Haunir is here cowering like a suckling infant, in a closet, Doc says.

What're you gonna do with her? I ask.

I watch Reyn find her position by the computer.

She's going on a trip as soon as Reyn is ready with a suitable destination.

"Reyn, he's got Haunir. He needs a star for her."

"Oh, send her somewhere good. Something preferably lonely and distant." Willa squints her eyes and wiggles in delight.

"On it. It'll take me a minute to run through the options. It'll have to be a planet one of the people on the market is from."

"Doc wants to know how long," I say back.

"I don't know."

Doc, you can bring Haunir down here and we can find Narp and Zo, if that'll help.

I've got enough people on my team to take care of Narp and Zo.

I shrug.

"You good here, Reyn? Doc is gonna bring Haunir down so you can give her a well-deserved vacation."

"And where are you going?" Willa asks. "I wanna be where the fun is."

"Doc thinks he doesn't need us to find Zo or Narp. I think we can be helpful. Or you can do what Doc thinks you're gonna do and be a pilot."

"Or I can do both. I'm multi-talented and I want to see those two pieces of walking dirt, squirm."

I look at my small team. We have to walk out of here since jumping isn't an option. I turn back to the corner Eton's sitting in, literally twirling his thumbs. "What are you gonna do, Eton?"

"This."

"Can you watch out for Reyn while you're in here?" Morren asks.

"Sure," he says, noncommittedly.

I look at Morren and Willa. I can't leave Reyn in here with him.

"Willa, would you mind staying here with Reyn so she can focus while Eton over there does what he does?"

"Yeah, I'll safe guard the hero and the zero."

"Oh, stop acting like you wanna be here," Eton argues.

"It doesn't matter if I want to be here or not. I am here. And so is your sorry behind. If I were you, I wouldn't be in such a hurry to get back to Base X. They don't take well to traitors."

"I'm not a traitor. They made me come. I was just fine."

"That's not how Chapis Kun Zo will see it."

"That's not gonna matter, cuz he won't be in charge. At least that's what this is supposed to all be about, right?" he retorts.

"Are you sure you wanna take him back to help repopulate your planet? I mean can you imagine more of him?" Willa asks seriously.

"Better than being populated with someone like you." Eton stands to his feet.

Willa walks up to him and stares him in the eyes. "What's that supposed to mean?"

"You think you're so smart - all you Baselonicans are dumb as the rocks and dirt you mine."

Her hands grip his neck. "Watch it, you spineless prick. We Baselonicans are also stronger. I'd like to think we are generally equals and if you were a real man, you'd know that. Take a lesson from Doc or Morren. Heck, just about anyone else you've been living with the past few months. Now, sit back down in your corner and shut up so I can do what I need to do."

I see Reyn smile at Willa's comments. I wonder how she put up with him for so long.

"I think I've got somewhere for her," Reyn says.

A light knock on the door makes us all turn our heads. Then I hear him, *It's me, Doc.*

I open the door and Haunir, arrogant and proud in her gray dress and powder-blue and white headdress, is being held in front of Doc. Two of his other team members are behind him.

"I've got a package." Doc pushes Haunir into the room.

"Don't think you're gonna get away with this." Haunir's struggling against Doc's brawn is futile.

"It's you. I remember you. But not fondly. Not fondly at all. I can't wait to see you go far away," Willa says.

"No matter what you do today, you'll still be nothing," Haunir snarls back.

"I'd normally smack the smart out of your mouth, but I don't hit kids, and I'm more evolved now." Willa turns on her heel, letting it grind into Haunir's small foot.

You're like one of the vermin on this planet. A pest that needs to be exterminated.

"Okay! On that note, she's set for the spaceship marked with this symbol." Reyn shows us what looks like a twisted seven and upside down two. "It should be near the end of the row on the right. All you have to do is strap her in and seal the door. I'll set it from here. Autopilot."

"What are you talking about? Where are you sending me?" Haunir's air of confidence is suddenly shaken.

"Somewhere you can't hurt anyone else," I say.

"Look. I'm sorry. I'm sure there's something I can do. Some arrangement we can make."

"Arrangement?" Doc asks incredulously.

"Really? You want an arrangement?" Willa asks.

"Yes, please. I know there's something I can do. Something I have that you need."

"Tell us where Zo and Narp are and maybe we can send you someplace not quite so far away."

"What do you mean?"

"Chapis Kun Zo and Director Narp. Now," Doc says, unwaveringly.

"I don't know where they went off to. But there must be something else."

"There's nothing else you can do. Reyn, program the coordinates for Haunir. She's ready."

"No! Wait. I don't know where they are, but I can get them to come to me."

"How?" I ask.

"They've invested a lot into this program. Zo will come if he thinks he can get his investment back, or more. Narp, he's trickier. He doesn't care about the money. He only cares about the power."

"Bastards," Willa says. "I say we send her off and find them ourselves. I don't trust her as far as I can throw her, even if she's only hip high."

"I swear, I can do it. I can bring them in. We've been talking about moving operations from Cuupton because of…because of you all," she says, looking at Doc.

"Keep talking. And you better make it worth my time to listen," Doc orders.

"We were supposed to meet during the after-market activities to discuss the final options for a move. We wanted a place where there wasn't much else going on, and that we could build an economy around our business."

Reyn stops and turns to look at Haunir. "You're sick, and all of you deserve to be sent to the furthest reaches of space. I will gladly program the coordinates right now, for her and the others. All you have to do is get them to the ship bay out there."

Doc only glances momentarily at Reyn. He won't be distracted. He wants Narp and Zo as much as he wants Haunir, and he's not willing to give up anything yet. He leans forward, still towering over Haunir. She's still too smug for my taste.

"You get them to come to you, then we'll talk about your options."

"No. I need a guarantee first."

"I guarantee that if you don't get them to come, you will be sent to the furthest place we can find to send you. That is the only guarantee you get," Doc says.

Haunir looks at Doc, neither of them blinking. After several moments, her eyes turn to the side. "Fine."

"What is your plan to get them to come to you?" Doc asks.

"In the event of a raid or other trouble here at the market, we are to follow specific protocol. There is a room here that is undetectable from the outside, and only those of us who operate the market have access."

"Wait. She's already lying," Willa says.

"Yeah. She said she didn't know where they were and that we had to bring them to her," Morren adds.

"I wouldn't be surprised if she's trying to lead us into a trap," I say.

Haunir's face tells us nothing. "Do you want me to take you to the room?"

I look at my friends around the room. We've come so far. I sigh deeply. "Reyn, program it for the farthest place possible. If she's lying, she goes there. If she's telling the truth, you can change it to someplace not quite as awful."

"Good idea," Willa says.

"Doc, we have pilots here and we have others who volunteered to help us. They can serve as a distraction to draw out Zo and Narp. There are also two who said they'd help Willa keep Reyn safe." I glance at Eton, but choose not to say anything about him. His thin middle finger is up toward me.

"What? You weren't supposed to -."

"I know, Doc. I know what you said, but I'm not gonna stand by and do nothing. We're going with you."

"Those who can fly will stay here," Morren says. "I'm coming too. Willa, you gotta stay with them. I'm going with Karana."

"You can't just walk up into the room with a big crew. They'll know something's up. We do have surveillance," Haunir says.

"That's what we have you for," I say.

"You're going to have to untie me."

"When we get there," Doc says.

"Willa, if they try to escape, you guys gotta go after them. Don't let them leave the atmosphere. And the two of you who are staying with Reyn, protect her. She has to stay alive. We all do. That includes you, too. Don't be afraid to defend yourselves."

"Right. We have a right to life, too," Willa says. "Despite what they try to say."

"We're good? Everybody knows what to do?" Doc asks before checking on Eton in the corner. "And you? Are you really gonna sit in the corner and do nothing?"

"I'm not doing 'nothing'. I'm waiting and I'm staying alive. That's what we're supposed to do, right?"

Doc shakes his head in disgust, grabs Haunir, and waits for his two guards to walk out in front of him.

"Wait!" I call out. "What's that?" I point to a small blinking light on the heel of her shoe. It reflects off the floor as she moves. "She's got something on her foot."

Doc turns her around and looks at her feet, noticing the soft pink reflection on the concrete. He picks up her foot and in the heel of her shoe is a small tracking device. Doc snatches it out.

"It's too late. There already on their way, if they aren't here already. You'll never get away with this. You'll never defeat us. See, we'll do anything and you – you stop, not willing to go all the way. It's why you're weak. It's why you're simple. It's why we control you."

Doc puts his large hands around her neck and pinches, catching her as she falls, passed out. He lets one of his guards hold her up. He peers through the window that leads into a larger lobby type area. The check-in area is ahead and then the spaceships are lined up.

"Reyn, can you look at what's happening out there? I can't see the area where the ships are."

"Yeah. Hold on. I need just... one... second... Done. Here you go."

Doc looks over at the screen Reyn turns toward him, studying each corner of the four-image layout. "Bring up the top right."

He studies it some more. "Something's off. Weren't the ships parked closer together?"

Reyn looks at the image he's looking at. "You're the only ones who came that way. We skipped that area altogether."

"Morren and Karana, I need you to call in my inside team to cover the area leading up to the bay and be ready to attack. I need them to have my pilots up front. I've gotta feeling they're getting ready to run."

"Got it," Morren says.

We close our eyes and I immediately hear, *Where've you been? We're out here not knowing what's going on! Did you get them?*

I try to answer the voices screaming at us, realizing we'd been so focused on Haunir and getting Zo and Narp we hadn't updated them.

We're safe. We've got Haunir. Everyone needs to maintain position, except Doc's team inside the market, I answer.

Send pilots up front. We must surround the bay and all areas leading to the bay. Be prepared for an attack from Zo or Narp, Morren says.

On our way, we hear back.

"They're coming. I'm listening for when they're in position," I say.

"Until then, we need to stay here," Doc orders.

Chapter Forty-One

"They're ready," Morren and I say in unison.

The sensation of butterflies hasn't left my stomach.

Morren and Doc hold up Haunir, who is now coming to. She's groggy as the two men hold her firmly. One of the guards pulls the door open and checks outside before giving the okay for the others to follow. The second guard checks again before I go out with two volunteers.

Doc, Morren, and Haunir continue toward the registration area and spaceship bay. I look down briefly with guilt for what I'm asking the volunteers to do, but we're all volunteering and trying to save our lives.

"I need you two to go to the middle level of the bay. Make sure you're seen. Draw them out. Don't be afraid to fire. Don't be afraid to stay alive."

They walk away toward the steps leading to the middle level. I spot Chapis Zo. He's trying to get into one of the ships.

The hatch won't open; the handle has been shot and damaged. He runs to another, this one with the windshield blown apart. He's running down, away from the bay and up the steps on the side. Brute is following him.

They're getting away, I send to Morren. *I'm going to find him and Narp.*

Wait, Karana. Be careful.

The two volunteers have made it to the middle level, and the sound of a bullet firing cuts the silence. It whizzes by the girl's head and hits the wall. They dive to the floor. I watch as they try to find the source of the shots. It's too late. The bullets are flying too fast. How am I going to get past them?

Willa and the other pilots scatter to find any available ships.

The girl my age glances toward me, then at the floor below. If she moves from her spot on the floor, they'll see her. She looks at me one more time, as if to say, 'run'. I shake my head no. She raises one of her thick black eyebrows before standing and running in the direction I need to go, drawing their attention and their fire. She's faster than I thought she'd be, and I hope I can keep up the pace to get far enough before they catch sight of me.

The shooting slows for a moment as several of the guards run toward space ships. Narp is getting away. I signal Willa. They can't let him escape. None of them can get away with this. I see Willa and her team running toward the spaceships, dodging the remaining guards firing back and forth with Doc's fighters.

Narp pulls a guard from a ship, shoving him to the ground before pulling down the hatch. I wonder where Willa is.

He's in a ship already. Hurry, I say.

On it, she sends back.

Good luck, Willa. I'll see you when it's done.

Bet your behind you will.

I hear the crash of a body against the rail and resist the urge to look or stop. I must keep going. Out of the corner of my eye, I see the guards brought by Zo, Narp, and Haunir running back the way I'd just come. They're firing again, their weapons raised at the same level as before. Doc's team is fully engaged but I don't know how I'll get any further without them seeing me.

I have to find Zo or else it will be pointless – everything.

I hear Morren. *Keep going, Karana. Keep going. We're holding them. You find him.*

I run around the corner Zo and Brute had gone around seconds earlier. The corner leads to a hall, with chipped, hideous lime-green paint and low lights. Doors marked in words I don't understand line the walls, one after another. I know he's not behind these. I slow my running and let myself listen to the Capellan. It reminds me of something I've been told many times, *Slow down and listen. Not with your ears, Karana. Not with your ears.*

I stop and slow my breathing enough so the panting isn't pounding in my ears and overpowering my other senses. The space between my brows begins to pulse as I listen from there, feeling the prana that flows through everything, even Zo. He can't control that. He's part of the flow and right now the prana leads me right to him. Brute is with him.

I shudder a bit at the idea of dealing with both of them as I check my hip for the gun. I need to draw them out somehow.

Did you find him, Karana? Morren asks.

I know where he is, but I don't know how to get him out. He's got that brutish monster with him.

Anyone with you?

Not anymore.

I'm coming.

No, Morren! You can't. You'll get shot.

You're right, big sis, I could get shot out here. I'm coming.

I stand in the hall, silently for a moment, considering Morren. *Okay. Hurry.*

Already on my way.

Of course he is. I lumber to the end of the corridor and look back. Morren has already made it to the other end of the hall. He could have been a great athlete had our world not been destroyed. He could have been a great many things.

I wave him toward me. *Be quiet.* In his haste, he's clomping down the hallway.

He reaches my side and I point toward the door just around the next corner.

There's barely anyone left in there, Karana. The pilots took off after Narp and the guards who left. It's a mess down there. I couldn't risk you...I needed to make sure you got out of here.

I'm sorry, Morren. Is Doc okay?

He took a bullet in the arm, but he'll be okay. Haunir, Morren says, shaking his head, *she got away.*

The pilots went after Narp, Haunir, and the other guards who tried to get away?

Yeah, they were hot on them. I didn't know Willa could fly like that. She spun out of there so fast. And she managed to wing two of their guys while going out – on purpose.

I smile, nervously, avoiding what waits around the corner, behind the door. I look at my brother. I don't want this to be the last time we have each other's backs.

So, what's the plan, Karana?

We need to lead them back to the bay. We gotta get them on the spaceship Reyn programmed. That means one of us, has to call them out and have them follow us back down the hall.

They'll be armed and Zo's guard is loyal as a dog, so he's gonna fight.

I know. Do you still have that one stink bomb Willa gave us?

Yeah. What do you wanna do with it?"

I look at Morren, and then to the door. *They aren't gonna come out anytime soon without a good reason. I say we give them a good reason. We plant it. You wait on the other side of the hall and fire, so they run back toward the bay.*

And I guess you'll be waiting for them there? he asks, concerned.

I will. You can keep them coming toward me. Just keep shooting.

What if they catch up with you? Morren asks.

Then you better be right on them. You're the fast one, remember?

From the look Morren is giving me, I know he doesn't like the plan. *You got something better?*

He searches for a moment before pulling the stink bomb out of his jacket.

Start walking away, Karana. Once this thing goes off, they'll be peeling out of that room.

He draws his gun and points it toward the handle.

Go. Now.

I walk away quickly before I hear the cling of bullet hitting the door. From half way down the hallway, I can smell the overpowering stench escape the room. It means Zo and Brute won't be far behind.

Their coughing is soon joined by a bullet ricocheting off the wall, and then the running of large men toward me.

I turn and lock eyes momentarily with Zo.

"It's that sneaky pola wannabe. Get her!" he yells to Brute.

They're both running toward me, and I don't see Morren anywhere.

You better be close, Morren.

A shot fires in the hall. It bounces off something concrete and Zo and Brute run faster.

I grab the rails and my feet pound the metal stairs, down toward the remaining ships. Crap! Only four left now, including the two damaged ones Zo tried earlier. Another one gone since I'd run after him. I survey the bay, looking for anyone else still left.

My foot slips on the stairs and I tumble the next six or seven steps, twisting my ankle and banging up the rest of my body.

I hobble to the nearest spaceship and crouch down. My hand settles in something wet as I ease around the side slowly. I look at my fingers. Blood. And then I see him. Eton. No. No. No. I reach my hand out to shake him. His hands still grasping at the handle to open the hatch. His eyes are drooped and slightly open. I shake him again. Nothing.

If he's out here, where's Reyn? Where are the ones guarding her? Where's Doc? Heck, where's Morren?

I'm right here. On the other side of Zo. He's looking for you. You gotta get him to come down the rest of the steps if we want a chance of our plan working.

I sigh deeply. *Eton's gone.*

Did he leave?

In a manner of speaking. He was trying to escape. His body is right here. He's not coming back home with us. I want to be sad for him, but there's no time.

No. We can't...can we? Is it possible to get home without him?

I don't know. We'll have to try. His prana isn't here.

Well first, we gotta get Zo and his guard out of here, Morren says. *Can you give them a clue where you are so they'll come down?*

I peek around the corner of the ship and give one more glance at Eton's lifeless body. I lower his eyelids. "I'm sorry, Eton," I whisper.

I come around the side of the ship and reach for my gun. It's not there. I reach on the other side, feeling around my body for where it could've gone. I must've lost it falling down the stairs.

I don't have my gun, Morren.

Where is it?

I don't know. I fell down the stairs, twisted my ankle, and got myself all banged up. The gun must've fallen out.

I slink back to Eton, feeling guilty and panicked as I check his body for a weapon. I find one tucked in his waistband. I go around the ship again and pull myself up to my feet, holding onto the ship to stay steady.

"There you are. The pola who thinks she's a princess."

Chapter Forty-Two

He's standing just twenty feet in front of me now. Only he and Brute remain in the bay. Standing on my ankle sends excruciating pain through my body, but I'll be damned if he sees me fall. I need help. A surge goes through my body from my head to my feet, and the pain dulls some, making it more bearable. I thank the Capellan and Selvedon. I can still feel her, and am thankful she hasn't gone anywhere yet.

Do you know where Reyn is, Morren?

No. I left her finishing up in the control room.

She couldn't have gone far. Hopefully, she's ready, wherever she is.

Out of the corner of my eye, I can still see the blood spatters behind the ship. Eton. If he'd only listened. But he wouldn't and there's nothing I can do about that now. I can't dwell on it. Not with Zo and Brute wanting more blood.

I spy Morren, but don't look directly at him. I can't give up his position to Zo and Brute. He's here; as sure as he's always been. We couldn't have gotten through this, either of us, alone. I know he's worried too. Worried about Eli and Lari, but mostly about Lari.

It'll be okay. We have one more thing to do, and we can leave here, I send Morren.

I smile smugly at Zo and Brute, mocking him. "I see you finally caught up with me."

"Yeah. Now you're gonna pay, for everything - what you did to me, for stealing my pola, for humiliating me at the market. You're gonna pay. Nobody does Kun Zo like that."

He's losing his cool. The ridges on his head are full of blood, throbbing.

He's not thinking clearly, trying to walk under water. His emotions are keeping him right where we need him.

It's just the two of us again, I send to Morren.

Are you sure you want to do this?

I am sure. I have never been so sure of anything in my life. I want to see him pay for what he's done and perhaps even suffer a little. I don't mind a healthy dose of karma, wherever it comes from.

In a matter of minutes we can change everything, freeing those on Cuupton and ending its operation as the center of the intergalactic slave labor market. Zo, like the others, must be dealt with.

But all I say is, *Yes.*

We do this together or it won't work, Karana. You have to trust me.

I trust you, Morren.

315

There is only one bay open and Reyn said she's programmed the spaceship already. It's a small pod and we get one shot. Do you think Reyn knows she has to be by that pod?

I smile. *That's right*, I think. *She's smart. I'm sure she's already down there, waiting.*

For a second, my stomach sinks and the nervousness settles in again. This is it. If we do this, maybe we can go home. We can see Tezzi and Dad. We can get to the other Immunes. Be safe. Rebuild.

Soon.

You have to come to me, Morren says.

I look Zo in the eye from a safe distance and begin counting in my head. *Three.*

I grip my gun tighter, so it doesn't slip from my nervous fingers when I land. I prepare to brace myself from the fall as well, as I try to keep my weight off the swelling ankle.

Two.

This better work.

One.

At the sound of my feet hitting the concrete hard behind them, Zo and Brute both turn to face us. I wince in pain as Brute reaches his hand out to grab my neck. I pull back and put my gun up, keeping out of the reach of his long arm.

"Oh, you think you're sneaky? You and your sister are in for a surprise."

"Not this time, Zo," I growl.

I keep my eyes on Brute, gun raised and poised to be used.

"This is it, Zo." Morren's gun is similarly positioned. "You're coming with us."

"Who's gonna make me?"

"We are," Morren assures him.

Zo looks around as if to suggest that the two of us are outmatched.

He lunges at Morren.

Morren steps back, nearly stumbling.

Brute takes advantage of my distraction.

I can't take him on body to body. He's nearly twice my size, and with Baselonican strength.

I point the gun at him and hobble back a few steps.

"You won't use that thing."

"Try me," I say.

I grip it with both hands and point it at the center of his head.

"You don't have the guts."

I cock the gun.

"Tell Zo to let my brother up."

Zo swings again at Morren.

Morren's cheeks wobble from the blow. Specks of blood pepper Morren's shirt.

Morren's gun is out of reach, at least fifteen yards away.

Zo kicks Morren in the stomach and lunges for the gun.

I take two more steps back. Brute matches me step for step.

I fire a single shot in Zo's direction, before returning my aim to Brute.

Morren gets to his feet, his eyes still unfocused.

"Run!" I yell to him.

We both turn to run but my ankle won't let me do more than hobble. It was too badly injured.

You have done so well. You must continue, Selvedon says. Her voice sounds weak.

What are you doing?

I have enough to give you strength to get through this. The swelling may still be there but the pain will be only mild. You must do this, Karana.

Wait. No. What are you going to do?

What I have left I am sending you, and when you are done I will move on.

You're leaving us?

Karana, it's not that way. I will simply move on.

"You have to run, Karana. I know it hurts, but this is our only chance." Morren intercepts my conversation with Selvedon.

The pain runs up and around my leg, throbbing and pulsing. Each step is like being stabbed.

But he's right. I'll have time to heal later.

Let me do this for you, Karana; for all of you.

No. I'll be alright.

Brute chases, angrily.

I turn back to see Zo almost at the gun.

I fire another shot in his direction, and the force of the large gun knocks me down.

Brute and Zo aren't stopping, and the pain that had receded previously had come back, agitated by the action. I wouldn't make it like this.

We need them to follow us, Morren says.

I know. I'm trying.

Let me help, Selvedon says. Her voice is weak but firm. *Don't deny me this chance to help save Cuupton and all the others; to right the wrongs done.*

You can't walk, can you? Morren asks.

You don't have time to waste. Take my help, Karana.

Taking her help means she leaves her body, never to return. It means saying good bye so that I can walk and run. I know it is bigger than that, but it doesn't feel fair.

Thank you Sel. Thank you.

My pleasure and my peace.

A powerful wave overcomes me, settling in the swollen ankle. The shooting pain and throbbing subside, allowing me to stand.

Selvedon helped me, I explain to Morren who looks confused.

We run to the other side of the parked ships. The smaller pod ship is hidden on the other side. And next to it is Reyn. I can feel the relief course through my body, but not enough to dull the sadness.

She's crouched down in a corner near the pod she's prepared.

"Up here, Morren. We gotta keep them coming!"

"You stinking humans won't get away with this. You won't get away period. Yeah, I figured out what you are. Diseased humans escaped your quarantine and think you can screw up my world too!" Zo yells from a couple vessels back.

"Who's gonna stop us?" I yell back. "You can't even keep your polas together!"

"Say it to my face!" he yells.

"You can't even catch up to a girl with a twisted ankle. I thought you were so big and bad."

"Bigger and badder than you or your brother!"

Brute is getting close. Too close.

Morren and I stop in front of a spaceship and get low. We need them both.

This isn't gonna work, if they aren't both here to get in the pod, Morren.

I know. We need help.

I try to see their shadows as they approach from the sides.

There is a heavy thud.

Brute's face lands near the ship and I step back, eyes wide.

Someone else is here.

"Oh! It's you. I didn't think I'd see you again," Zo calls out to whoever just knocked Brute out.

"Good. After today, I have no intention of ever seeing you again." the familiar voice says.

"You think I'm gonna let you come back to my home after this?" Zo says. "He's my best guard. Get your lazy behind up. You're embarrassing yourself," he says pushing Brute with his boot.

"He couldn't have been too good. And no, you don't have to let me come back. It's not your home anymore, Zo. It is being returned to the people, and to the legitimate leading family. Your time is up, and you are no longer welcome on my home of Baselonica Xuna," Lari says.

"Ha! I'm the one holding the gun, you wannabe queen."

"That's okay. It's already in motion. Your clan is already out. The people in the mines are free and, trust me, you don't want to know what they'd do with you. So, you can kill me, but what you knew as home is no more."

"Come one step closer, and I will kill you. And believe me, it would be a pleasure. Then I'll kill that conniving vixen Karana and her hapless little brother," Zo says loudly.

"You'll do none of those things," Eli says.

"Oh look, it's the tentacled walking slime lady again. I thought I got rid of you already."

"You may leave now, or suffer the consequences. It is your choice," Eli responds calmly.

"Damn right, it's my choice. It always is. And I choose that you don't get to choose what my choices are!"

I can see Eli's tentacles flowing from her head. They are a reddish tint. I know she's angry, even if her voice is still even and measured. She's coming around the front, where we are. I offer her my gun, but she ignores me.

I don't know what she's planning, as she casually looks down and locks eyes with me, shielding her thoughts.

Then she's gone, reappearing behind Zo. Before he can react and face her with the gun, they're both gone.

Seconds later Eli is back, kneeling beside Brutc who's now wriggling and holding the back of his head. She's gone again.

She's back and looking around for any other stragglers that might need a ride.

I hear the banging of fists on the heavy clear material on the pod. Reyn is gone. I look for her and find her standing, near a panel. She looks at the pod, number six. She puts something into the computer on the panel and the pod starts up. Zo and Brute, crowded in the single passenger pod, struggle with the door releases.

The pod begins to hover and move to the open lane for take-offs and landings.

Zo looks at Reyn and fires at the glass, hoping to break the bullet proof material. Soon it will be too late. He moves quickly out of the path of the ricochet, but it bites his shoulder. Brute bangs on the shield, in vain.

Reyn presses another button and waves her hand at them.

I can barely see them leave; only a streak of light is left in their path as the hyper-drive sends them out, and into the deep.

I fall back to the ground, eyes facing the ceiling.

Chapter Forty-Three

It's been two Earth weeks since we've been back. I was forced to stay off my ankle and let it heal, in yet another cave. But I'll take this cave, given what's outside is a tropical paradise.

"You finally awake?" Morren asks, handing me a cup of coffee and a bowl of what looks like oatmeal.

"Yeah. Today is the day."

"I don't understand why she isn't drawn here." Morren is still bothered that it hadn't been cut and dry.

"My guess is that she can't jump. And without Dad, how would she get here."

We hadn't talked much about Dad since coming back. He'd never left the compound we escaped. It had been a lifetime for Tezzi but only a little over a year for us. I know for her she'd grieved already, but Morren and I are still processing that whatever goodbyes we'd given that day in the compound were the last for Dad. Tezzi is all we have left. We'll rescue her friend Karren, too. She must also be an Immune.

"I'm nervous, Morren."

"Is that why you're eating that oatmeal so slowly?"

"I'm not eating any slower than you're drinking your cup of coffee." I take a sip of the coffee sitting beside me. "Bleh. No cream or sugar?"

Morren rolls his eyes and doesn't bother answering me. He just folds his hands around his mug and takes a slow drink.

"She might be able to jump, but after all these years, she may be too weak," he ponders.

"It could be. Or they could be drugged. I guess it won't matter. We'll all be together soon."

"We've been gone ten years. You know, Tezzi is older than I am in human years now," Morren says wistfully.

"I know. I was thinking about that. I'm ready to find out what she looks like, meet Karren, and thank her for helping our sister through this. I don't know what she'd have done all by herself.

The spoon falls into the half-eaten bowl of oatmeal. My nerves won't let me finish it or the coffee. I don't need caffeine on a day like this.

No matter what happens, we're bringing them back. They'll join us here and bring our total number to a hundred and forty-four. We need every one of us to make this new world work. For the first time since I can remember, I feel safe. Tezzi deserves to feel the same.

"The sun is breaking along the horizon. That's what we agreed to last night. Let's confirm where she is, and that they're ready so we can go."

Seated across from each other as we'd done so often on Cuupton, Morren and I create a link to Tezzi.

Tezzi? I call out.

There's no answer.

T*ezzi?* Morren calls out.

We're here. We're here, Tezzi answers

My heart skips and my breath catches in the back of my throat. It's really happening.

Are you on your way? Karren asks.

Yes! We're coming for you. It's time. I know my emotions are effusive.

I'll let them hear us count-down to get them.

Why don't you lead, Morren? You always land much better than I do.

Morren and I stand, he reaches for me and grabs my hand.

Three.

It's really happening.

Two.

Ten years we were gone.

One.

Your review of this novel would be greatly appreciated.

About the Author

Bernette is a multi-genre writer and creative with a passion for creating and inspiring positive change in people. She lives in the metro Atlanta area with her family.

Website: BernetteSherman.com
TikTok: TikTok.com/@WriterandCoachBernette
Instagram: Instagram.com/IAmBernette
Facebook: Facebook.com/IAmBernetteSherman.
Other books: BernetteSherman.com/Books-by-Bernette/

Characters

Morren and Karana – Brother and sister from Earth.

Tezzi – Morren and Karana's younger sister

Eli – Alien from the planet Eliatar, living on Earth

Reyn and Eton – male and female Immunes from Earth

From Baselonica Xuna (Base X)

Willa Zouxia – female alchemist from Baselonica Xuna.

Curly/Lari – female from Baselonica Xuna who helps Morren and Karana

Chapis Kun Zo – Ruler of Baselonica Xuna

Goede – female from Baselonica Xuna who aids in preparation of Karana to meet Chapis Kun Zo

Brute – Chapis Zo's right-hand bodyguard

From Anfar

Director Narp – Bureaucrat and regular leader of the Sovereign Goyar activities on Anfar

From Cuupton

The Capellan – non-physical conscious being that resides in a physical host

Doc – A leader of the Comrades of Liberation and one of the hosts for the Capellan

Selvedon - A leader of the Comrades of Liberation and one of the hosts for the Capellan

Haunir – Runs the slave labor trade market

Surek – Cook for the Comrades of Liberation

www.ingramcontent.com/pod-product-compliance
Lightning Source LLC
Chambersburg PA
CBHW030924260626
47169CB00002B/375